"Equal parts muscle and magic, Red Wood isn't your average police consultant. And *FEAR*, Book 1 of *The Red Wood Chronicles* isn't your average debut novel. M.J. Hook casts a powerful spell in this spirited tale of mystery, demons, and the dark arts. Highly recommended."

Larry Hinkle, author of *The Eris Ridge Trail* and *An Hour Before Dark*

"Hook's writing is a perfect blend of earthy magic and supernatural realism. It's impossible not to drown in the depths of his intricate plots and become enchanted by Red Wood, the giant and snarky hero."

Lily Clemons, author of *Necromancer's Empathy*

FEAR

CHAKRA DEMONS

THE RED WOOD CHRONICLES – BOOK 1

M.J. HOOK

SERIES DEDICATION TO KATHY WYATT

Your friendship was my first best, and for that I am eternally grateful.
Thank you for introducing me to the famous monsters.
So bummed I missed you.

BOOK DEDICATION TO EVERETT FORSYTHE

Said I would, knew I could, so I should.
Thanks for watching over my shoulder.

A SMALL MORSEL

When I first met Travis "Red" Wood, he was thirty-three. The encounter was brief, but by the end, I knew he and I shared a spiritual connection, a fantastical bond that has grown stout over the past few years. We've become very close comrades, and while our relationship evolves, I continue to learn more details about my spiritual buddy and his magical, chaotic life.

A six-foot-eight, proportionally muscled, 280-pound man with red bushy hair and a sense of humor that tames the ominous first impression, Red possesses a shambolic backstory—rich with detail and plagued by mystery. Delving into Red's historical particulars, I've realized that many of his tales contain too much information to include in these chronicles. But I still wish to share them with you.

So, I've created a means to distribute these added tales on m'blog at www.mj-hook.com.

As Red's journey continues, I promise to post interesting, and often humorous, recollections about his past, his training, his unique friends and companions—but never any spoilers.

Well, maybe a betokened morsel of a hint; toss you a few bones to scry some possibilities.

'Nuff said, except *thank you* for joining me on this journey.

My hope is that by the end of *FEAR*, you will be an enchanted member of m'crew.

Hook
May 2026

Behind the secrets of nature remains something subtle, intangible, and inexplicable.
Veneration for this force beyond anything that we can comprehend is my religion.

– Albert Einstein

I've been walking behind you
Since you've been able to see
There's never been any reason
For you to think about me

– "Never Been Any Reason," *Flat as a Pancake*, Head East, 1974
Track 44 from the *Soundtrack from M'Life* playlist

TABLE OF CONTENTS

THE ROOT CHAKRA

SANSKRIT NAME
Muladhara

LOCATION
Base of spine, perineum

PURPOSE
Survival: Provides a base or foundation for life and helps one feel grounded, able to withstand challenges. The root chakra is responsible for the sense of security and stability.

MANTRA
LAM – "I AM"

MUDRA
Connect thumb to pointer finger.
Place hands on knees. Palms down to facilitate rooting to the ground.
Palms up to harness fresh energy and find balance.

ASSOCIATED COLOR
Red

ELEMENT
Earth

PRIMARY CRYSTALS
Red Jasper, Hematite, Red Tiger's Eye.
Secondary Crystals: Fire Agate, Black Tourmaline, Black Onyx

SPIRITUAL DEMON
Fear

1

TUESDAY, EARLY MORNING

I WAS BORN *in Lake Michigan.*

For some reason, my blood mother, Jenny Blatt, pregnant and in a frantic rush, drove her pickup off the Mackinac Bridge into the great lake. While the truck began its descent into the chilly water, I popped out of Jenny, then popped out the truck window to start my trip to the surface.

Several people driving on I-75 that morning witnessed the accident. One man, Dr. Bill Wood, stopped his car, ran to the broken side rail, and jumped into the water to save the occupants.

As he swam down to the truck, something rushed up and bumped him in the face.

That was me.

Dr. Bill loved telling the story.

"Once I realized it was a baby, I changed direction and swam up for air. Backstroking toward the concrete footer under the bridge, I got to where I could stand up and see he was a newborn baby boy—born in the caul. I took the sac off, allowing him to take his first breath. Seeing the cord and placenta attached, I went into doctor mode."

He tied off the cord with a wet shoelace.

"Amazing," Dr. Bill would say, "this big boy came out of such a tiny woman. His real father must have been a giant."

My mother couldn't confirm or deny the fact. The small woman, Jenny Blatt, drowned.

Dr. Bill rode in the ambulance and made sure I settled in at the hospital.

He went back to the bridge, watched them pull the truck out and ID my dead mother, then followed the police to her remote cabin near Garnet.

Other than her name and address, they found no indication of who she was, nor where she was from or who my blood father was.

"There was a trunk full of money and a box labeled FOR THE BOY that contained some used toys and a pack of newborn diapers. That was it. One toy was a tiny, plastic red-haired troll doll," he would add. "I asked the officers if I could take it 'for the boy.' They looked at me strange, but didn't object once they had it documented."

In Michigan for a doctor's golf retreat, Dr. Bill called his wife, Tina, back home in Colorado Springs and told her what happened. Since they could not have any children and had talked about adoption, he put an idea in her head.

"I told her, 'Shoot, I already feel like the Lady in the Lake gave him to us, Hon. Like Excalibur.' Something very magical about that moment when he bumped my nose."

Tina flew up to Michigan that evening.

After an extensive background check on Dr. Bill and Tina, the court agreed that they could temporarily foster me in Michigan. Tina rented a small apartment in Grand Rapids, while Dr. Bill headed back to Colorado Springs to work. He would visit every weekend.

After three months, the court found no evidence of who my blood father was and had no luck finding any relatives of Miss or Mrs. Blatt.

Dr. Bill and Tina Wood became Dad and Mom.

With the completed adoption, they took me back to Colorado and formally named me Travis, after my new mom's father. Because of my brilliant red hair and my way-above-average physical size, eventually everyone just called me...

• • •

"Red?" Benny's voice squawks from my phone, steering my attention back to the road and call. "Earth calling Red Wood. You there, buddy?"

"Sorry, oh mighty detective. I was woolgathering," I huff with a fatigued voice that should sound exhausted to my friend, adding a heavy sigh for punctuation.

"Yeah, I do that too when someone tells me they have a dead body I need to see. Happens every day, as a matter of fact," Benny laughs, ignoring

                                M.J. Hook

my weary feint.

When Benny Rogers calls, it undoubtedly concerns a crime scene the Colorado Springs homicide detective needs me to check out. Homicide means at least one body. The invite means supernatural misdoing may be involved.

"So, you need me now?" I attempt a tone of reluctance this time. Driving home after a long night of training with my apprentice, Jabari Le Roux, has me tired physically and spiritually. I want a shower, a meal, and my bed. Not a case of paranormal malfeasance to work on.

"Yes, and good morning. Great way to start a chilly November day, and I would like you there before stuff gets tagged and bagged. I'm heading up right now. Scenic turnoff, Fountain Creek side of the pass, just south of Waldo Canyon. Pull in at the exit."

Duty calls.

• • •

The creek culvert where we stand is a tree-filled, rocky area that stretches across from the highway to the base of the foothills traversing up Ute Pass. Fountain Creek runs deep from the mountain runoff, giving the tranquil scene a soothing, trickling soundtrack to complement the view. The fresh snowfall would be icing on the visual cake, but the morning vista is tainted by crisscrossed yellow crime scene tape surrounding a corpse.

With no fresh prints in the virgin snow around the victim, an investigation team member starts melting the white stuff with a heat blower.

The body, a girl, naked and posed in the starting position to run a race, remains isolated inside the confines of the yellow tape. Her feet on their balls, arched to lift her heels—one foot below her raised butt, the other set back—dig into the dirt like a natural starting block. The back, starting with her butt, remains perfectly level to the ground up to her shoulders, held in place by her two extended arms, palms flat, not on fingertips. Her head tilts up to look toward an imaginary finish line with cloudy, lifeless eyes. The face of what might have been an angel in life—young, sweet, and innocent—displays inert regret frozen in death.

Someone went to a lot of effort to show off their victim. It leaves me feeling colder than the November morning temperature.

The snow-glazed pose is a curiosity, but adding to the weirdness are what appear to be short table legs attached to precise parts of her body.

FEAR

Two identical metal legs, one stuck behind each ankle, match the two on the backside of each elbow. A larger, wooden leg appears to thread into her tailbone, which matches another leg screwed into the back of her head.

"What's up with the furniture accessories?" Benny asks.

"No idea... yet," I say, shaking off the chill as we move around the scene.

Flipping back and forth between normal viewing and my spiritual sight, or what I call *3E*, I had seen nothing from the parking lot down to the creek that would suggest magic was involved. No sign of residual energy from a curse, spell, or enchantment.

Using my *ajna*, or third eye, allows me to see the true nature of things, an amplified sight that displays the spiritual core of my surroundings. Auras display the radiant colors of emotion and intent of people, as well as the primal spirits of all living matter—animals, plants, insects. Years of grueling practice trained me to focus on what's important while masking out distractive noise.

Using 3E also increases my other five senses, allowing me to capture a clue that may not be obvious on normal sensory levels.

It reveals the world as it truly is—matter, energy, elements—mingling together in a spectrum of universal magnificence that can cause tears of wonder, and horrors that would make bladder and bowel release instantly.

Most importantly, the sight displays magical energy, which I am currently looking for. Magic always leaves some sort of residue, whether it be a cast spell, blood (which holds a living being's energy for a time even after death), a binding, or something hidden by a glamour—an illusional construct to mask a sorcerer's misbehaving.

Viewing the girl's body, I see nothing to suggest sorcery. No residue of an arcane sacrifice. No blood anywhere on or around the body. The girl has a pentacle tattooed on her right shoulder, which is why Benny contacted me, but the tatt is not fresh.

One thing I can see suspended above her head is the girl's *baddoon*, her soul bag, twisting and floundering like a large, glowing larva stuck in a bird's beak. The girl's spirit fights to retain life, while its glowing root attached to the crown of her head stretches and kinks.

After a peaceful death, the soul's essence inflates the baddoon, its aura adjusting to the death and appearing like a rainbow-colored balloon. The spirit sack of the deceased tethers to the crown of the physical body. Once

M.J. Hook

the passing of the soul registers and the moment is accepted, the connection dissolves, allowing the spirit to journey on to the Universe.

With murder, or even suicide, spiritual anger and regret hold onto the mortal vessel.

Wanting justice, revenge, or a second chance at life, the spirit struggles until the energy deteriorates and the grip releases, sending the departed into a universal purgatory, something like a crowded train station during rush hour. Or, if the energy is determined to stay near friends, family, or the murderous jerks that checked their ticket, the spirit reattaches to a familiar place to haunt the living as a ghost with baggage.

The girl's baddoon appears to be on a train to ghostville as it twists and expands. A fury of color, its aura glows with frustrated rage, a brilliant distortion within the confines of the tarnished bag. My sight fills with the kaleidoscopic palette of wrath and regret: a rainbow covered by mildewed clouds of gray, the formations tainted with green-molding remorse, surrounded by brown-infected edges of disappointment.

"So, still no idea about the table legs, Detective, but her spirit has a story to tell," I say to Benny, in my for-his-ears-only voice.

"She got one of those, whadya call it, *balloon bags* hanging on?" Benny replies. He glances at me—one part hope, one part curiosity.

"Yeah, she does, and it ain't pretty. I don't see any sorcery involved in her death, and it's obvious her murder didn't happen here. No blood. Hopefully, I can get the story from her spirit, but I need to start story time now."

"Let them clear the snow. We found some tire tracks up behind the convenient blind spot in the turnoff. Also found some sweet footprints coming down the trail. Guy must have carried her, so the extra weight made accurate impressions. Just need to see if they match what's around the body."

Benny enjoys finding blatant evidence. It makes the hard but rewarding job of catching the killer that much easier. By communing with the victim's baddoon, I can normally put a name to the bad guy, if they knew them, and a location for evidence to make the arrest faster.

"We got footprints, Detective," the tech inside the tape yells to Benny. "Looks like a match."

"Good. Cast a left and right and take lots of pics," Benny instructs.

"Yes, sir."

Benny pulls me out of earshot from the investigative crowd gathering around the tape surrounding the body.

"I'll get people to pull back once the plaster's poured. You know the drill, wear the footies and gloves and touch nothing that's, uh, real. Physical." Benny hands me a pair of elastic shoe covers from his coat pocket. I wear my own leather gloves, which comfortably fit my hands.

"You ever tire of explaining why I get special treatment with your dead bodies?"

Benny smirks. "With my success rate finding sicko bad guys, I don't need to explain."

I'm attempting to place a cover over my left boot when the elastic breaks just as I clear the heel.

"You really need to stock up on some larger booties for my size 15 feet, Detective. One size does not fit all." Using a quick adhesive spell, I fix the break, then successfully cover the other boot without mishap.

"That would be a special order. Next time, I'll bring trash bags and bungee cords." Benny pauses, looking up the trail to the highway. A loud voice, heavy on the nasal, is shouting orders.

"Eddie Munster's here. You need to get in there and do your thing."

Eddie Munster, aka Edward Hinkle, is the COSPD lead forensic investigator. The man is good at his job but lacks the social skills to maintain friendly relationships. Dead bodies don't talk back, so Hinkle naturally enjoys their company. I will admit, he is good at listening to the stories their remains tell.

As the Paranormal Specialist for the department, I've worked my way to the top of Eddie's shit list. One time, I correctly interpreted an investigation that Eddie misdiagnosed, and since then, the PS has been able to inspect crime scenes, including bodies (with a no-touching clause), before Dr. Hinkle gets involved.

Following the same path in toward the body that the tech made walking out, I approach the girl. Stopping beside her head, then kneeling, while spreading my arms up and out, I open my palms as if preparing to conduct an orchestra. This is assuming my *paranormal posture*. The pose allows officers to see my hands, a ruse while I extend my cog coil from my stomach toward the tortured soul inside the baddoon.

My cognitive coil is another bonus of being a well inked and linked wizard to Gaia, the Earth Mother. By reaching out with a cog coil, I can connect to another's spirit, alive or recently deceased. It is a tool to share and

M.J. Hook

sometimes influence energy. Normally, the communion starts with a gentle introduction. But sometimes, when someone is freaking out and needs to get their shit together to avoid, say, an oncoming car or a gun-toting idiot, introductions vanish.

The baddoon is pulling harder against its binding. There will be one more lost soul with major unresolved issues if I don't make contact soon.

Since forensics frowns on enchanted circles drawn around their crime scenes, I have learned to communicate with departed spirits without the protection charmed circles offer. Most baddoons rarely lash out, but in case one does, I have other tricks up my sleeves that can subdue it momentarily.

Like, right before the tether breaks. It's a great opportunity to discuss options with the frantically departed.

In a hushed voice and using my spiritual power language, a Donegal dialect of Irish Gaelic, I invite my power to the energy surrounding the soul bag in a spiritual request for welcome.

"Cuir failte romham, le do thoil."

Every wizard, witch, sorcerer, or sorceress has a language that complements their spellcasting. This gives intent and meaning with words to link energy inherited in the caster's blood. Latin is a popular one to roll off the tongue. Those with knowledge of their lineage may use a common tongue, or beef up their studies to learn Sanskrit, Egyptian, Ethiopic, and other ancient lingo. It took little time for me to discover mine. As I had the same ginger locks as my blood mother, my teacher for the subject kept me dialed in to the Northern European languages. Mine became obvious as I spoke a simple flame spell to light a candle and ended up setting the curtains across the room on fire.

The connection in place, I introduce myself to the girl's energy using spiritual telepathy through my coil—speaking between souls.

"Child. Please share with me your anguish. Show me your story so that I may relieve your suffering and free your spirit."

The twisting bag o'soul stops its movement and vibrates, a posturing that allows me to connect my coil and pass through the spiritual membrane. As the power from the bag's aura blends with my energy, the girl's desperation yanks my core and drags me in.

Her story begins—a ribbon knotted in terror.

A brief life unraveled by evil.

2

TUESDAY, EARLY MORNING

THE SEVERE VIBRATION hits my coil with spirit-shattering intensity.

I call it the violent verve.

Imagine every negative feeling—knowing your life is about to end after whatever vile pain and suffering an executioner's torture inflicts—converting and amplifying into a fierce ball of spiritual fear and anger. Sharing with that energy could crush my soul, forcing me into a fog of eternal spiritual dementia. Once the link breaks, I would fall into dead space, an empty consciousness with no memory—a driverless vessel doomed to crash.

A big suck-all of nothingness.

Having shared with several tortured baddoons, I am prepared for the verve, buffering the severe emotion and physical torment with magical constructs learned in training. I allow the waves to pass, then use my energy to calm the spirit's despair.

I am here. Thank you.

Another wave rolls over me, this time visuals of the girl's life are revealed, a foothold of focus on her energy core to explore her life thread. I exist in the ribbon of her memories, all seen through her eyes.

I am here to help you.

The next wave advances, slowing and surrounding my presence, feeding off the peace I offer, seasoned with my living soul—delicacies for a recently dispatched victim.

Thank you. Please, show me who you are.

The energy bands into a single cord of the girl's life. It resembles a shiny ribbon, a strand of film containing all the moments of her existence. I accept the invitation and fall into her story, which immediately displays a series of violent images. Her murder. I help her push past the moment, allowing myself not to focus on details.

That comes later.

Show me who you are? What's your name?

Without a proper circle for protection, I do not allow her spirit to speak with me. Words have power, and while I am sharing my energy with her agitated soul, her spiritual voice can spank me something serious. So, I encourage visuals. It's a pain in the ass because it takes longer for the departed to tell their story, but my sacred butt remains unscathed.

Her life rewinds, traveling through her thread, passing the day of her murder, then weeks before, stopping at a moment in a mirror. The girl's smiling, her energy lit up with a rainbow of excitement. She looks down at her hands.

She holds a new driver's license, issued in August. The girl's identification is now part of my memory—17-year-old Theresa Barlow of Woodland Park.

Thank you, Theresa. That is a wonderful moment. Understand, to reach the Universe, you must...

The image warps, spinning into a funnel of chaotic recall. I push energy to calm her while making a gentle request for detail.

You only need to show me who did this to you so they are held accountable.

The thread spools forward, slowing down.

Theresa is trying to start her car. Trying again.

"Caw pwoblem, T'wesa?" I hear a man's voice, distorted by a vibrating tremor. She turns and sees an overweight man walking across the lawn towards her—his body covered in shadow. He gets closer to her car. The shadow turns into a jerky silhouette with violent, rippling edges. The shadow deepens to a total darkness.

Something is not right.

Theresa. I offer a gentle yet firm spiritual nudge. *I need to see him.*

"Hi, Mr. H," Theresa replies with familiarity. Her voice is clear. The man reaches her car window, his chubby body completely masked out of the scene. A twitching silhouetted mass of emptiness. A twanging chord of sound fills the viewing as he talks, syncing with the visual distortion.

The tone reverberates through my coil and shakes my spirit. Minor

M.J. Hook

aches emerge throughout my body. I force myself to ignore the irritating pain and focus on the memory.

Wait, please. The name? Where is that sound coming from?

The dark shape moves to the front of the car and opens the hood, then moves under it. The distorted voice continues its staticky discord.

Theresa tries to start the car.

The amplified twang ruptures again as the form approaches her window. Mr. H is obviously talking, but all I can hear is the single chord of distortion. My spirit reacts again, pain coursing through the link. I try to adjust the connection to minimize the feeling as the jagged silhouette, an empty jittering hole, waves for her to follow. Theresa gets out of the car.

Walking next door to the garage, his form remains a mess of garbled blackness while another thrum resonates to twist and curl the static edges.

More pain. It's not her agony, but mine.

Please. Theresa. Wait.

I'm tempted to enforce more control, but I still have no identification for her killer. More control could break the link.

She approaches a workbench in the back of the garage, then something hits the back of her head.

Complete darkness.

Forward. Then light. Her last moments display like a twisted homemade horror flick.

Theresa. Please. Take me back…

She wants me to see. I feel her spirit's determination. The documentary of her death punches fast forward, not giving me any opportunity to interfere.

Fluorescent lights on the ceiling cause her to squint. They make her head hurt worse, so she shuts her eyes. Something fills her mouth, muffling her as she tries to speak. She can't lift her arms, feels something tied around each wrist keeping them spread wide. As she lifts one, it pulls the other down. Her back aches as she tries to lift her legs. Her ankles are tied together the same way as her wrists, but lower, causing her lower back to grind against the corner of the surface she's tied down to.

I don't feel her pain. I don't feel her fear, but I acknowledge both through her soul's impression of the moment. Like a spiritual Geiger counter, the colors of her aura allow me to detect the physical and emotional levels of distress.

She turns her head and opens her eyes and sees the woodblock table she's trussed to. Lifting one hand, she sees the rope on her wrist. The lead going under the table goes taut as it pulls down her other arm. She looks left, right, and notices the room. A workshop, tables with tools, pegboards with more tools hanging on hooks.

She lifts her head. It hurts. But she needs to see, to understand, how her legs and back drape over the large table's edge.

She thrashes and screams. The thing stuffed in her mouth muffles her efforts. Her tongue feels the cloth as she tries to push it out. A rag. Her thoughts recognize the taste of bleach as she attempts to swallow. Moving her mouth, she feels something stuck on her face, holding the cloth in.

Thrash. Scream for help. She twists. Scoots down. She feels her feet touch the floor. The corner of the table is digging into her mid-back. She squirms and slides down more. If she can get on the floor, maybe…

Someone grabs her hair and slides her back onto the table. She screams, more from fright than pain. She arches her neck when they let go.

I see the silhouette; another chord of distortion plays as it speaks in garble. The form's edges ripple with the vibration. The pain I feel is almost crippling, the tremors shaking my spiritual core, a shudder quivering my bones. I try to listen, hoping to hear words from the killer, but the only sounds I recognize are Theresa's muffled screams.

The form moves around the table to her legs. It holds a knife in a shallow grasp. It cuts off her pants. Theresa fights, and the knife cuts her leg. The form stills, and again the voice answers with warped words. The pants are off, then it cuts off her panties with two swift cuts. It cuts off her shirt, her bra, until she is naked except for the shoes and socks on her feet.

The twitchy blackness paws her body. It grabs her by the hips, pulls her closer to the edge.

It enters her, ripping away her innocence. She screams and chokes on the rag in her mouth. The darkness stops thrusting and grabs the tape around her mouth. She feels the adhesive pull on her skin as the cloth lifts from her throat. The violation continues.

Exhausted, she yields. Her body submitting as the void continues to defile her, groping with dark and empty hands. The thing finishes as tears fill her eyes and drip down her face.

I view the torture in a matter of seconds. Her memory zipping by holds me in shock. The garbled visual and sound of her assailant has me baffled, angry, causing me to lose focus. Then the shared link staggers as my spirit

M.J. Hook

and body falter from the energy the killer's next strum releases.

I force myself to hold on, ignoring my pain. My energy centers on her core as I push to calm the girl's spirit.

Child. Listen. This memory is unnecessary. Help me find this…

The memory moves forward. The void defiles her again. She lies still. Defeated.

Forward again. The empty hand holds something above her face, a long piece of tubing. Maybe aluminum. It is hard for me to identify the material through her tears before the distortion pulls it away. She struggles, thrashing against restraints as it pulls her body completely up on the table.

The knife reappears and cuts open her wrist.

She screams, then screams again as the trembling darkness feeds the tube into her arm.

Darkness.

The next view is from her baddoon. Her spirit looking down as the obscured killer disembowels her corpse. Blood and guts surround the table…

Please stop, child. I see it. I see it all. Find me, find my embrace.

The scene disappears as I apply a compassionate energy. She has shown me enough. Her neighbor is suspect number one, and hopefully the crime scene is in his house or in a workshop he owns. Benny can figure that out. It is time to urge this girl to release.

I will find him. I promise. It is time for you, dear Theresa, to let go. Review your life's blessings and accept alleviation.

I watch as her lifetime passes. She travels her ribbon of existence. Joyful moments with family. With friends. Love.

Her energy consents; she frees the tether.

The Universe accepts as I break the link.

M.J. Hook

3

TUESDAY MORNING

MY HANDS TREMBLE as I lower my arms. The link to Theresa's spirit felt like an hour in the electric chair, but I know it was only a long minute for the few people watching me. My body is in pain. Muscles ache in hypertrophic agony. My spirit's unaligned, creating a vertigo wave in 3E.

Switching views, I kneel and focus on my breathing.

Feeling better, I examine the girl's legs and arms. I can see bulges where the tubing threads under her skin to hold her limbs in position. Between her breasts, a sloppy incision runs down her stomach. It protrudes and creases from the rude sewing job. The stitching used to seal her up is clear, like fishing line.

"Oh great, the illustrious Matthew Hopkins is here. Hope you haven't exorcised any evidence from my crime scene."

Edward Hinkle, forensic virtuoso and irritating as gout, announces his arrival by referring to me as the 17th century witch hunter. After watching Theresa's murder, anything Mr. Ed has to say will be lame, but a welcome and familiar lame.

"Find any devil marks yet? I understand the girl has a pentagram carved into her back."

I stand up, feeling my legs react with an unfamiliar tremor to match my hands. Shaking off the anxiety, I turn and raise an intellectual eyebrow to my lab coat adversary.

"Sorry, Eddie," I say, using Hinkle's non-preferred given name, "but that's a pentacle. A pentagram has no circle." I test my 3E, finding it still giddy, but keep it on long enough to smile and witness Ed's aura peeving.

"Toe-may-toe, toe-mah-toe. You done?" he asks, waving off my comment with a gloved hand.

"Also, Ed, it's a tattoo. But I am sure after hours of study, you would have figured that out."

Hinkle, standing at the edge of the tape, barks a laugh.

"Good one, he-who-should-not-be-named. You've had your five." Hinkle finishes his sentence by punctuating the air with a latex-thumb swipe. "Time for science to do its job."

"The scene is all yours, Herr Dippel." I wave Eddie in, using the name of the German scientist who inspired Shelley's Frankenstein.

"Sorry, Wood, my science is real, non-proto."

A brief wave of admiration that Eddie knew who I was talking about quickly passes like bad gas.

I take one last view of the body. That's all it is now. Evidence. The baddoon is gone.

I accomplished guiding Theresa to find peace in the Universe. Now it's time to get Benny involved with finding the murderer. Though I have enough information to catch the killer, my confidence wavers thinking about the weird anomaly while trying to see and hear the bastard. The blaring chord of sound that caused me varied physical and spiritual distress bothers me.

An extra mystery I need to figure out.

Looking around for Benny, I spy him standing over by the trail leading up to the parking lot. Holding his hand out to shake, he greets a petite Asian woman with a short wedge of black hair wearing a fashionable blue winter jacket, jeans, and hiking boots. The neon green backpack hooked on her shoulder makes me wonder if she's a kid.

Benny's hand hangs useless as the woman replies with a bow.

Watching my friend wipe his hand on his pants and attempt a bow of his own, followed by a pant hitch and a shoulder roll inside his oversized overcoat, helps relieve my nerves from the trauma of communing with Theresa's spirit.

Benny looks like a Robin Williams doppelgänger, only with his hair in a jarhead crop. His manner of dress is consistent come rain, snow, or shine—a wrinkled taupe Columbo-style coat covering a matching wrinkled suit and a scuffed pair of Doc Martens. The cherry on top of the detective's image is his voice—a deep southwestern sort of drawl. Aware of his eclectic

                    M.J. Hook

aesthetic attributes, Detective Benjamin Rogers pulls it all together as a focused, witty, tough-as-a-rhinoceros cop.

I hear Benny say, "Sorry. I can't dance, can't carry a tune, and burn water trying to boil an egg." He and the small woman are laughing as I walk up.

I grip my left wrist where I would wear a watch if I owned one—a coded move to inform Benny that we need to talk sooner than later.

Benny acknowledges with a nod, then introduces the woman.

"Travis Wood, I would like for you to meet Inspector Emiko Omori of the Fujiyoshida, Japan, Police Department."

I give a casual bow of greeting.

"Ko-nee-chee-wah," I say, my pronunciation intentionally awkward.

The inspector smiles, an attractive cherub face complemented by two astonishing copper-colored eyes. She immediately starts speaking her native language. My hand goes up to halt her mid-sentence. Even though I understood some of what she was saying, I never like to reveal cards at first meetings.

"Sorry, 'hello' is the only word I know. I sure hope you speak English."

"Yes, I do. Well, so I'm told," she replies, with a hint of accent.

Benny butts in.

"The inspector here is part of the Sister-City Program; we send people to Fujiyoshida to shadow a common profession, they send someone to us. All city departments do it. This year COSPD was chosen to receive."

Turning his attention to Hinkle starting to inspect the body, he continues.

"Inspector, you arrived just in time for a Rocky Mountain homicide. Guy that found her spent a long night playing Dungeons & Dragons with friends up in Woodland Park." Benny points north. "Pulled off here to drain his dragon, uh, relieve himself, early this morning on his way home and spotted the victim. Called 911 around 6 AM."

"Thank you, Detective," she says, then turns back to me. "What position do you hold at the department, Mr. Wood?"

"I'm a consultant."

"You are hired to…?"

"The young girl has a tattoo of a pentacle on her back. I'm called in to determine if there may be any occult connection to the murder. If so, it may help with clues. If not, it will save time not spent looking for any."

"I understand, thank you." Inspector Omori turns and follows Benny to the body.

Viewing her aura in 3E, it displays the restrained flux of someone guarded. It also conveys a subtle shine of inquisitiveness. My sight quivers. I follow, going back to normal view to conserve energy.

"Have you deduced anything, doc?" Benny asks Hinkle, who's examining the handles attached to her ankles.

"Hard to estimate her TOD. From initial viewing, the body has had some serious work done to it, indicated by a long, vertical incision down her abdomen. The stitching is crude. There are other incisions on her arms and legs. Mostly hidden from view. May be others. These handles," Hinkle lifts a handle just enough to lift a foot, "appear to thread into bone, but we'll need to get her on the table to confirm. Not sure what purpose they serve."

"Excuse me," Inspector Omori says.

Hinkle turns to look at her. "Who are you?" he asks, sounding irritated by the interruption.

Benny makes quick introductions. Hinkle continues when Omori steps forward, raises her hand like a child in a classroom with an immediate answer, and announces, "I have seen handles like that before."

She has everyone within earshot's attention.

"Not on a dead body, but on a, how would you say..." She stops, muttering in Japanese, then continues in English.

"The figures made of wood that have strings attached." Her hand holds an imaginary item that she tilts left and right.

"Do you mean marionettes? Puppets?" Benny asks.

"Yes. But no. In Japan, we have performances called *bunraku*. Puppets, as you call them, but no strings. Some are small, others are as large as people, or larger. They're made to move by more than one person, using handles like that." She points to the body.

I remember seeing that. While studying sigil development near Osaka, I saw one of these performances while walking through a park. The puppets were quite tall, and the puppeteers were all dressed in black, hiding their identities while they manipulated the figures onstage.

The coincidence sends a shiver up my spine, like a shark racing to the surface to snatch a seal. I couldn't see the killer during Theresa's spirit recall because the bastard didn't want me to. The jaws of happenstance chew on my brain as I try to focus on the discussion.

"So, each handle is used to move a limb or the head?" Edward asks with genuine interest.

M.J. Hook

"Correct. The performers remain hidden so the puppets stand out. Sometimes the handles are more complex for more detailed movement. Those," she points, "are a basic placement."

Benny huffs. "Well, it's a lead. Thank you, Inspector. Edward, send me your initials as soon as you document them. Excuse me, Inspector." Benny puts a light hand on her elbow. "I need to chat with Red, then I'll take you down to the station to get you settled in."

"Red?" The inspector looks at me with questioning eyes.

"Sorry. That's Mr. Wood's nickname."

Omori looks me over, starting from my face. She lowers her eyes to my feet, then slowly lifts her eyes back to stare into mine, almost two feet higher. A small chuckle escapes her lips.

"Red Wood. I have family that live in northern California. I visited them a long time ago, and I remember seeing the redwoods. Your nickname suits you."

"So I've been told. It's a pleasure meeting you, Inspector. I hope your visit to Colorado Springs is productive as well as enjoyable." I bow.

Returning the bow, she says, "It was nice to meet you."

• • •

"I'll catch you at High Plains as soon as I get her settled in. I'll get a uniform to tour Omori at the station, then head over," Benny says, referring to the coffee shop in Manitou Springs where we meet frequently to discuss cases.

"Sounds good. Sooner the better. I can text you the girl's info." I'm impatient.

Benny waves me down.

"I'm right there with you, buddy, but solving too soon raises flags. And a text from you is no justification for a warrant. We both know the drill."

I nod to validate my friend's concern, then shake my head with anxious impatience.

"Benny, I saw what the killer did to her."

The detective looks at me with sympathetic eyes.

"I know what you're feeling. You know who he is and want to nail him now. I do too. But by the book. I'm glad there is no supernatural involved, but you know how much I appreciate *your* help. What did Conrad say? 'The belief in a supernatural source of evil is not necessary; men alone are quite capable of every wickedness.' I've learned from you it's necessary to believe in the arcane shit. But truth is, humans can be monsters."

As Benny walks away, I wonder if some arcane shit is about to hit the fan.

M.J. Hook

4

TUESDAY, MIDMORNING

I'VE ASSISTED DETECTIVE Rogers with several cases since we first met four years ago—the night of Benny's wife's murder.

Shit, "murder" is too banal a word for it.

Celia Rogers left life in a brutal, unworldly sacrifice. Her slaughter would have made the strongest man release his bladder and puddle in a piss-pool of fear. We both watched it from opposite sides of the warehouse. Benny, gun drawn and puddled in a corner, was out of his league for action and explanation. He witnessed me handle the demon and its controller, dispatching them both with a similar magical brutality. Benny would have shot me, the strange fire-flinging giant with bushy red hair, just to relieve his anguish. Fortunately, he removed his finger from the trigger when he saw me run to Celia's body on the altar to help her.

Because Celia's evisceration was fatal, I approached Benny. Coiling him calm, I touched Benny's spiritual points to relieve his catatonic fear. And to lower his gun. Then he broke down, crying for his wife.

The revelation of their relationship shocked me, but with only a matter of time before other officers arrived on the scene, my reaction was unimportant. Benny would have to explain to them what had just happened.

A story that would not involve the *real* arcane shit.

Entering the detective's mind, I added a mask to his memory. I hate doing memory swipes, and with the death of his wife, I knew whatever I did would never hold. Too much emotion involved. Once the genuine memory was pieced together, it would crash and burn his brain. The mask I placed was only a bandage to hide it.

To manifest what Benny would tell the officers, I cast a mending spell on the sorcerer's body, making it whole. With my remaining energy, I layered a mental construct on top of the mask in Benny's head. Think of it as splicing new footage into a movie: a mental edit. Instructing Benny to shoot the bad guy sealed the story. Exhausted, I left as flashing lights filled the warehouse windows.

I showed up at Benny's house the day after Celia's funeral and removed the mask from his memory. The visual and emotional reality of what had happened caused Benny to piss himself while we faced each other in his doorway.

Benny was given two months of mandatory leave, so I spent the next few weeks making it my mission to explain the light and dark sides of magic to him. After accepting his recovered memories of that night and watching me do simple spells, it did not take long for the detective to believe.

Benny's eyes were opened to a new sort of *bad*.

"Shit, Red. The people I go after are fucked up. Either in their head or in their heart. I call them evil for what they did, but your shit means adding a fucked-up spirit to the list."

I liked Benny, enjoyed his problem-solving mind, which was bundled with a sense of humor that made me laugh—something I don't do often enough.

The experience in the warehouse, though, led him to a black period. His depression and drinking ended on the day he considered suicide. It took him an intense moment to say "screw this," clear the round, and put the safety on his Glock. He spent the last few weeks of leave sobering up and working out his body to purge his remaining depression and self-pity.

We became friends with similar professional interests. Benny looks for bad guys who kill people, while I look for bad types that kill, curse, or manipulate people using bad mojo.

Benny set me up as an authority on the paranormal. I delivered a truthful, slightly embellished resume of my educational experiences to justify being onsite to examine a murder.

Like this morning.

After leaving the crime scene, I drive down the pass, pull into Garden of the Gods, and pick a parking spot. Finding a nice rock to sit on, I take time to meditate, then think.

M.J. Hook

In appearance, the murder displays no magical influence. So, capturing the killer means following Benny's rules—get the information and reverse engineer it to justify a capture. But the distortion of the neighbor's image concerns me. Had Theresa's spirit been so disheartened by the betrayal to cause what she saw and heard to warp out?

No. She heard what he said in life. She saw and knew him. That means something else was involved.

But what?

My body and spirit are still feeling the bruises left behind by that loud, twanging thrum the sketchy void emitted.

Phone in hand, I tap an explanation of what happened to Donum's private bulletin board. Maybe someone else has experienced the same dynamic or can give me some sort of explanation.

Donum—an international coven of unique practitioners blessed with Gaia's gifts—maintains a private online presence. We consult with each other frequently while accomplishing our coven's mission of snuffing out the rotten eggs poisoning Gaia's spirit, Nature. The light will always have a dark, and the dark makes Donum itch like a nasty rash.

● ● ●

High Plains Brewer is a coffeehouse and café in Manitou that serves a great mug of coffee and incredibly healthy breakfasts all day.

The owner, George Frillman, is a dead ringer for the High Plains Drifter, Clint Eastwood. In looks and voice, the man is the actor's younger twin and No. 1 fan. The shop's adorned with posters from Eastwood movies. On the wall by the cash register are three photos—one of a young Clint Eastwood, signed "Thanks for the coffee, brother. Clint." Next to it is a picture of George, about the same age and in the same pose. Below the pair of handsome prints is a picture of Clint and George, both older, standing outside the coffeehouse with their arms around each other, smiling like two brothers having a joyful reunion.

I've known George and his family for years, my parents having taken me to High Plains for Sunday breakfast frequently when I was a kid.

Once I introduced Benny to the café, he made every excuse to return. The food is delicious and the coffee exceptional, and watching George act like Clint Eastwood is a highlight of my friend's day.

Benny enters, sees me in our usual spot, and rushes over.

"Me, first," he says as he sits down. "I've got an officer doing research on the puppet show angle. I asked Omori to fill him in with details. Hinkle has moved the body and hopes to give me autopsy details later this afternoon. Moving the girl, he mentioned that there appeared to be some tubing material inside the body that allowed the killer to pose her. He determined that the initial rigor TSD estimate would be late yesterday afternoon. We also got some fingerprints."

Josey, George's daughter (named after the Outlaw Josey Wales), walks over to take our order. George named all four of his kids after Eastwood film characters.

"Hi, Red. Your usual?" Josey asks. My usual is a cup of dark roast.

"Please."

"Detective?"

"Benny, please, Josey. I don't call you *waitress*. I'll take the unleaded with cream on the side."

"Sure thing, detect…, uh, Benny. Be right back." Josey leaves.

"When did you start drinking decaf?" I ask.

"Since my doctor told me my blood pressure could be read with a seismometer. I just need to start exercising again, then I can fill up with my regular cup of rocket fuel. And don't tell me you got some magical, natural plant pills I can chew on to fix it. No shortcuts."

"I understand. I admire your stubbornness. Let me know if you change your mind. Now, if you're done, my turn."

"You have the conch."

I slide a piece of paper over to Benny's side of the table.

"The girl's driver's license info. Theresa Barlow. Turned seventeen on September 10. Lives at that address in Woodland Park. I looked it up. Based on my visual, the killer is her next-door neighbor, in the house on the west side. Number 209."

"Gawd, man. It never ceases to amaze me." Benny shakes his head in disbelief. "I wish I could take you on every case we get. Make people think twice about committing a crime in our town."

I knew what Benny would ask next, so I continued.

"Nothing on the neighbor, other than he is pudgy and probably used a tool from his garage to knock her out. I couldn't tell where he did his—" I stop, needing to discuss what I'd seen and heard. "Something weird happened this morning. The view distorted, and I lost control of her spirit.

     M.J. Hook

I saw what he did, Benny, and as it played out, the distortion increased. Benny, this guy's twisted. There might…"

Benny, acting as if he already had several cups of rocket fuel, interrupts me.

"Of course he is. But no details unless I ask. Let Hinkle figure the details out, and we can let the evidence explain it. Hopefully, the prints belong to the killer and are in the system."

The coffee arrives, delivered by Inspector Harold Francis Callahan, aka owner George Frillman.

"I know what you're thinking. 'Did he bring six creams or only five?' Tell you the truth. In all this excitement, I kind of lost track myself." The impression of Eastwood as Dirty Harry is, as always, dead on.

"I'll never get tired of it," Benny says, laughing. "Good morning, Inspector Callahan."

"Detective. And just so you know," still talking as Callahan, "it is now afternoon. Sure hope you're better at catching killers than telling time. Christmas is coming up. Maybe Santa will stick a watch in your holster."

Benny continues laughing while I place a hand on my face to hide my impatience.

"George," I say in greeting, still wanting to finish my discussion with Benny.

"Hi, you two. Solving a crime or just wasting time?"

"A little of both," Benny replies.

"Well, good luck. By the way, Red, the wife was asking about you the other day. Wanted to know if you would like to join the family for Thanksgiving next week," George says.

"Tell her thank you. I'll let her know by the end of the week," I say with dismissive agitation.

"Uh. Ok. Good. Hope you can make it *this* year. You two hungry?"

Benny stops laughing as a text pings on his phone.

"I'll take the Beguiled Bagel, mushrooms on the side. To go." I need to eat.

Looking up from his phone to George, Bennie says, "Think I'll stick with coffee." Then looks at me. "Hinkle's got some stuff to show me. I need to go sooner than later."

George leaves to fill my order.

"Did Dr. Eddie actually say anything? Or is it the standard *must show, can't tell* message?" I ask.

"Same as always. Whaddya think of Inspector Omori? Turns out she's an Olympian. Competed in Judo. She went on and on about visiting the Olympic complex and museum."

"Appears to be competent. Can I finish?" I say, with as much irritability as I can muster without causing a scene.

Benny, preparing to sip his coffee, puts the cup down and gives me a look worthy of a Munch painting.

"Sure, buddy."

Benny doesn't always understand my realm of sleuthing, but I feel an urgent need to explain what I saw. "Look. Something about Theresa's spirit, what that poor girl went through, all the distortion and spiritual distress I experienced. I think there's more to it than just a murder, Benny."

He gives my short, fractured rant a considerate pause.

"Can't say I understand, Red, but I think on some earthly plane of reasoning, I do. Murder comes in all shapes and sizes as society unfolds into numbness. Always hard to figure out any reason for it, only the killer's messed-up justification."

I shudder, remembering the vibrating emptiness of the killer's lack of face and the devastating twang of a soundtrack. Thinking about it reminds me of the pain residue in my spirit that I keep trying to ignore.

"I'm not being clear. This was more than a violation and murder, Ben. I can't explain it, but after everything he did, killing her was probably a blessing. I know that's twisted to say, but she would not have stuck around long had she lived. Putting bracelets on this guy won't be enough. I need to go check him out. Something in my gut screams it's...."

"Red," Benny interrupts, again. I stop him with a palm.

"I know. Your rules, Benny. And right now, your rules suck."

                    M.J. Hook

5

TUESDAY AFTERNOON

RELIEVED AS I am that there is enough information to find the killer, my nerves remain sparked. A bad fuse in my gut keeps blowing every time I think sorcery is involved with the girl's murder. I wanted to say more before Benny left. Even with his minimal knowledge of bad-guy magic, talking possibilities with him helps me troubleshoot my faulty doubts and come to some sort of fix.

I figure once he finds the murderer and thinks magic is involved, he'll text me a 911.

Pulling up to the Crystal Heights gatehouse, I notice Boris sliding open the window, which means my simple wave will not suffice.

Boris VanVoorhies, Crystal Heights's gatekeeper, custodian, and warden, is the most stoic person I've ever known. Tall, thin, and always dressed in a nice dress shirt and tie, he has the personality and constancy of a concrete pillar. The man never smiles, never cracks a joke. Pure business. His aura never changes; his voice and mannerisms are as reliable as the Earth's rotations.

He had a full bush of styled hair when I hired him eight years ago. Now he maintains a precisely shaved power donut around his head. His hole-of-dome normally shines like a freshly waxed car.

I enjoy the opportunity to throw occasional puns his way, attempting to see what a grin would look like on his undertaker face.

"Afternoon, Boris. What's going on today? Did the Crystal Crew misplace your locks?"

"You must mean keys, Mr. Wood?" he replies with literal understanding. "And no, nothing is missing. Just need to give you the Thanksgiving week schedule for myself and the Crew." He hands me a typed columned page. I glance at it and notice one bother.

"Boris, you're here every day. Vacation means taking time off. You never take time off. Do I need to give you a forced leave of absence?"

"No, sir. I have a vacation planned at Christmastime. I'll be visiting my sister in Boston, so I elected to work this holiday to give the Crew extra time off."

The Crystal Crew is Boris's team of efficient minions. They clean the residents' snow-covered roads in winter and assist with several handyman chores needed on the mountain. Because they take care of *his* mountain, Boris takes care of the Crew like they are his family. And, although I own Crystal Mountain, he honors and maintains the 788 acres, ensuring the well-being of all residents, wildlife, and nature.

"Good to hear, Boris." I hold up the schedule. "And thank you for this. I'm heading up for some much-needed sleep."

"You look a bit weary, sir. Hope your efforts are successful."

I roll up my window and drive off. Boris knows my odd hours, but I can't recall ever hearing him comment on how I look. I check the rearview mirror and see dark circles of fatigue under my eyes and write it off as a polite observation.

Scout—my father's 1974 International Harvester Scout II Traveler, and now my enchanted ride—drives up the mountain while I nibble on my bagel and consider thumb-twiddling variations I can perform at home until I pass out.

No need to clean the place. I have always been a creature of anal-retentiveness, rarely leaving a mess. The messes I do leave, my housecleaner, Lois, will come in and take care of. Occasionally, there are odd jumbles of objects left out—feathers, sticks, rocks, piles of ash, or strange powders— that cause her eyebrows to raise, but she knows I enjoy the outdoors.

The one room Lois does not have access to is my bottega.

Opening the hallway door reveals the utility closet where she keeps her supplies. After saying some special words to release the hidden lock, the closet guts slide over and reveal my spiritual sanctum.

I built the bottega, my fancy name for a workshop, directly into the mountain. It, too, remains immaculate, unless I'm working on a case.

             M.J. Hook

Which I am. I need to, but I'm forced to wait.

The shelves built into the east rock wall display various-sized mason jars, metal canisters, sacks, baggies, cans, and tubs. Each one is labeled with whatever ingredients are inside—dried herbs, powders, minerals and gems, liquids, dried parts of animals, insects, and other substances I use to make foundations for certain spells and potions.

Many of the ingredients read like stuff in a witch's cupboard from a horror film: moon salt, acid grip, brain crystal, dying breath, widow juice, dried bat wing. Other items are traditional staples of a caster's pantry: lavender pulp, cinnamon, brindledust, dung fungus, maiden's eye, and dried rosemary, to name a few.

Having a mother with two green thumbs, I learned to appreciate the value of fresh, organic ingredients at a very early age—long before "organic" became a shopping buzzword. I also discovered that I lack the green thumb she possessed. I used my adoption as an excuse. My mother grew many of the plants I used to train with, developing her own fascination with plant properties and preparation for my studies. She taught me things she had learned from her own experiences.

I really miss her presence.

For many ingredients, I have a network of witches, herbalists, and botanists, plus geologists and metaphysical practitioners I contract for specialized materials.

Impatient with waiting, I continue my tour to declutter my thoughts.

The south rock wall has shelves holding my weapons. Assorted knives and clubs, many of them enchanted, rest in slanted foam shells for easy view and grasp. Other weaponry displayed gathers dust but looks impressive. To the right of the shelves hangs a large patterned tapestry that holds no special meaning, other than behind it is the hidden door to my vault. Through it and down several steps is a large, heavily warded cavern where I keep dangerous objects collected from the magical villains I've encountered in my work.

There's a lot of crap down there I need to sort out, but not today.

The west rock, also carved out with shelves, holds the books, scrolls and manuscripts I have collected over my years of learning and dealing with magic.

One shelf holds my personal journals. Since I discovered my powers as a kid, the habit of writing about my experiences has never left me. The older spiral-ring books lie stacked to the left. As I grew older, I used composition books, labeling each one with dates. Once I started taking cases, I came up with titles to label the covers.

Needing something to do, I grab a new book, label the spine "The Odd Baddoon," then date it. On the title page, I write *Theresa Barlow's Baddoon – Weird Distortions*.

I learned early that staying organized saves time when you need to find something in a matter of seconds. If I have OCD issues, fine. I consider it a blessing. My friend Sena, a *bruja* living in Mexico, told me I should use a laptop for all my efforts. I told her that computers crash and need constant protection from my spiritual energy. She told me I could back up the information to an external drive and save it offsite. I told her that if there is a power failure, all I need is a candle, a spell to light it, and my books.

Driving down the mountain to an offsite location is a waste of time, and wasted time can cost lives.

The laptop and cell phone I use are for Donum business and researching important things like coffee, who's playing what music and where in town, or the weather. Besides, if I don't constantly protect my electronics, magical energy can fry them in an instant.

I check my phone to see if anyone in Donum replied to my post.

Nothing.

Flipping to the first empty page, I make notes of the baddoon experience, adding details, including a small sketch of the distorted-void killer I saw. I scribble the edges of the character to enhance the static effect I witnessed. With nothing else left to add, I put the book back.

To keep my thumbs busy, I sort through supplies, checking to see if anything is low enough to reorder or make.

After an hour, nothing screams empty enough to start a list. Jabari does a good job keeping stuff stocked. I wish she was here right now. I could call her, but I know she's sleeping. Waking her up would only cause an argument.

An argument sounds good right now.

Grabbing a clean rag and charmed wood polish, I approach my altar centered in the room. Divided into three sections, the table functions as blessed space to perform spells, as well as an extra-warded surface to protect and contain cursed objects. The central area is a large piece of black laurel where I do most of my casting. Burned into the center is a beautiful wheel showing the four directions, the four seasons, and several runes that

M.J. Hook

help with protection and success. In the middle of the wheel is a stylized pentagram representing the five elements: Spirit, Air, Fire, Earth, and Water.

To each side of the main surface, smaller pieces of African blackwood attach directly to the laurel. Each surface has smaller, runed circles for containment and protection.

The table is spotless, but I clean it anyway.

Behind the altar is a six-foot circle of copper tubing etched with protective symbols and embedded into a polished oak riser. Entwined inside the tube are cords of iron, silver, gold, and bronze. Each piece has special protective symbols and runes etched on their surface as well, adding security for casting summoning spells, or defense if some unlikely force gets past all the wards protecting my cabin. I doubt it could happen, but I've learned doubt kills more often than foresight.

Staring at the copper coil reminds me of the similar tubing the killer void started pushing into Theresa's arm.

The bottle of polish cracks in my grip, the liquid drips between my fingers. Anger at my clumsiness builds. A dark emotional cloud fills my mind, which is never healthy for a practitioner of magic. Emotions are one of the key ingredients that influence the intent of a spell. Negative feelings breed dark results.

I loosen my grip, wrap the bottle in the rag, and notice a minor cut on my hand. My yarrow paste for healing is in the kitchen, so I go to my workbench and grab a tin of bandages. The first one I find shows a picture of Garfield preparing to eat a whole pizza.

The dark cloud diminishes. I smile and chuckle at myself.

"Nothing you can do about it now, Red, so get back to twiddling." I clean up the mess, polish and energize my altar crystals, then recharge all the wards surrounding my cabin.

Still feeling antsy, I remove the seal skin cord around my neck, then uncinch my leather totem bag attached to it. I lay the bag on the altar and remove the contents to check and recharge. Two small vials, one filled with minerals and herbs for warning, another filled for protection. My tattoos gifted to me by Gaia do a great job for both purposes, but it never hurts to have more.

I shake out the three blood beads, two made from the blood of my adoptive parents, one made from the blood of my mentor, Dr. Tinibu— the one who saved me as a kid by figuring out my powers and teaching me how to use them. Tinibu taught me the art of preserving the power of unconditional love inherent in the blood from loved ones. Charged, the beads are like a backup battery for my spirit.

The last item I take out is a small, plastic troll doll. The only item I have from my blood mother, Jenny Blatt. Dad grabbed it from the chest of items she had allocated for me. It's ugly face and mop of red hair is my only link to her. When I bless it, then charge it with power, it keeps me rooted to Gaia. At least that is what I feel, and that impression keeps me grounded.

Done, I decide to visit with Marlow, my rescued pet mountain lion. Goofing with my cat would be a pleasant distraction, but my shoulders slump in disappointment when I discover his empty pen. The kibble I put out last night is gone, so he's probably off hunting rabbits.

Walking a few circles around the front room, I stop and look out the window and admire the red and pink sandstone of Garden of the Gods. The winter sun enhances the brilliant colors reflecting off the rock formation, appearing like some ancient dorsal ridge of a buried dragon.

Taking a deep breath, I realize I have not slept for the last thirty hours and decide to get some rest. A nice dream kicks in just as Mork chimes, "nanu nanu," on my phone. Benny's text tone.

Killers name is Thomas Hutchins, left his prints all over the handles. Girl's neighbor. U nailed it. Getting warrant and squad together to fetch the asshole. Will call when Tommy is wearing bracelets.

Too eager to fall back to sleep, I brew some coffee and decide to give Scout a bath, a blessing and recharge while I wait for Hutchins's capture.

                    M.J. Hook

6

TUESDAY, LATE AFTERNOON, BENNY

"YOU READY?" BENNY asked Omori.

"Yes," she replied, holding her New Nambu M60 up beside her cheek.

The tactical team was in position around the house, with two Woodland Park detectives lined up down the entry steps behind Omori. Three tac officers stood on the other side of the door, one holding a battering ram in his hands.

Benny knocked on the door, firm and loud. Any harder and they might not need the ram.

"Thomas Hutchins, this is Detective Ben Rogers with the Colorado Springs Police Department."

After waiting a too-long minute, Benny banged the door again.

"Mr. Hutchins? We need to ask you some questions about your neighbor, Theresa Barrow." Benny knew that if Hutchins killed the girl and was inside, hearing her name would likely trigger a race out of the house.

Benny also knew the team would never let him make it to the finish line. Checking the doorknob, making sure it was actually locked, he nodded to the brute holding the ram.

"Third time's a charm. Knock it in, Jeff."

Jeff took the battering ram and gave the door a solid slam on the lock assembly. Splinters flew and the stained glass mounted in the center of the door shattered. The tac team rushed in, the first one being the team leader, speaking into his comm piece, letting the rest of the team know their visit had started.

FEAR

Benny, Omori, and the WPPD guys followed, staying behind the team as its members yelled "clear" while searching the rooms. The house was dark, so Benny flicked light switches on in the rooms deemed free of scum.

"This is a pleasant home, Detective," Omori commented, looking at the modern decor of light fixtures, furniture, and decorations. "It would appear Mr. Hutchins is a family man," she said, pointing to a large, framed family portrait in the living room: a man, his wife, a young boy, and a younger girl.

Benny took a picture of the portrait with his phone, then more pics as each room was lit up.

"It may have been a pleasant home, Inspector, but now it's really going to hurt property values."

"In Japan, houses with violent histories, what you may call haunted, are very popular to own."

"Let's just hope that there is only one ghost occupying the place. If this creep killed any more kids, I'll—"

"We've got a body in the basement," came over Benny's earpiece.

"Shit," Benny said.

 M.J. Hook

7

TUESDAY EVENING

I LOOK AT the text from Benny.

Too much to text. Coming up to your place. Damn sure hope you have fixins for a stiff mule

• • •

Grabbing copper cups out of one cupboard, then vodka out of another to make Moscow mules, I cannot ignore the tone of disappointment in Benny's text. When Benny drinks, which is rare, it's to release tension. He normally celebrates a good job by eating waffles, horn blowing the capture, and then going to bed.

Pulling the ginger beer from the fridge, I spend too much time finding the perfect lime to cut. As I grab a knife, my memory flashes to Theresa's arm being sliced open, the distorted void hovering over her body while the twanging chord of sound filled my head.

Snapping out of the moment, I find the lime in my hand demolished, its juice dripping between my fingers onto the floor. Throwing it into the trash, I move to clean up the mess.

Something to do.

Benny arrives, walking through the door with no fear of being turned away by my wards. He wears an enchanted coin on a necklace I gave him to allow access. Pointing his finger at the two copper cups on the bar, he says, "Mule first, then talk." I finish pressing the mint leaves into his cup.

He drinks in several continuous swallows, draining it to replenish what confidence he may have lost during the arrest. Handing the cup back to me for another, he remains quiet while the mule soaks in. Benny walks over to the couch and sits down with a lead weight in his ass.

"Hutchins was dead when we got there, Red. Suicide. Took aluminum tubing, like what Hinkle found in the girl's body, and noosed himself on the basement rafters. Stretched his neck something twisted. Damn."

I let Benny talk, not wanting to interrupt him with the news that I am aware of the tubing in the basement.

"There was a note on a desk in his workshop downstairs, with all the receipts for the tubing, rope, tape… all the shit he used. He also left a bloody pile of guts stinking on the floor." Benny stops to drink another kick from the refreshed mule I bring over.

"What did the note say, Benny?" my impatience gnaws on my nerves like a persistent beaver with perfection issues.

"Yeah, the note." Benny pulls out his phone, calls up his photos, and swipes until he finds the right one. He hands the phone to me. "Here, you read it. I need to use the can."

I zoom in to read the last words of Thomas Hutchins.

I know what I did, but don't remember doing it. I just remember. The stuff I didn't buy is here, her blood is here. So it's real. I am so sorry T. I know your parents will never forgive me. I can never forgive myself.

I read it a few more times, trying to find meaning. Remembers, but doesn't remember? Stuff he didn't buy?

"Fucked-up suicide note," Benny says, draping his coat on the kitchen counter. "We compared the writing with some other stuff we found. Kind of shaky, but I guess when you are planning to turn yourself into a human mobile, it'd be hard to keep your hand steady. It matched enough. Her guts were there. The blood, her blood, covered the floor. We did a quick scan, trying to see if there was any obvious evidence that he had done it before—body parts in the freezer, panties in a special drawer, maybe a necklace of ears—nothing."

Benny finishes his drink and beelines it for the bar.

"Did the guy live alone?" I ask.

"No. Married, two young kids. They're out of town, visiting the wife's parents in California. He flew back early for some work, according to his wife. She's flying home, leaving the kids out there. She knows he's dead and that it's bad; no discussion of the whys and what fors. Not the fucking, fucked-up details. By all the evidence gathered so far, the guy seemed hardworking and clean nosed. Found his passwords in his office. Got on his computer and did a quick check on his history and found no searches on how to kill, gut, and stuff a girl and turn her into a sculpture. He was honest about needing to come back for work. Calendar showed a meeting that he obviously missed earlier today. No porn. No trophy pics that we could find. Nothing." Benny grabs some mint to press into his drink.

"You got a picture of him on here?" I ask, holding up the phone.

Benny sits back on the couch, muttering through his thoughts.

"There's stuff on there you don't need to see. You don't want to see. But yeah, I took a few."

I wanted to tell Benny what I had seen through Theresa's spiritual replay, but he was right. I certainly did not want to view the remnants.

Swiping through his pics, I expect to see a face in silhouette. Instead, I see a normal framed picture of a chubby man surrounded by an attractive wife and two kids. I zoom in on Thomas Hutchins. His body shape matches the trembling void. The build is right.

"Any chance I could go up to the house and look around?"

"Huh, why y'assk that? We caught the guy."

Benny, now standing at the bar, is halfway through his third drink. Mostly vodka, and a splash of ginger beer. His words are becoming slurred, and his volume increases to braying level. Any attempt to explain the distortion I experienced would fall on fuzzy ears.

"Just something I want to check out."

"Not for a coupla days, but I can asss Hinkle's peopless if he saw sometin'. Make me a lisst. Heyyyyy, y'all never told me what viced yer balls s-so bad dis morning."

Benny's body weaves, a subtle back-and-forth that will increase to waves as he takes another pull from his copper cup, drinking to deal with today's events. Something about this case certainly has *his* balls in a vice.

"I'll tell you about it in the morning, Benjamin. Right now, I think it's time to put the mule in the barn for the night. Let's take you back to the guest room. I got an enormous pile of hay for you to lie on."

"Assss-hole. Muleses sleep standing up."

"Good luck with that."

8

WEDNESDAY, EARLY MORNING

BENNY PASSES OUT quickly, giving me time to take a two-hour nap, then eat a loaded salad to restore my power reserve before I climb into Scout to drive up Ute Pass to Woodland Park.

I did not expect too many people to be out in the frigid temperature gawking at the crime scene at three o'clock in the morning, but with official vehicles still parked in the driveway and along the curb, the house remains lit up like a beacon. A few neighbors still stand across the street, gazing at the scene with mugs of steaming drinks cuddled in their mittens and gloves—the self-selected diehards hoping for informational scraps to throw up on the neighborhood social page before going to bed.

I continue to drive by and notice that Theresa's house, sixty yards to the west of her killer's, remains lit as well. Several cars parked out front probably belong to friends and family attempting to console the grieving occupants inside.

The street slopes and curves down, passing dark and less curious homes. I park Scout in front of one house that appears to be asleep for the night and eat a homemade shockra bar for an extra boost of spiritual energy.

Made from an assortment of high-protein foodstuff, powdered amethyst, zinc, and clear quartz, the bar's ingredients are blended in a large pot filled with honey and mashed dates to bind the mixture. After panning the mix, I set them outside during a full moon. Once the moon hits its apex and I cast a spell of healing and energy, the bars are baked, cooled, and bagged.

It's a chore to make a batch every month, but the payoff is worth it.

Especially with the schedule and magic output I tend to maintain.

With no way to walk to the killer's house without the gawkers noticing my presence, I cloak myself with an invisibility spell. My magic battery will keep me hidden for an hour or more if I don't need to use any other enchantments. I pocket a few more bars, just in case.

The tech van backed up to the house is in front of the garage door, which is conveniently open. Even in the low light, I recognize the workbench Hutchins led Theresa to before knocking her out. I step around the evidence tag on the floor next to a stain I assume is blood.

The door into the house is slightly ajar, so I ease it open to see steps going down and a short set going up. I listen to locate voices; the only ones I hear are coming from the basement.

Great, the one place I need to see during my visit.

The steps look sturdy, but for a six-foot-eight, 280-pound giant, being invisible doesn't mean my steps won't cause squeaks and groans on the trip down.

Three vehicles parked out front means at least three techs inside.

Not blessed with enough patience, I remove and hide my boots, then step onto the landing, place my feet on the outside edge of each step, and slowly make my way to the basement. I have plenty of time to listen to the three forensic investigators discuss a date one of them went on the night before. The conversation and their research activities make enough noise to cover the minor groans my steps make.

"Well, I told her that my work means odd, spontaneous hours, so if she doesn't mind meeting for breakfast or my leaving in the middle of a movie, I would be interested in seeing her again," the first technician says. She appears to be the only woman of the three techs working the room, being shorter and curvier than the other two.

I take the last two steps and move off to the other side of the basement.

Hutchins's body is gone. The three techs look like they are finishing up.

Bagged and sitting on the floor in front of the workshop area is the spool of aluminum cable. The room's lit up with the too-bright fluorescents in the ceiling above the worktable. Their obnoxious light enhances the white coveralls the three technicians wear as they putter around the bench on the far wall.

"Good luck with that," Tech Two says. "My dates try to deal with it, but calling at four AM to see if they're up for coffee gets old real quick."

         M.J. Hook

The concrete slab around the workroom is stained red from Theresa's blood. Dried pools remain under the table where her piled entrails had been. A chill wraps around my spine, shaking with the visual of her murder.

"I'm done," Tech Three chimes in. "Let's exit this popsicle stand."

I ignore their prattle and explore the other side of the basement. A man cave of sorts for Thomas, decorated with a large flat-screen TV, mounted on a stand against one wall, facing a ratty couch and a mix of loungers. The other wall displays several framed photos of him with family and several fishing photos of Thomas holding prized catches. In every shot, he's surrounded by at least one friend or family member, everyone smiling and enjoying the moment.

At the back of the room sits a washer and dryer near a door that leads out to the backyard. The walls of the basement are taped and partially painted, but the ceiling still shows rafters except above the laundry area. Several sheets of drywall lean against the slanted wall where the stairs ascend. Thomas appears to have been a do-it-yourself type.

Tech Two closes a tackle box of supplies and announces he's done. He grabs several evidence bags and heads up the steps. The others gather their stuff and turn off the overhead lights. Tech One grabs the bag holding the aluminum and follows Tech Two up the stairs. They leave the light on at the top of the stairs, so I'm not in complete darkness.

I remove my veil and listen while they walk around upstairs turning off lights. Once I hear the garage door closing, I turn on the fluorescents above the worktable and step back and observe the workroom in 3E. Not sure what I am looking for, but the gnawing feeling that some type of magic was involved still chews my gut.

Theresa's blood twinkles throughout the room. The residue of her life's energy still pulses in every spot, pool, and smear. Her spirit departed, now one with the Universe, will cause it to evaporate soon. I dial the sparkles down to look for other signs of magical remnants.

Nothing.

I'm prepared to give up when I spy a small glow of energy up on a rafter above the worktable. Probably the rafter Hutchins used to hang himself on. Careful not to step in any of the blood on the floor, I move to the edge and climb up onto the table's surface.

It's a sigil of some design, marked on the wood. Small, scripted in Theresa's blood, made with a minimal amount of magic. I put out my palm and say "*Sféar tine*," creating a small orb of fire I gently push toward the mark.

In magic, sigils are symbols crafted by a practitioner that represent a desired outcome when activated. Devising a given symbol entails varied and precise constructs for each mark made. The practitioner recites their intent while drawing each line in ink, chalk, or, in this case, blood—the most powerful medium to use. One can place the sigil on almost any surface. However, it will be ineffective until triggered—usually by fire—which releases the magic.

My preference when igniting someone else's sigil would be to draw a protective circle on the floor, creating a magical barrier of containment to sit in, so when I release the magic, I'm certain to remain unscathed. But messing with a relatively fresh crime scene makes magical doodles tough to explain. Benny would know and understand my reasons for taking precautions, but he would still give me a severe tongue-lashing.

Besides, once I burn and release the sucker, there may not be much of a crime scene left.

My tattoos of protection glow. A secure warmth releases around my body. As my burning orb moves closer to the sigil, my totem bag trembles against my chest. I magically shade my sight, like putting a welder's mask on, to make sure any major explosion will protect my spiritual and mortal sight after the sigil detonates.

My fiery orb is close. The first licks of heat burn the mark. The blood used to draw it bubbles. I push the small flame up to complete the burn, and a sudden flash and pop erupts, like a cork from a champagne bottle.

"What in Lamashtu's madness—," escapes my lips as I remove the cover from my sight.

A message appears before me, floating on the air in a twinkling script of spiritual calligraphy.

On your mark Travis Wood

     M.J. Hook

9

WEDNESDAY MORNING

BENNY WALKS INTO the kitchen, and I hear him beeline to the freshly brewed coffee. I'm sitting in my leather chair that faces the wall of windows looking out over the foothills. The view is an ignored background to my thoughts.

Benny sees me and walks over.

"Thanks for putting me up," he says like a chipper squirrel.

"I put you down, mule. Never seen you drink so much, so fast before. This case hit a sore spot?"

Taking a sip, he closes his eyes and ignores my question.

"Your coffee is like ambrosia. What country this morning?"

"It's a Harrar blend from Ethiopia."

Benny enjoys another sip and sits down on the couch.

"Yes, something about this case has the hackles bursting through my collar. Can't explain it, so the only excuse I can come up with is just how weird it is." Taking a larger gulp, Benny dictates a checklist.

"First, the girl, where she's posed and how she's found. If the guy wanted to put on a show, why not just leave her up on the turnoff? Still hidden, but found quicker. We got a break when dragon dude chose that spot to take his piss. The girl's unstuffed, then restuffed with all that tubing shit, then accessorized with table legs. Hutchins's prints in the system for a DWI a few years ago are all over them. Who does that? And the evidence—no attempt to cover it up, like he wanted to be caught. But *no*, he remembers he can't remember, but remembers anyway and gives himself an aluminum necktie." Drinking a few more sips, the wrinkled detective sighs. "That covers most of it. I keep going back to the girl. How he posed her. What the fuck was that shit about?"

"I've got more weirdness to add to yours," I mention, with reluctance.

"Everything on your side is weird, but that's what makes a seven-foot giant so endearing."

"I'm only six-eight, Detective, and there were some things I didn't get the chance to tell you about the baddoon reading. Some things I saw and heard."

Letting Benny know the girl had been alive through most of her violation and torture, I follow up with the distorted details I observed—Hutchins's jerky silhouette and the matching twang that vibrated the visual and racked my body with pain.

"You've never experienced that before?" he asks.

"Never. I've also never lost control of a viewing. Granted, the void discombobulated me, but there was also a spiritual disruption that vibrated through my connection. Kept me off balance."

I take a desperate sip of coffee from my mug before the memory causes me to shake off another traveling back chill.

"Looks like we've both had a rough time with this case. The only good thing is it's over. I need to clean up and get to the station. I promised I would show Inspector Omori how we fill out paperwork here in Colorado. Nothing like sitting in front of a monitor all morning."

"Benny, wait. There's more."

His phone chirps just as I am about to reveal my clandestine visit to Hutchins's house.

"Rogers," he answers. I know it's work-related. It's always work-related.

After a long silence, I notice my friend's shoulders sag with the weight of the world.

"I'm on my way. Have Williams bring Omori with him." Benny pockets his phone, releasing a long, frustrated sigh.

"There's been another body found, Red. Same shit with the table legs."

The news lifts my ass out of the chair and over to the kitchen to drop off my mug and get ready to leave.

"I'm going with you," I tell him as I retrieve my coat.

"Nuh-uh. You can follow. I'll text you the address. I need to apply my game face. Talking to you right now would only delay the application."

M.J. Hook

"Benny, I went to Hutchins's house this morning."

The detective puts his mug down on the table, making sure it is in place before he launches off the couch to meet me toe-to-toe. I've got to give him credit. At just under six feet, he can emote a menacing presence by puffing himself up next to a colossus like me.

"You did what?"

Before I can answer, he shakes his head and hands, as if denying a scoop of horse shit for dessert.

"You know the rules. *Our* procedure. You put this case in some kind of jeopardy…"

"Benny," I interrupt his rant with a voice of force. "I found something. Something dealing with magic. Something dealing with me. Personally."

His blustering stops. The blank stare makes me wonder if he might request a shot of something in his coffee.

"Fuck. I'll drive. You talk."

Benny remains quiet as we drive down the mountain. Considering his anger with what I did last night, and adding a slight hangover and a big pinch of confusing revelation that magic is involved, I know it's best to stay quiet until he's ready to listen. We exit the gate and hit traffic before he greenlights my mouth to speak.

"Start with your visit to Hutchins's house," he says while accelerating the car onto the highway.

Reassuring him that no one saw me, I explain finding the sigil and the cryptic message left for me in the basement. Benny stays quiet as he drives his Pontiac, flashing and blaring, through stoplights, around ignorant cars, and on the interstate shoulder. Taking an exit, we speed into a neighborhood, where he turns off the noise and slows down to watch for ignorant pedestrians.

I finish my discussion with one last thought. "The message stating, *on your mark*, most likely explains why Theresa's body was in the race-start position."

"Shit," Benny says, followed by a quick sigh. Then his interrogation starts.

"First, any idea who's doing this?"

"No. Been racking my brain trying to figure that out."

"Why you? Better yet, how you? You don't know these people, right? Hutchins? The girl?"

"No."

"Then how did Hutchins know you would show up and wave your wand over the scene?"

I don't use a wand, and Benny knows it. But I understand his jest, and I have been wondering the same thing myself. Only a couple of conclusions came to mind this morning while I stared out my window drinking coffee.

"First, I don't think Hutchins killed her." My statement causes Benny to brake the car hard in the middle of the street. The wheels squeal against the concrete.

"Now hear me out, Detective. Think about what he wrote, about not remembering. Sounds like a case of possession on some level. Some spirit takes control of his body, but he's still in there, forced to the back row of his eyes' theater to watch the murder play out. Spirit leaves, then Hutchins is left to face everything he did, or didn't do."

Benny shakes his head and starts driving again.

"I guess it makes sense. Guy gets a spiritual roofie, wakes up, and realizes the violation," Benny says. He slows the car down as we approach a park.

"But again, how are you connected? How does he know you?"

"Because I know you is my guess. I get called to a murder scene and find some weirdness afoot. I'm going to investigate."

"Well, Sherlock, put your hat on and light your pipe. Your second clue is just up ahead."

M.J. Hook

10

WEDNESDAY MORNING

THE SMALL BOY grips the baseball in his right hand, his arm cocked and ready to throw. His left hand, covered with a baseball glove, stretches out in front of his small body. Standing on the outskirts of a playground on the northwest side of the Springs, the posed boy is ready to throw the ball. Only the child is dead, an isolated effigy sculpted in position by an unknown killer. Small green handles drilled into position, just like on Theresa Barlow's naked body, confirm that the same twisted artist is involved.

One difference: The boy's clothed except for shoes and socks. A Rockies baseball cap sits on top of his head, lifted in back by the handle threaded into the skull.

"Jogger spotted him this morning at 5:43. Thought it was a statue. On closer inspection, he realized it wasn't. That's when he called 911."

The officer reads his notes to Benny while I stare at the child using my sight.

The baddoon attached to the small corpse thrashes in anxious spasms; the sack glows with a spiritual intensity radiating fear and terror, much like Theresa's. Standing outside the yellow tape, I can already feel the despair pulsing from it like a cranked-up subwoofer.

"Poor kid. Can't be older than ten. Maybe younger." Benny turns away and looks to the street that runs beside the park. "Hinkle and his crew are here. I can't let you in until they initially process the area." Benny scours the ground, frowning at the wet grass around the body. "Won't be so lucky for footprints."

FEAR

"I need to get in there, Benny. The kid's soul is in turmoil. I need to find out who did this, then set him free." I push against the tape.

"There's no sign of any occult activity. There's no reason for you to even be here."

"Then I'll make a reason."

"No Red, you can't!"

While walking up to the body, I had pulled out my sulfur crayon from an interior jacket pocket and drawn a pentagram on my left hand in case this moment was necessary. Benny reaches out to grab my arm, but he misses as I stretch my palm out toward the cold child. Flaring my fingers, I say, "*bog an áit*," causing the mark to flame and disappear from my hand.

"Red, what did you do?"

"Detective, I believe you'll find a pentagram drawn on the back of the boy's neck. Easy to miss. I'll approach from the backside, and I brought my own booties to wear." From my coat pocket, I pull out a couple of plastic bags that I grabbed before we left the cabin.

"Damn it, Red."

"Just keep Hinkle benched until I'm done."

Benny turns away, mumbling obscenities before calling over an officer to monitor me while he hustles to delay Hinkle's approach.

I slip on my gloves as I approach the boy. The body faces the street some sixty yards away. Behind him are large boulders sticking out from a small hill. The murderer would have brought the child in a vehicle and carried him to this spot during the night, the path conveniently blind to camera surveillance.

I step over the tape and make a straight approach to the boy.

The top of the faux pentagram peaks above the back of his shirt. The glamour will wipe off easily once Hinkle has the body on a table.

Seeing extensions of the heavy aluminum tubing exiting the small heels and sticking into the ground to hold the body in place forces my fists to clench in anger. *This child may have been alive, like Theresa, when the killer started his sculpting.*

I close my eyes and speak a quick mantra for strength before focusing on the small, thrashing baddoon. As before, no signs of magic reveal. No blood.

Squatting rather than kneeling to avoid leaving unneeded impressions in the wet grass, I reach out with my coil. Instead of halting the violent

     M.J. Hook

movement, the baddoon moves like a freshly caught bass trying to return to its water of life.

As I connect to the boy's spirit, I send a wave of calmness. The thrashing stops as the sack vibrates. Sharing our energies, the verve hits. I'm thrust into a nightmare mashup of frightful visuals and sounds—twisted memories of the child's life where mangled faces scream and growl. Rotted arms with clawed hands reach out to grab the boy.

Betrayal often causes distortions of reality when a young soul dies.

I'm already regretting this viewing, but if I'm involved with this boy's death, I need to suck it up and do my job.

I'm here to help. My name is Red. I know you are confused and frightened. I can make things easier, but first, I need to know your name. Can you show me your name?

I fall into his ribbon, the memory of his life. While giving the child spiritual encouragement to bypass the recent horror and find a moment to identify himself, I choose to listen in case his reveal is in words, not images.

A woman's voice fills the vibration. *"Jimmy!"*

Your name is Jimmy. Thank you, Jimmy. I know this is difficult…

But before I can ask Jimmy's soul to take another step for identification, he carries me to the murder, where another distorted void fills the vision, the same twisted sound of a perverted instrument twangs in a single, fractured chord. My body feels severe pain. My spirit hangs in a tight web of distress as I hear Jimmy scream, *"Mommy, no! Mommy, stop! It hurts!"*

A jittering black hand forces an aluminum coil into the boy's bound arm.

"NO-O-O!" The boy's scream breaks through another thrum of the gnarly tone. The painful memory forces his spirit to release a wave of terror through my cord with a god-swat of energy.

Jimmy's baddoon releases, sending his soul off to haunt someplace familiar, an irritating existence on a miserable, unearthly plane. As I watch his spirit soar, my own sinks in defeat.

"Mr. Wood, are you alright?"

I snap back to reality with my butt cold and wet. An officer standing behind the yellow tape looks worried, asking again if I'm OK. Behind him, I see Benny with Inspector Omori, wearing an Olympic Museum snow cap, walking up with Hinkle, who's carrying his metal case. Everyone seems concerned, but not necessarily for me.

"Way to go, Wood. Don't think we have enough plaster to cast your ass.

Can't wait to type your fuck-up in my report. I told you, Rogers, one day this oaf would make a mess of my crime scene." Hinkle waves his hand as if I were a prize on a game show. "Welcome to the day."

"Shut it, Eddie," Benny says.

Standing up is difficult. My limbs shake and ache with the effort. I retrace my steps to get outside of the tape.

"You OK, Red?" Benny asks, his tone tainted with more regret than concern.

I hold up a finger to ask for a moment, shakes rattling my body. My spirit is on a spin cycle and my footing uneven. Ignoring Benny, I approach Hinkle with fierce determination, making his five-foot-six strain to meet my six-eight stare.

Eddie loses his vibrato posture to a nervous chihuahua twitch.

As I grit my teeth to hold back a major rant, a spout of bile burns up my throat and rests in my mouth. Swallowing my words tastes worse than the bitter acid.

"Edward," I say, using Hinkle's formal first name, "I apologize for my mishap. I know you have made several compensations for my contributions. Many, I remind you, have been helpful to the PD. But, I'm afraid my emotions took over my common sense this morning. Type it up if you must, but know I am truly sorry."

Hinkle looks at the boy's body, then back at me.

"I'll keep it out of the report, unless your ass print winds up being an obstacle. Next time, wait until the area's processed before you stomp the scene. You know the drill." The crime scene investigator pauses, looking back at the boy. "This type of shit is enough to rattle anyone's cage. Including mine. Thought we caught the bastard, unless there's a club out there for this type of shit."

Hearing the forensics investigator express perplexity is almost a surprise.

"Thanks," I say, keeping my anxiety in check. I wave to Benny to join me.

"Now I know something is wrong—you apologized to Eddie. Spill it."

"The boy's mother did that to him."

Benny's eyes bulge in disbelief.

"What the fuck? Did you get a location? A name?"

"Boy's name is Jimmy. That's all the ID I could glean. That same voided figure with the plucking soundtrack was present. Jimmy's soul was too

        M.J. Hook

traumatized to control. The hurt. The betrayal. It was too much. Wasn't able to stay connected." My body vibrates. Before it was dread, now it's anger.

Anger is a feeling I can use. Keeping my emotions just this side of rage helps me to focus, allowing my blood to simmer and stir my mind and body to action. I rip the bags off my feet and stuff them in my pocket.

"You need to go have some early morning cocktails at home," Benny suggests, half-joking.

"No, I need to figure out what's causing normal people to do evil shit to innocents. I put that pentacle on the boy as an excuse, Benny. But I'm wondering if it's a reason. You send me any information Eddie finds, and once you figure out where the boy lives, I need to be there pronto."

"It's hard to ID kids, Red. Usually have to wait for a missing report."

"The kid's mom did this to him, so my guess is it will be the father or another relative filing that report. She's probably... aw damn." I stop, knowing that once Jimmy's mother snaps out of her possession, or whatever it is, and realizes what she's done, she will not hang around with the living for long.

Just like Thomas Hutchins.

"Damn what?" Benny, for once, waits for me to finish my sentence.

"Look, she did it, but she didn't. Not with her own free will. Like I'm guessing with Hutchins. Something spiritually and physically strong is forcing these people to kill."

"You said possession before. Could they be hypnotized?" Benny asks.

"No. Even under hypnosis, the subconscious is going to have serious issues with doing something bad, like killing your own child. It would break the mesmeric influence. This is some kind of spiritual sabotage, like possession, but the spirit holding the reins is highly versatile as well as powerful. If it were a common possession, I would have been able to read it on Hutchins or Jimmy's mother. But this void, this presence, blanks out. It's..."

I stop and remember one of the first rules of examining a crime scene.

"Blanks out what, Red?"

Impressed once again that Benny wants me to finish a sentence, I switch to 3E and start walking over toward the crowd of gawkers gathering on the outskirts of the park. Benny follows.

"Criminals like to watch, Benny. Sometimes, they like to observe the crowds admiring their work. This guy is an artist in need of an audience."

Benny understands my line of thought. "Good thinking. You point, I'll catch."

11
WEDNESDAY, MIDMORNING

POSSESSION WILL DISRUPT a normal aura with a visual blanket of spiritual mold. The denser the mold, the more dominant the possession. The gallery of viewers on the edge of the park shows no sign of being infected—normal auras colored with curiosity and concern glimmer around the crowd.

No one appears weighed down with a spiritual mantle of ill-intended fungus.

Benny approaches a couple of officers and points to the neighborhood across the street, letting the uniforms know they will need to go door-to-door and ask if anyone saw or recorded anything this morning. Still using my sight, I look at the privacy wall enclosing the homes where he's pointing, the backsides facing our direction, when I notice a dark, twisted anomaly standing on the back porch of one home.

I continue turning, forcing myself not to stare. A second glance shows me an abyss in the shape of a man holding a mug of coffee. The emptiness against the colorful view looks like a black hole in a vivid galaxy of animated color.

My head twist continues and stops at the park's public restroom.

"Hey, Benny," I say, grabbing my stomach to show discomfort, "keep your eyes on me. I spy with my eye a bad guy." Benny wants to whip around but maintains focus on me.

Pointing to the restroom, I say, "Gonna hit the head, open the door and disappear. This thing is not in your realm of jurisdiction to capture. I'm hoping it won't see through my veil and know I'm after it."

FEAR

"Shit" is Benny's response.

"Exactly," I reply and two-step it to the building, still clutching my gut like I'm holding back a flood.

The door's locked, so I pick it with a simple Air spell, then swing it open. The door blocks the thing's view of me as I walk in, disappear, and then step back out before it closes.

Trying to maintain 3E while under a veil uses a lot of energy, especially after it was damaged by the loud thrum in Jimmy's baddoon. I switch sight to normal and see a man standing on the back deck, dressed in a bathrobe and holding a mug. His morning hair sits on top of a face that is smiling at the scene in the park. His eyes glance to the restroom I am supposedly relieving my guts in and do not follow me as I run across the street and up the grass strip. I hide behind the neighboring wall.

I jump, catch the lip of the wall, swing my leg over, and then lie flat for a moment, switching views to get a read on the *Void*.

Need to call it something.

As I stare at the static emptiness drinking coffee, the name sticks. There is a small undulation of color in the man's aura, which grows and shrinks. The possessed vessel is probably trying to regain control, but the Void appears to put a lid on the man's spirit with very little effort.

When I switch back to normal view, the goofy grin on the man's face pisses me off. The Void is obviously happy with his artwork across the street. I wonder if the man's spirit is aware of the artist's efforts. He continues to observe the forensic team, occasionally looking over to the bathroom to see if I've finished my paperwork inside. His grin spreads wider.

Asswipe may be a better name for this arcane creep.

I stand up on the wall and walk toward the grinner's backyard. Just past the privacy fence dividing the yards, I lie down and swing my legs over. After a short hang time, I drop and station myself in the yard's corner.

I thank Nature it didn't snow last night, so the ground won't show my enormous feet leaving prints. But it is wet, and the grass is long enough that stepping through the yard could telltale my approach. I turn slowly and face the grinning figure.

I have no plans for how to snare this thing—I don't know what it is exactly. But capturing it should be a Containment 101 lesson. It's an evil spirit or demon of some type, so sticking it in a containment field should give me time to hold it, identify it, release the vessel, then dispatch it with

     M.J. Hook

an added spell of hurt to make a point.

If only magic like this was really that easy.

Taking large, quiet steps, I walk up the side of the yard beside the fence and am out of the Void's view. The deck blocks our lines of sight. Noticing that the space between the slats could still show my approach, I stay veiled and walk slowly across the lower patio until I am directly under the man's figure.

The next part is tricky, but pulling evil spirits out of human vessels has been part of my repertoire for years.

Removing a small notebook from my jacket, I pull the top page from the clipped papers inside. Unable to see the containment sigil drawn on the paper, I know the first five pages are prepared for just this purpose. I lick the backside of the paper and stick it on my palm, lifting my hand and aiming it just under where the human vessel stands.

Next, I pull my phone out, making sure it's silent, unveil it to see the screen, and text Benny:

Make some noise

I wait, but my anger at what the shit stain above me has done to two innocent kids makes it difficult to stay calm. Blasting it to oblivion would be a quick solution, but since it currently possesses an innocent bystander, I chill my fury.

Within a minute, I hear Benny yelling at the crowd to get back, then a cruiser siren turns on to enhance his orders.

I whisper *"bog in airde,"* lighting the paper and activating the sigil to manifest. The circle of containment glows in midair above my palm. Spreading my fingers enlarges the pattern, allowing me to size it directly under my target.

I push the spell up. The encircled runes float just below the decking.

Quietly, I say *"ceangail agus teacht le chéile."* My words allow the energy to course through me and transfer the runes through the deck.

As the pattern emerges topside, I ignite the spell, evoking a containment wall around the circle. I hear a satisfying scream as the mug hits the deck.

The siren stops as I run out from below, dismiss my veil, and rush up the steps to the upper level.

Switching to 3E, I see the Void pressing its empty hand against the restraining walls of my trap. Normally, touching the sides would inflict a type of electrical shock to whoever or whatever's contained, but the Void just looks at its empty, sketchy hand and starts laughing.

"You play a great game of catch, Travis," it says in a voice backtracked with the strange twang I heard in Theresa's and Jimmy's baddoons. "I didn't expect you to catch the ball so soon."

"What are you?" I demand, not wanting to join in the wordplay related to the dead boy's pose.

The Void squats down, leaning its back against the charged field.

"Travis, Travis. I should take offense, but I guess I'm considered a *thing*. Not a person. Certainly not a place. But I come from a place, Travis. A place a long way away from Col-o-ray-do. Came all this way to meet you, Red. Mind if I call you Red?"

The subtle twanging noise plays as he speaks. With every fourth or fifth word, the chord plays and sends a shudder through my body, touching the edges of my spiritual core. It hurts. I turn off my 3E, and the noise ceases. The robe is sizzling where the man's back rests against my containment wall. As the Void leans the head back, the hair sizzles and sparks, ash floats around the crown. The eyes look up at me, wide and content. The stupid grin glares with perfect white, pearly teeth.

Stupid discussions take time—time needed when trying to escape. I've monologued myself out of several situations, usually by playing into the bad guy's ego. This thing knows me, and as much as I want to learn the how and why, it's already murdered two kids to get my attention. It's got me in spades. Now it's time for some arcane justice.

"Enough with the talk. Time for you to no longer exist," I say, preparing for a quick exorcism and spirit-annihilation spell combo.

The man stands up, rigid and without effort. A patch of his hair is on fire, the front of his robe collapses around his hands, and the back material burns to floating ash. The smile is gone, and his eyes roll up into empty black orbs. I switch back to 3E to monitor the Void's movements. The empty silhouette vibrates inside the containment.

"You don't want to do that, Red. Tear me out of this mortal and my hooks will rip his body and spirit to shreds. Try to dismiss me, and all that'll remain of poor Wayne here is a pile of mortal goo inside a pocket of charred pelt. Besides, we're not done playing."

As it talks, its chords reverberate through me. My containment spell

     M.J. Hook

shakes as its voice gets louder. The twanging of misfit tones bangs against the protective walls. My legs tremble as if the bones inside my hips and legs are shattering—an earthquake within my stance. I fall to my knees and attempt to cast a reinforcement spell on the containment. I'm shut down again as it speaks, playing another spiritual chord of destruction.

"You see, Red, I've got many games for you to play. To test your will and shit. See what activities push your panic button. Tickle your terrors. Wobble your willies. We've just met, and you want to kick me out of your sandbox? Too bad for you, 'cause I kick back. Hard."

One last blast of vibration rocks my soul, pulling me down to my side, causing my arms to fail. I try to cast more power into my containment, but my body locks up. My spiritual senses shut down. My sight returns to normal viewing. It's quiet as I watch my spell crumble apart beneath the man. The deck dissolves in a circle as his body falls through and hits the pavement below. I scoot myself to look over the edge, then hear the voice from the Void.

Above me.

I look up and see a distortion in the air. It takes effort to switch my sight back on. The Void is there, like a ratty scrap of black carpet. A large, floating, single cell of dark emptiness.

"Do you like my song, Red?" The Void pauses. A small ripple of sound fills the air. "I know what we can play! You'll love this one, Red. Let's play hide and seek. I'll hide."

The Void floats over the wall toward the park. I watch it through the slats as it spins itself into the body of a woman spectator across the street. She grabs the man next to her and locks lips in a passionate kiss. Then it twists out of the surprised woman, jumps, and spins inside an officer near the crime scene. He puts his hands on his knees and gyrates his butt against another officer next to him. The shocked officer staggers back and trips over the tent they are putting up around Jimmy's posed body. As the tent collapses, the Void slams into Jimmy's body. The lifeless form lifts and falls, causing Eddie Hinkle to stagger and collapse on his ass.

The Void stops in midair, and I swear it gives me a wave with a static black corner before heading over the rocky hill. Unaware but confused spectators gab in its wake.

I lay my head down on the deck in defeat. Why didn't it just kill me? What am I to it? What the fuck is it?

Questions fill my head, each one causing a tremor to rack my body with pain. Normally, I would be angry. And I am. But something else is knocking my anger to the side.

One last uncomfortable thought, one last shake of pain before I pass out.

I'm terrified.

12

WEDNESDAY, LATE MORNING

"PLAY GAMES? THE fuck you say." Even over the phone, Benny's voice sends jolts of pain through my head, his frantic tone lethal to my already aching eardrums.

"Look. You see me up here?" I wave my hand again, still too shaken to stand up. "You need to send an ambulance. This guy just fell about ten feet, and he ain't moving. Neither am I, but I'll be gone before they arrive."

"I'll come get you. I'll let everyone know I'm going to start the canvas and will start with that house. Say I found the back gate open. Meet me there, and I'll help you to the car. *Then* I'll call an ambulance."

Butt-dropping down the steps is rough, but I am walking by the time I hit bottom. The man, Wayne, has a pulse, but his legs are in terrible shape. A bone sticking out of his right shin, his left leg broken and bent the wrong way at the knee.

I meet Benny at the gate and tell him to go on and help the guy as I veil myself with what energy I can conjure, make it into the back seat of his Pontiac, and pass out again.

I wake to see us driving up the switchbacks to my cabin.

"You've been unconscious for a while," Benny says when he hears me groan.

"Yeah, seemed appropriate. Did you get Wayne an ambulance?"

"He's alive and will probably spend the next year dealing with surgeries and therapy. He's gonna have to make up his own story about what happened. That hole in his deck was beyond my imagination to come up with a theory for. Almost home."

Once I get inside, I head to the kitchen to eat a shockra bar and pour a cup of coffee. Benny sits down and listens to my story about meeting the Void.

"Has anything you've ever encountered broken out of one of your circle thingies before?"

"Nope."

"Has anything you ever fought before brought you down like that?"

"Nope."

"You got any idea…"

"Nope." I interrupt his interrogation. "No idea what I'm dealing with. No idea what games it wants to play, and no idea what it will do next or why. The only thing I know is that it's here to mess with me, and unfortunately, it's using you because we're friends and you deal with murdered folk."

"Well in that case, partner, you and I…"

"Nope," I interrupt him again. "There is no you and I. We need to distance ourselves. I don't want you involved with this shit. If there is *another* murder like the other two, you let me know, but I will not come to the crime scene with you. I'll be around, but on my terms. My rules. You understand, Detective?"

Benny stares at me like I just broke his favorite toy, undecided whether to beat me over the head with it or start leaking tears.

"This thing, this Void, will continue to use you to get to me. It may hurt you to hurt me, and I don't want, or need, to worry about that. Better we keep a distance."

Benny bows his head, then nods it with obvious regret.

"I'm picking up what you're throwing down, Red. But we still need to communicate. I may be unable to arrest this thing, but you *know* I can help you figure out how to hunt it. It may be supernatural, but it *definitely* sports an ego. All egos need to feed. Let me at least help you figure out how to put it in your sights."

I smile at my friend, then nod.

"Agreed, just as long as you stay out of my sight."

He wants to talk ideas, and all I want to do is sleep. I tell him to leave and that I will call him later.

With little sleep the night before and my body feeling like it survived a drop from an airplane onto concrete, I look at the wall clock and notice

M.J. Hook

it's only ten-thirty in the morning. Grabbing a jar from a kitchen cabinet, I twist off the top and take three healers—pills magically made for immediate healing of spiritual and physical aches and pains. Chasing them with several glasses of water, I can already feel a kick of relief.

I head to my bedroom, take off my boots, and collapse on the bed. Thoughts of my encounter with the Void invade my thoughts, making it difficult to rest. I hear soft, familiar footsteps walking down the hall. A furry head noses itself under my hand as I scratch Marlow's ears. My 150-pound mountain lion purrs as he licks my hand.

Sharing his company and spirit is soothing. He lies down beside my bed, and we both fall asleep after a hard morning hunt.

• • •

"Hey, Teach? Red? Oh, Mr. Woo-ood!"

The voice forces my eyes open to see Marlow crouching at the corner of my bed, growling in his playful mountain lion way, preparing to jump on Jabari—my apprentice, student, and decent sparring partner—who is flat against the wall by the door. Her eyes, wide open and beautiful on her ebony face, alternate their stare from Marlow to me and to the door.

"I thought your name meant brave," I mutter, sitting up.

"It does, and I am," she says as Marlow whips his tail, preparing to attack her.

"You're also born under a rich Fire sign, which makes you a warrior."

"Teach, I'll throw down with your mountain cat here, but I know if I hurt him, you won't be happy." With that, she straightens up and prepares to cast a spell at my kitty.

"Marlow, chill," I say, and he relaxes, turning to me with a *yeowza* roar for breaking up his playdate.

"Look, Teach. I like Marlow. He's a cool pet, but playing with him is hard. He bites, scratches, and makes me bleed. And that's just when I feed him."

Bringing myself up to sit on the edge of the bed takes effort. My legs feel as if I climbed Everest this morning. The muscles in my stomach and groin feel like I fell off the peak and hit every crevasse on the way down. When I switch to 3E, the auras from Jabari and Marlow glow without glitching, but my spiritual senses overall give me a wave of off-world vertigo.

To hide my discomfort, I grab Marlow by his cheeks and speak baby talk to his majestic face. "We're just gonna have to teach Jabari-boo how to play with you. Ain't we, pal?" I scratch his body as he rolls into mine, pushing me back down on the bed.

"I thought we had a lesson now. Why are you still in bed? You're always ready for a…" Jabari's rich South African English takes on a teenage trill as her eyes blossom with anticipation. "You got a case, don't you? What is it? Give me the details."

I push Marlow away. He purrs as he rubs up against Jabari's long legs, pushing her back against the wall. She gently grabs his tail and lets it travel through her grip.

"No," I say, standing up, thinking how nice it would be to start the week over.

"Aw, come on. You said I'm ready."

"I said 'almost ready' and that we would explore the idea after you receive your Third Mark blessings."

When Jabari Le Roux attained her spiritual sight, her ajna, she was four years old—early by most reckonings. Normally, viewing Nature in its full glory is stimulus overload for a child. But for Jabari, it was like having an internal tablet to play with. She learned on her own how to turn it on and off. Once she told her parents that she could see and talk to dead people, they contacted Dr. Tinibu, my original mentor.

He taught her the preliminaries and traveled with her around the world to learn from others, much like he'd done with me. Jabari took to the craft like a fish to water, excelling in many disciplines and arts. After her First Mark blessing—the first ceremony, when an apprentice is buried to await tattooing of the Elemental Runes of Identity by Gaia (the Mother, Mother Earth… she goes by many names)— Jabari arose with the Fire blessing predominant. That's fairly common, but her markings labeled her for defense, which is rare.

I bore similar marks after my first blessing.

Soon after she received her Spiritual Runes of Identity in the second ceremony of blessing, Dr. Tinibu brought her to me for training. Once a student, now a teacher, I took on Jabari as my apprentice in the art of magical fighting and protection in the name of Gaia.

Some days, it feels like the fighting she's excelled in is the art of verbal warfare.

"I am ready, Red. The other night I knocked you down so hard that the remaining leaves on the aspens fell, tucked, and rolled to safety." Just over six feet, the 19-year-old is built like an industrial smokehouse—framed in muscle, reinforced with shapely curves, with a foundation in magic that challenges my knowledge frequently. She could slaughter, skin, cut, smoke, and serve up any side of badness to cross her shadow. But…

"You don't have the experience yet. And this case… this case may even be above my pay grade."

We walk to the kitchen and prepare a late lunch while I tell her everything that's happened since she left me rolling in a pile of golden leaves two nights ago.

After popping a cherry tomato in her mouth and chewing on it along with her thoughts, she dishes out an idea. "Sounds like a trickster spirit. I mean, the thing wants to play games with you, Red. And to break your containment circle, it's got some major mojo to throw down."

I slowly smile. "You may be right, Jabs. Maybe you *can* help me with this case."

Her magnificent smile shines with joyous anticipation as she wags her butt like a dog expecting a treat.

"Start researching trickster entities. High-level spirits that have some immunity to low-level magic, possess rather than shape-shift. Adorn themselves with a high-frequency soundtrack capable of subwoofering a person's bones to jelly."

Her wagging stops. She arms herself with a salad fork, her smile flips, and a vicious tongue-lashing begins.

"That's not what I meant by helping, and you know that. I want to get out there and fight."

My sigh is exaggerated but warranted.

"What is the first rule in fighting, Jabba?" She hates it when I call her that.

My apprentice knows when to curb her emotion and refocus. Putting down her weaponized fork, she takes a deep breath and replies, "Know your enemy."

"Exactly. This Void has murdered two innocents. Three if you count the neighbor, and maybe four if Jimmy's mother follows pattern. Brutally using the victims' trust to trap them, then inflict violation, pain, and death. People will remember the possessed hosts as killers, and that is all kinds of wrong. You will help me do the research and figure out ways to put this thing down.

Understand?"

"I do. And you're right."

"Thank you," I say, then take another bite of salad.

"Just... just, please consider having me along when you throw down with this scab of darkness. OK?"

I add a small smirk to my chewing, which brings the magnificent smile back to her face.

"That's right," she says, picking up her fork and twirling it like a well-balanced knife. "Know your enemy and where its butt is so you can kick it with an ass-driving boot of magical righteousness." She spears her salad and nails a healthy bite of confidence.

Being a teacher has its blessings and curses, but when your student displays enthusiasm doing necessary grunt work for a greater good, that's pure magic.

     M.J. Hook

13

WEDNESDAY AFTERNOON/EVENING

WE BOTH HEAD to my bottega. Jabari takes her laptop to her corner, where she has her own table to mix and practice potions and spells and, like right now, do research.

While she boots up, I grab several books from my shelves that I hope will assist in her search. Setting them down next to her, I grab the journal I filled in earlier and complete my notes about everything that happened this morning. Finished, I write a phone number on a scrap of paper.

"Go through my notes and merge them into a *very* short summary. That's Basil Rusu's number in Amsterdam. It's past his bedtime, so he's probably awake. You can call, but he won't recognize your number, so he won't answer. Introduce yourself in the message, mention my name, and tell him you are doing research for me and need his all-knowing help. He won't call back, so call again and repeat. If he doesn't call back, start texting."

"Who is this guy?" She asked, looking at the number as if it were a dark hole.

"He's the Research and Acquisition Director at the Jaager Library in Amsterdam. An incredible storehouse with documentation and information that dates back long before Khufu wore diapers. Just make sure you let him know you're working with me. I am one of their principal benefactors, so I get special treatment. Give him your summary and let him go nosing around his shelves."

Jabs looks up, cocking her head like a puppy that just heard a loud fart.

"Benefactor, huh? I know you don't enjoy talking about how wealthy you are…"

"Correct. I don't. Now focus. Give Basil a call and hound him like a Baskerville. Once he gets the scent, take a whiff yourself and see what you can hunt down. The sound the Void releases is on a spiritual level but can still be noticed when the sight is off. I need your help to buffer that crap and put it down before anyone else gets hurt."

"Yes, sir," Jabari says.

I turn and walk to the door, waving my hand. "And if you hit anything near a bullseye…"

"I know. Call you."

"You rock, Jabari. Thank you."

"Where are you going?"

"First, I need to realign myself with meditation. Then, over the hills and far away, to Grandmother's house I go," I reply.

• • •

The Oracle, the woman I call "Grandmother," is one of three Ancients I have met personally. Our first meeting was during a mission to rescue her in New York City. Her family, which belongs to the Ute Mountain Tribe, asked for my help to retrieve her from a warlock and his business associates who had kidnapped her, enslaved her, and forced her to use her all-seeing talents to make money—one of the many elements of power that turn people, magical or not, to the dark side.

Breaking through the warlock's wards was easy. We found her and her captor in a luxurious underground suite. While I took care of the wielder of dark stupidity, Kog Lehi—the Ute warrior who recruited me—picked up the frail body of the Ancient and carried her to safety. In the alley behind her prison, she asked Kog to let me carry her into the sunshine.

As the firsts rays of light touched her body, the emaciated figure in my arms filled with energy. She transformed from a mummified waif into a beautiful, elderly dame in her eighties.

"Good morning, Grandmother," I said.

Patting my arm, she smiled. Her eyes, appearing brown at first, turned a bright crystal blue as we stepped fully into the sun.

"It is, my child," she said. "It's been too long since I have felt Father's touch upon my face. Thank you, boy. Take me home."

Home for her had been a small house in Victor, Colorado. But she had been captive for several years, so, fearing for her safety, her family placed her in the penthouse of the Golden Eagle Hotel and Casino in Cripple Creek.

I step off the elevator, the wards protecting the floor open for my welcome. Kog greets me at Grandmother's door. He is one of the few people I look up to, only because he is four inches taller than I am. His biceps are probably four inches larger, too. He crosses his massive arms and gives his guns a small flex to welcome me. His face, lined with scars from fights he refuses to discuss, tilts down to give me a gander. The single long ponytail hanging over his arms is as black as the dark eyes boring into me.

"Hey Kog, you look healthy. Whatcha benching these days?"

"My father's tractor," he says. Tipping his head to the door to her suite, he continues, "She's expecting you."

"Of course she is. Thanks, brother. Good catching up with you." A smirk forms on Kog's lip. The guy is tough, formidable in any situation that requires a physical altercation. And though he might fight like a grizzly, I know he has the heart of a teddy. The man keeps pictures of his beautiful family in his wallet, which he is happy to show you while still displaying his resting going-to-fuck-you-up face.

I step into the Granny Suite and smell the distinct aroma of white sage. The front room is sparse, with only a rug and two large pillows in the middle of the wooden floor. The drapes surrounding the large window are open, allowing the last of the day's light into the room. I walk over and look out at the former gold mining town, now a hub for mountain gambling and entertainment.

"You bring trouble with you today, child." The soft voice touches my ears with a chilly whisper of caution. I turn and see the Oracle sitting on a pillow. She's good at masking her presence. Even with 3E, I would struggle to notice her.

Her dark hair, tied into two braids resting on an ample chest, has fewer strands of silver than I remember. The light from the autumn sunset dances on the reflective highlights of each fold in her silky, turquoise robe. Her eyes need no light to shine as they stare at me with a bright, celestial blue gaze.

She offers the other cushion for my seat, which is not my first choice in chairs, but I accept with a small grunt of effort.

"It's nice to see you, Grandmother. And yes, trouble."

"You only visit when you have an issue to discuss. One day, come and visit when you have no burdens. We could enjoy a delightful meal of elk steak together." Her smile is warm and inviting. After returning from New York City, she insisted I visit often, which I did at first. She claimed my aura was grand to observe, but my past and future hid from her sight. A refreshing anomaly in her life as a seer.

A frustrating disappointment to me as an adopted child.

"You're right, and I apologize. It's rare that I don't have a couple of burdens weighing on my shoulders. The one I carry today…"

Her hand raises to stop my voice as her eyes glow with the azure light of divine observance. My presence becomes a captive to her stare.

"Something has changed about you, Travis. I now see glimpses of your moments before and those to come. The veil that keeps you in umbra, hiding your past and future, is now fractured. The entity you have encountered is responsible." She stops but keeps her raised hand in place. Tilting her head to one side, she draws out her silence, then tilts her head again, as if listening to conversations. The radiance in her eyes increases, filling the room with a soft glow of blue.

"It has followed you here. My miners have seen it. Drawn to it, they are. It is playful. It is evil. Its purpose… another's." She finishes as the glow from her eyes dwindles, blanketing the room in common dusk.

Her raised hand moves forward and touches my forehead, touching my ajna. I feel her dive into my spirit.

Since she could not read me before, this news gives me a glimmer of hope and fear at the same time. The mask that has kept my birth, my lineage, in shadows has always chafed my ass. Same thing with my future, cloaked from any type of scrying.

Hearing her convey this news fills me with expectation as her touch propels me into a light trance. Her spirit probes mine for a brief, gentle moment. As she finishes, I feel my pores open, establishing a film of sweat upon my whole body, as if I just broke a fever.

"You must leave, child, and take the cursed thing with you." Her announcement is calm, without threat. I had expected a reading about myself, but that will obviously be for another visit. I know she means business.

"I will, I promise. But can you tell me what it is? It has done evil things, and I need to stop it before it hurts anyone else."

The Oracle takes a deep breath, closing her eyes on the inhale. As she exhales, her lids open as two frosted orbs of fatality. This is not a good look for her.

                         M.J. Hook

"It is ancient. It is a piece of original chaos. Darkness gives it strength. Fear gives it life. You… give it purpose. Deny its intent."

The sun sets as if a bucket of cold water was dumped on its last bit of radiance. The outside flares with neon lights from the casinos and theaters, casting the Oracle's room into a kaleidoscope of noxious, shifting color.

She blinks once, returning her eyes to their normal crystal blue.

The door to the suite opens. I turn to see Kog's silhouette fill the entrance while blocking the outer light with his bulk, which saves me from a glaring retina shot of pain.

"Time to go," he announces with a steady growl.

"Wait." I turn, wanting more answers, but Grandmother has already left her pillow.

"What, no goodie bag of bones?" I say to the empty cushion.

• • •

Riding down the elevator, I consider the charm of information the Oracle dangled before my spiritual eye. I've known her for almost eight years, and in all that time, she could never get a bead on me. Then today, she threads the insight, a sphere of my past, on an alluring bracelet, then refuses to hook it on my wrist.

The doors slide open, the muffled cacophony of gambling noises coming from the casino side of the building. I head to the hotel lobby, then recall the mention of her miners.

When the Oracle returned from captivity, her sight violated by men and women of power to gain more power, she considered revenge as a morning-after pill. Moving to Cripple Creek, she discovered an abundance of gold miner and gambler spirits hanging out around the casinos. Using her ancient magic, she interviewed several of the spirits, helping many to wind their way to the Universe, but others who wished to stay, she recruited for what she called "justified possession."

Covertly inviting many of the men and women who abused her talents to a Rocky Mountain gambling getaway, she had the spirits possess and milk them for major losses, mostly through donations to local tribal charities. For the few she really despised, after depleting their accounts, she offered the press compromising Cripple Creek "Thank you for visiting" photos that wrecked their prestigious reputations. Revenge complete, she now allows the miners to find and possess other mortals with bad intentions for a gentle fleece or a major flock. Punishment delivered, local charities get a boost, local businesses get a boost, and the miners' hungry spirits are satiated.

It's wrong, but after Kog showed me dossiers on the particular entities the miners put their axes to—wealthy pedophiles, unscrupulous lawyers, scoundrels in business—I backed off. No deaths, no one innocent hurt, and probably several innocents saved in the future. I let it go.

The Oracle claimed her miners were aware of the Void. The damn thing followed me here to Cripple Creek, which worries me as much as it pisses me off. If I find one of the miner's souls, maybe it can tell me what the Void is. Even show me where it is.

When I turn back toward the casino, Kog and a few of his larger native brothers greet me with a wall of Red Rover.

"She told you to leave," Kog says, with no invite to come over.

"Look Kog, she told me a lot of things but nothing to help. I'm leaving with more questions than answers. So, I promise not to bother her anymore. I just want to visit with one of her minion miners." I hold my position, keeping my finger in a fist, rather than poking Kog with it on his massive chest.

"Already causing problems in town. You leave, problem leaves. You come back when it's gone." Kog pauses a moment, then relaxes. "Please."

"Well, if you're going to be polite about it." I turn and walk out, deciding that a throwdown with friends is not on my agenda. Big friends, too. Plus, I'm a guest in their house. The only thing accomplished with a fight is a big bridge burned and another point for the Void.

Stepping into the parking lot, I make my way to the back of the lot where I parked Scout. A few cars away, I hear Scout honk, his way of letting me know that something's not right.

I spy with my magic eye four hooligans looking at my ride as if it's possessed. None of the figures appear as the Void, but listening to their conversation, I'm guessing the floating parasite of mayhem is involved. I keep my sight active in case it shows up.

"Don't lean on it. You'll set off the alarm again," Hooligan One says, wearing a sweater that looks stitched together with navel lint.

"Right. This piece of shit is too old to have an alarm system. Probably just bad gas," Hooligan Two replies, his bald head adorned with a pair of stupid turquoise earmuffs.

"Hey!" I shout, just to get them to stop talking crap about my ride.

M.J. Hook

All four look up and see me as I pass under one of the lot lights.

"Guy said he was big, but that dude is huuuuge," says Hooligan Three, wearing a snorkel coat probably snatched at a shady surplus store. "I don't know, Dex."

"Shut up. The guy paid us good money to put this guy down. More when we're done. Get ready." Hooligan Four—Dex, obviously the sad wardrobe gang leader—is a head taller than his buddies and dressed in a mismatch of workout sweats and a puffy winter coat. "We'll start with his piece of shit car, then finish with his face."

They really shouldn't talk about Scout like that.

14

WEDNESDAY NIGHT

NAVEL LINT AND Earmuffs stand on each side of Scout. On the driver's side, Navel Lint holds a crowbar, while Earmuffs keeps his hands in his coat pockets on the passenger's side. Snorkel Coat, gripping a hammer, and puffy Dex, holding an attitude, both meet me behind Scout's tailgate.

Dex, who looks like he might have some hardy muscles under his inflated coat, laughs and leans against Scout's rear end.

"Mister, you must've really pissed off the wrong people," he chortles.

Before addressing these dopes, I look around, hoping to glimpse the Void. If cold, black, and empty is watching, it's out of sight. I turn off the 3E and stare at Dex.

"If you're looking for help, dude, ain't no one going to save your ass." Dex's confidence in his band of ill-dressed hooligans is obvious. He appears to be the only one with a puffed chest of assurance. The other three keep their eyes on him, not me.

"Who paid you?" I ask.

"Nonaya business, dumbass," Snorkel Coat chimes in, pissing Dex off enough that he slaps the arm holding the hammer, which falls to the pavement with a loud, embarrassing thump.

"Shut up, idiot," Dex says.

Earmuffs, on the passenger's side, pulls a screwdriver out of his pocket. He adds a big grin to his bald head as he brings the point near Scout's door.

"Enough of this," I mutter, then shout, "Scout!"

Scout's horn honks like a trumpeting elephant. The lights flare bright as both side doors of my ride open fast. Navel Lint gets a solid hit. The crowbar in his hands pushes up and slams into his face. Blood erupts from his nose and gushes over his ratty sweater as the crowbar and his ass hit the ground simultaneously.

Earmuffs takes the full sweep of the passenger door, which lifts him from the ground, forcing the back of his head to hit the light pole next to Scout. The clang of his head hitting metal rings out across the parking lot.

Dex pushes off Scout's rear to see what is happening behind him as Snorkel Coat bends down to retrieve his hammer. Scout's tailgate slams down, pushing Dex into Snorkel Coat, causing them to hit the concrete. Both try to stop the fall with their face, which elicits a duet of swearing.

"Careful, buddy, you might dent something," I say. Short, happy honks and flashing lights are the reply I get. My enchanted ride enjoys a good fight, warded to the hilt against corrupt magic and spelled with decisive protocols that deal with defensive and proactive driving. At some point in our journey together, Scout developed a sense of humor.

"What the fuck, man?" Dex, his puff deflated by my ride, is having a moment of despair as he gets up, wiping blood off his forehead.

"You shouldn't have insulted my car, Dexter."

As he spins around to face me, my fist slams into Dex's stomach. He bends over to consider a second look at his dinner. I allow him a moment of gag before pulling him up by his hair to make eye contact.

"Where are you supposed to meet the guy for your bonus payment?" I shake Dex around when he doesn't answer. It's fun to watch the rest of his ego turn into humble pudding.

"OK, OK, stop. The guy told us to work you over, then bring you and your car up to the MK gold mine parking lot to get a bonus."

I let Dex go back to his knees. I drag his fellow hooligans around to the back of the car parked next to Scout. Scout opens its tailgate so I can grab some zip ties, courtesy of the Colorado Springs PD. I zip all three pairs of hands behind their backs, then their ankles.

"A big Native American man will be out here soon to carry you boys to the trash bin. Be polite and thank him. If you're lucky, he may not break any bones on your way there." Kog knows everything going on in town.

Dex, watching me wrap his cohorts up, finally finds a backbone behind his yellow belly and takes off running. I pick up Snorkel Coat's hammer and give it a toss, hitting Dex just behind the knee. He falls with the grace of a

                    M.J. Hook

hobbled stork.

"Argh," is his response to my fine throw.

I walk over, grab his puffy scruff, and haul him to the driver's side of Scout, open the door, and toss him up into the seat.

"You drive," I say.

"What? I don't know how to drive a stick car," Dex says, choosing a phrase that exemplifies his worldly base of gearhead knowledge.

"I wasn't talking to you, puff boy." I close the door, and Scout starts the engine as I climb into the passenger seat.

"How is this possible?" Dex squeals as Scout shifts and drives us out onto the main drag of the mining town.

"Smart car. You've heard of those, right?"

Dex goes quiet as we head out of town and ascend to the gold mine entrance at the top of the hill.

"Scout, pull into the Heritage Center. Dex and I need to have a little chat." My ride takes a left, drives into the empty parking lot, and parks.

"Dexter? You ready to listen?"

Still confused by Scout's independence, Dex peers up at me with the dazed look of an intoxicated monkey and nods.

"Good. I'm going to get out and make my way on foot up to the tour building. You are going to wait here for a few minutes, then Scout will drive you up there and park. You will stay in the car until the guy you are supposed to meet shows up. Stay in the car. Make him come to you. Understand?"

Dex nods. It doesn't matter if he listened or not. Scout's understanding is all that's important. The passenger door unlocks so I can get out and relocks as I hoof it up the hill.

The Mollie Kathleen mine facility is dark, with a few spotlights mounted on the buildings scattered around the lot. I stay in the shadows, approaching the mine from the back side. The scaffolded tower housing the elevator that takes tourists down a thousand-foot shaft stands like an erector set dinosaur. I move up behind it and dilate my eyes to examine two cars parked in the lot. Next, I switch to 3E and look for signs of anyone, or anything, hiding.

Nothing.

Scout pulls off the highway and drives through the entrance, slowing as it drives through and parks near the main building with the most lights. A few minutes later, a large sedan pulls in, drives around the car lot and pulls up next to Scout, driver's side to driver's side.

FEAR

I make my way to the two cars, keeping my eye on the sedan's driver window until I'm tucked behind Scout.

Gloves off, I prepare the only spell I can think of that will hold the Void long enough to cast something more significant for containment. The sedan's driver window lowers. I zoom in using my sight and see the Void jittering inside. Aiming both hands at the open window, I yell *"Reo"* and will the elements of air and moisture through my hands, creating a blast of freezing rain that rips through the opening.

Scout pulls away quickly as I bombard the driver inside the sedan. I continue the blast on the outside, shattering the windshield to finish filling the front seat with ice. Colorado is a dry climate, so moisture can be a rough resource to pull out of the air. Fortunately, there is plenty of snow around the lot, which dissipates with my spell.

I blast apart the passenger window and finish making the inside a solid block of ice.

The Void is silent. Still.

Spent, I fall to one knee to catch my breath.

The possessed man, frozen solid inside the car, is still alive. Yank the possession and dispatch the shit stain, I know I can resuscitate the guy. But I need to move quick.

Scout pulls up, and Dex jumps out.

"How in the hell…" His comment cuts short when the ice cracks. The demonic twanging resonates inside the frozen trap. I turn off my 3E to avoid the debilitating pain I know will follow.

"Get back in the car, Dex," I shout. He runs toward the highway. Scout takes off in pursuit. The delay in action pushes me to react. Not that I had any plans to begin with, but I thought the ice would hold longer.

Stomping my right foot down, perceiving the earth underneath the car, I emit a quake of power. The force pushes a column of dirt up underneath the sedan, causing the car to launch several feet off the ground to rest on the large pillar. The effort weakens my spirit.

Dismissing my fatigue, I pull my karambit knife from its sheath inside my jacket and slice my left palm deeply. The blood drips as I invoke a jet of flame through the cut, aiming it at the base of the column. Reciting a powerful spell of containment, I move around the column. My blood and my words stoke the fire with intent. The scorched earth burns like blazing lava, creating fiery runes of restraint.

                    M.J. Hook

I hear the ice above me break and shatter. A frozen block slides out of the window and hits me, causing me to stumble.

My misdirected blaze hits the column of soil, knocking a chunk out of its side. The car's weight breaks the platform edge, causing the sedan to slide backward. The rear bumper slams into the ground, causing more ice to break.

The glowing circle, incomplete, begins to fade. The cut on my hand cauterizes as my spell dies.

"So much for improvising," I say to no one as I run off to the side to find the Void, switching on my sight. My legs tremble as the demon's tone vibrates in the air surrounding me. I stagger, then step on ice and slip. I tuck my shoulder so the fall turns into a roll, rotating my body into a squat.

The Void twists out from the man in the car, then launches out of the sedan's window. Its dark form drags across the parking lot. Unlike this morning, the shit stain's not as animated—no frolic in its departure. Thinking it's injured, I chase it, my tattoos energizing with magical intent and protection. The Void falls to the ground and drags itself into the ravine by the mine's large entrance sign.

Slowing down, I prepare another blast to freeze the demon. Worked the first time. Just put more layers down and turn it into a Voidsicle.

A bout of laughter erupts behind the sign, followed by a strangled scream. Turning my sight from 3E to night vision, I stop on the edge of the ravine to see Dex on the ground, his eyes startled. His hand grips a rod of rebar, thrust completely through his neck.

"Not again," I grumble, realizing the Void made Dex do it.

I switch to 3E and prepare to blast the Void, but it's not there. I run out onto the highway, looking for the vibrating piece of shit. Scout pulls up beside me, thinking I may give chase. My shoulders slump as I pat the hood.

"Thanks, buddy. Meet me by the tipsy car."

As Scout backs up, I turn around and see Dex's baddoon slowly inflate with his spirit.

"Just a night of fucking messes."

The baddoon lights up, twisting and glowing like an animated Christmas tree covered in mud; his spirit needs attention. Dying by unintended suicide would put any soul in a state of panic.

To be out of sight of travelers on the highway, I pick up the body and carry it into the parking lot behind the mounted sedan. Out of Scout's boot,

I pull a small spray bottle filled with an enchanted mix of paint and spray a circle big enough to contain me and the baddoon. Unlike chalk, paint is handy on a rough surface like gravel.

Unsure if evil, black, and twangy is nearby, I need assurance that dealing with Dex's soul will go uninterrupted.

Kneeling inside the circle, I touch the paint, directing a surge of energy into it. A protective wall of magic surrounds me and Dex's floundering spirit.

Building my will and intent, I coil into Dex's spirit and am surprised how easily it accepts my presence. Since there's no mystery to solve, I have no reason to relive any of his past.

With brief discussion, I bring him around to his life thread and send him on his way to the Universe.

Normally, I do not make it a habit to help every soul bag I see, but I know I'm responsible for Dex's death. The Void may have put him down, but my trip to Cripple Creek set him up.

I scrape the paint to break the circle, and my phone rings.

Kog's name appears on the screen.

"So, I guess Granny told you to call," I answer.

"Tell me what needs to be done," Kog says in his gravelly, put-out voice. I apologize, then tell him where to come and the body count, and I let him know one body is probably still alive—sitting in a partially frozen sedan with one end several feet in the air.

"Be careful with him. He's in a fragile state. Thanks, Kog, and please let the Oracle know I'm leaving now."

"She knows," he says, then hangs up.

The driver of the sedan is leaning back, staring out the windshield. His frosted hands grip the steering wheel hard. He sees me and begins babbling questions only someone in the same state of shock would have answers to.

"Hang tough, buddy," I say, not caring if he hears me or not. He has a heartbeat, and I have a splitting headache.

He screams, then checks his pockets. He must have found peace of mind, as he returns to a quiet prattle. With what little energy I have left, I push air under myself to reach the open window and touch his forehead.

"*Codladh*," I say, putting him to sleep.

I climb into Scout and take the wheel. For the drive back, I need to feel like I am in control of something, even if it's for only an hour. The cut on my hand is sore. I pull a jar of enchanted yarrow paste from a kit I keep in

Scout and spread a large glob on the singed wound. Wrapping my hand in a rag, I grab the steering wheel and drive.

Almost home, I pass by the turnoff where the Void left Theresa's body, and my phone chimes.

Think we found the boy's house. Heading there now.

Benny adds the address.

"Yep. One fucking mess after another."

15

WEDNESDAY, RANDY SHURTER, BENNY

DRIVING HOME FROM a five-day elk hunting trip, Randy Shurter was feeling the black cloud he'd left behind in Colorado Springs. Its reappearance cast a shadow on the good time he'd had with his buddies. They drank, smoked some weed, told the same old stories that evoked stupid fits of laughter.

All the married guys, including Randy, talked about how great things were with their families. He knew a few of the guys were probably lying to keep face and not throw a pile of used toilet paper on the fun. Randy boasted about how wonderful his wife, Darlene, was and how much fun he had playing with his son, Jimmy. It was all true until about a month ago.

Darlene wasn't happy, and she spelled out a long list of whys to Randy one afternoon while Jimmy was at a playdate. The main gripe—not spending quality time with her and the boy—summed up the long list of itemized gripes.

He made efforts, but nothing seemed enough. When the hunting trip came up, Darlene started talking about therapy as he packed his truck. He agreed as he hugged her goodbye, almost adding that it would be good for *her* to go. Fortunately, he bit his tongue, hugged James, then left.

Randy started the trip happy, the home-front frustration left in his rearview mirror. The first day of hunting was cold, and he saw nothing to shoot at. A couple of the guys scored some nice racks, and the night ended with a drunken laugh-a-thon. By the fourth day, everyone had fulfilled their tags.

Everyone but Randy. All he nailed was a sour stomach and a constant barrage of texts from Darlene with links to therapists she wanted his feedback on.

Wednesday afternoon, he texted, telling her they would discuss it when he got home. She did not reply.

Later, he called and left a message to say he would be home late.

Again, no reply.

He began texting, saying he looked forward to seeing her and James. Packing up his gear, he believed his intent, texting to let her know he was looking forward to going to a therapist and turning things around.

Halfway home, he stopped to drain off the afternoon lunch of beer and filled up with gas and frustration over her lack of replies. Nothing, not even a message covered in the hearts and smiley emojis that she used in every text bubble.

Pulling into the city, Randy decided that it was Darlene's fault his trip sucked.

The upstairs lights were on as he pulled into the drive. He grabbed the meat his friends shared with him and tossed it into the garage freezer. Grabbing his gun and ammo, he left the rest of his stuff to deal with tomorrow. He walked around Darlene's car, seeing it parked at a weird angle that put him out of joint. Randy went into the basement. He walked over to the gun cabinet and noticed the guard was unlocked.

"Fuck, she'll be adding that to the list," he mumbled while putting his rifle into its slot. Then he noticed his break-action Mossberg was missing.

"Where the hell?" he said, then looked around downstairs.

"Darlene?" He yelled upstairs, getting no answer. He headed to the stairs, still yelling up to his wife.

"Honey, did you or James get into my stuff down here?" When he reached the landing, the smell in the house turned rank, like putrid elk guts. Randy walked into the kitchen dining area and found his shotgun lying next to Darlene's body. Her head was splattered all over the room.

•••

"The 911 came in at 9:13 PM—husband came home from a hunting trip to find his wife shot and his nine-year-old boy missing—her body's in the kitchen surrounded by blood, and, uh, entrails." The officer squinted on the last word, as if it hurt to say it.

Numbness washed over Benny's emotions as he listened to the report

                    M.J. Hook

and reviewed pictures on the officer's phone. Most of the information was relayed on the call to the scene, but this brief came with visuals.

Most of her head splattered on the walls. But no obvious cuts on the body. The entrails...

Inspector Omori had shown up with John Williams, the officer he assigned to escort Omori the day she arrived. Both were standing nearby to hear the report. Benny noticed they seemed friendly with each other, the distance between their bodies thin. He figured they might hold hands soon.

First responders continued to isolate the scene, the tape going up like cheap front yard Christmas decorations, wrapping around the evergreens and front deck. Benny stepped away and watched the effort on the extended driveway, staring at nothing.

He could only see the small pile of guts pictured on the kitchen floor inside.

WEDNESDAY, LATE NIGHT

I ARRIVE AT the same time the forensic van shows up, so I park down the road and make my way on foot to the house. Switching to 3E, I look for the Void. Keeping my sight on for long periods of time would exhaust what magical energy I have, and the trip to Cripple Creek drained most of my battery.

But this thing, the Void, whatever it is, is following me. I need to keep my sight on frequently. I eat a shockra bar and take off on foot toward the crime scene. I'm pretty sure the Void will look for a front-row vessel to occupy.

I mentally run through spells and counter moves to consider, but my meter is low. I doubt my efforts. Probably should have grabbed a couple more bars.

The house is a one-story structure with a basement, sitting on a large, unfenced property. I run around the back and see lights on upstairs. Downstairs lights show through the ground-level windows. On the other side, a row of blue spruce runs down the long driveway.

A familiar aura catches my attention.

Oddly, Benny is standing away from the activity buzzing around the house.

"The house is only a few blocks from the park," I say, pushing through the pines behind Benny. He goes rigid, then jumps a half circle to face me, fumbling with coat buttons to reach his shoulder holster.

"Damn it, Red."

"Why aren't you in the middle of the mess? Not like you to be a wallflower."

"Because," he starts, then walks around to shake off the hunching monkey on his back. "Because we have another clear-cut case of murder-suicide here, but I know it's not. You know it's not. And I don't know how I'm supposed to think about that. This supernatural shit's making it hard to fill out the paperwork and feel justified in a job well-done."

Benny stops and looks into my eyes. "This poor woman is going to go down in history as a piece of scum, and according to you, she was just a puppet, a plaything for some Grimm character no one can see."

I want to apologize, but I don't know where to start. The detective's eyes are open to the supernatural. Confirming that this puppet master is pulling strings to get my attention only makes matters worse. Nothing I say at this moment is going to help Benny deal with his inner demon.

And this demon is mine, which makes it even harder to speak.

I can only do something.

"I need to get inside, Benny. If the woman's spirit is still there, there's a good chance Jimmy's spirit is in there as well. Right now, I can't make things right here, on our plane. I can at least make it right for her and the boy."

Benny looks at the gaping front door of the house. The forensic crew is still getting their gear together by the van.

"You think that *thing* might be in there?"

Switching on my sight, I look around the area for the quivering black hole.

Nothing.

"Be my first guess," I say.

Running fingers through his hair, Benny makes a loud *grmph* and starts walking to the house.

"Look, I know you want to get in there, but this is going to be tough to justify. It's a deranged Pollock painting in that room. I'm going to need to escort you in there, understand?"

"Yes."

Walking up the steps, I continue to doubt the plans running through my head to deal with the Void. After the events in Cripple Creek, I realize I don't know how to contain the entity. I don't know what I am dealing with.

My primary concern must be for the mother and child. Fairly sure the

M.J. Hook

boy's spirit would run home to haunt, and if the mother's spirit is still there, I can at least settle that account.

"What's the mother's name?" I ask.

"Darlene. Darlene Shurter."

We stop outside the door as an officer steps out.

"Detective! We're about to start. The husband, Randy Shurter, is in the squad car finishing his statement with my partner." The officer points to the vehicle. Two silhouettes sit in the front. "Guy was sitting outside, holding himself together when we drove up. Inside…" He turned to look through the door. Speechless.

"Yeah, I saw the pics," Benny says. "Look, I'm escorting Mr. Wood in to look around. Keep everyone out. We won't be long."

"Yessir," he says.

Benny pulls out booties, handing a pair to me. They go on without ripping.

Walking up a short set of steps, we run directly into the scene. Filled with the stale crimson smell of bloody death, the air is hard to breathe,

"If this was what it appears to be, Red, I could stomach the mess. But it's not. Right now, I want to puke a surreal chunk of denial."

The body, head mostly missing, and shotgun lie on a floor covered in blood. A pile of guts lies under the table. The table is also covered in blood, with ropes tied around the table legs. A spool of aluminum tubing rests on the cleaner side of the table. There's blood and brain matter on the wall and the vertical blinds covering the door leading out to the back.

It's a mess, but not my concern. Again, I switch to 3E as a wave of weariness flows through my body. I need a decent meal and sleep. A complete reboot.

After adjusting my filters to mask out the blood flares of energy, I witness an unfamiliar sight—Darlene's baddoon slumps by her body, showing no agitation or frustration. A spirit wisp, a ghost moving at great speed, is whirling around the baddoon, entering the bag by slicing a spiritual gash in the side, only to create another gash to exit.

"Jimmy came home. The boy's spirit is here, terrorizing the mother's soul. The energy is traumatic. Disruptive."

"Is the killer here, Red?"

Shit.

I scan the area and see no sign of the Void. I dial in tighter to look for any magical markings and find a small rune written in blood next to the woman's hand, her index finger coated.

"No, but I found another sigil. This might leave a mark."

"What? Wait!" Benny shouts as my palm extends to release a small fiery orb at the sigil. Inches from the floor, sparkles of energy lift, like floating ash. The orb ignites the rune, and with another sparkling pop, a flashy message appears.

On your mark
Catch me if you can Red
Hot deck strike one
Cold Dex strike two

"Damn it," I say as the message dissolves.

"What?"

"I'll explain later. I need to take care of these two." Focusing on Darlene's baddoon, I stretch my coil over the bloody floor. As I touch the moping sack and connect, I can feel her spirit's despair. The vibration we share causes Jimmy's spirit to pause its attack, creating the opportunity to encompass Darlene's spirit and connect to her soul.

A spirit crying takes the vivid colors of an aura and douses them with spectral sludge. Detached from mortal emotion, the pure spirit displays immaculate energy. Emotions gone, the vitality of spirit will run positive to negative.

Darlene's spirit, burdened with the guilt of watching herself kill her son and now being pummeled by his dazzling ghost, looks like a compost pile.

I take a moment to attract her energy back and share my vibe.

Darlene, my name is Travis. I am here to help. I am here to let you know what happened was not your fault.

The energy builds, the colors flare, filling the bag with rage. A scream vibrates throughout her soul, creating an environment I'm used to working with. I have her attention.

Darlene, I need you to show me before. Before the bad. I want to see what possessed you. What smothered your love as a mother? I see your spirit, Darlene. It was not you.

Pushing through the turmoil of what happened here in the room, I offer trust, vibrating confidence and hope.

 M.J. Hook

The spirit video rewinds.

She and Jimmy are laughing, running down a racetrack. Another runner runs by, but it looks like a movie. Next, I see pictures of athletes, backlit, larger than life. I recognize the display.

I understand. You are at the Olympic & Paralympic Museum.

The two are in a large room, watching fireworks on a large screen. Darlene sees a black hole in the screen. She stares a moment longer, and there is something darker inside the hole, movement. The creature has a form.

I hear the Void's twang. The rift fills Darlene's spirit with sadness. Despair. She's lost.

Darlene closes the trunk of her car. Gets in the car. Jimmy is crying. She tells Jimmy they are going to go home to build something. Difficult to hear as the chord plays louder.

Darlene checks the rearview, all I see is the Void in place of her head. I try to sort out the Void's presence, but through the memories of the dead, I have no side glances. Just forward and reverse, and the controls are sensitive. The remote is in the hand of the spirit whose thread I am viewing. I can only suggest what button to push. And although I can hear the Void's destructive tone, it does not hurt my spirit or body. Feels more like an itch.

Not sure what it means, but I make a mental note as I continue to watch.

The scene moves forward. They stop at a hardware store. The thing that is not Darlene leaves Jimmy in the car to play on her phone. She buys supplies. I watch the spool of aluminum coil and a bundle of rope cross the store scanner.

Darlene, I have seen enough. That was not you. That was something else. You were there, but your soul, your consciousness, was imprisoned. Jimmy is here. He needs you. Your love. Your guidance. Feel him.

Using a soft vibration, I move her past the memory and show her the ribbon, the shining thread of her life that embodies her soul. Darlene's conscious and subconscious, the filament of her spirit filled with the experiences of her mortal coil. The link to the Universe. Her link to Jimmy.

This is your path, Darlene. And look, next to it, very close to it, is another. That's Jimmy's path, but he cannot find it. You are his mother, and he needs you because he's scared. He needs you to walk him down that path, his path, the one next to yours.

Her spirit vibrates softly, like the purring of a mother cat to her kittens.

FEAR

I'm going to let Jimmy in here. With us. With you.

The soft vibe turns into a slightly agitated quiver.

He knows that was not you. Help him remember before. Take him down the path. I will help you calm his spirit. It will be hard. I need your strength, your mother's energy, to do this. If we fail, Darlene, his spirit will remain here. Lost. Frightened.

Oscillating between agitation and a rhythmic pulse, her spirit grows in strength. In radiance.

In love.

Here he comes.

A small thread of spiritual coil shines like a glowing lure, an invitation for Jimmy's spirit to join. His energy works its way in, allowing Darlene to soothe away the quivering vibrations of anger. She joins with his energy, reintroducing the boy's connection to his spirit, allowing Darlene to merge with her son and lead them both to the Universe.

I promise to find the demon that did this. I doubt they can hear me, but I need to say it.

I break the link. Tears flood my eyes as I look at Benny. For once, he's speechless as I turn and leave the house.

Benny chases after me. I hear him tell the officer at the door to get busy with the scene; the techs are walking up, dressed in white coveralls, carrying their cases of tools. I walk off into the grass to avoid them.

"Detective, what should I do?" I hear Omori ask. I walk too fast to hear Benny's reply. My mind races with everything that has happened in the last two days. I check my phone to see if I missed any messages from Jabari. My frustration spikes when I find nothing.

Not a damn thing to reveal this shivering, empty fuck of death.

"Damn it, Red, will you stop and talk to me? Don't make me take you down. You know I can." Benny huffs his threat to me, trying to catch up. I stop.

Humor is powerful magic. When faced with fear, doubt, even anger, cracking a joke can add levity to a negative curse of emotions. I try it, if only to achieve some focus.

"You and what army?"

"Oh, I would cheat and just shoot the back of your knees." He catches up, his forehead shining from the effort. "That way, I would at least get you down to my level."

　　　　M.J. HOOK

"Fair enough." Finding it difficult to focus, I feel the need to unburden the thoughts running through my head. "Look, there's a lot I need to tell you, Benny. A lot has happened today."

"Then tell."

I let him know Jabari is doing research, then I tell him about my trip to Cripple Creek. Benny is aware of the Oracle, but not the details of my past with her. When I explain she's got a bead on me, he speaks as if reading my mind.

"So, this Void thing. It somehow, what, cracked your spirit force field?"

"That's as good an explanation as any."

I continue with meeting the hooligans and getting the one named Dex to go with me to the gold mine. After telling Benny what happened to the boy, I jump to the sigil I just read.

"The thing came back here and added to the message. 'On your mark,' with Theresa in the racing stance. Then 'catch me if you can,' Jimmy playing catch. It did not expect me to find it so soon on the deck. Then *it follows me* to Cripple Creek. It's following me, which means it may hurt you, Jabs, anyone I know, or cause them to hurt someone else."

Benny puts his hand on my arm. "So, what makes this bad guy so different from any of the other ones you've encountered? Shit, remember that cursed dreamcatcher thing, caused all those students to have nightmares, and you just…"

"Benny, this thing, this Void, has me in its bullseye. It started killing before I was even aware of its intent or its presence. The damn thing wants to play games, and I have no conception of what it even is, what rules it exists by. In just two days, *two days*, five people are dead, the husband is probably a nutcase. Its link to me has led it to devastate three families so far. On top of that, it's powerful. I don't know how to hold it, let alone put it down." My body shakes. A cascade of unfamiliar emotions flows through my psyche and pushes me to my knees.

"I feel wrong. Unbalanced. Desperate."

I want to vomit.

"Woah, hoss. I've never seen you like this before. What's going on?"

I look up at Benny, his face barely lit by the amber streetlight, and I fess up.

"I. Am. Afraid."

"Uh. Um." Benny continues to stare at me, the machinery in his head working hard not to blow a gasket.

Or maybe that's just what's going on inside my head.

"Shit, Red. You've just done the impossible."

I try to figure what unattainable feat I may have accomplished as I stand up and check my nerves.

"What's that?"

"I'm speechless. I have absolutely no idea how to respond to the guy who whacks demons, trashes altars of necromancers, whispers to ghosts, and smacks around vile sorcerers, and now, this same guy is dealing with a demented ink spot that's making him piss in his size 20 boots."

I smile. On an unmagical level, the crap Benny deals with—gruesome murder, pointless death, psychotic killers—he totally understands my moment of weakness.

"Well, when you put it like that… and my boots are size 15."

"They're huge, regardless. But you're the only one who can fill 'em. Even if I struggle to believe in your world, Red, I sure as shit believe in you. So, choose: piss or sweat. Go home first. Eat some of that healthy crap you prefer to stuff your face with, stay away from the coffee, curl up with your cat, and sleep. Decide what fills your Doc Martens in the morning."

• • •

Scout gets me home. I notice Jab's car is gone, and I worry.

Inside, I find a note on the counter from her.

Found several possibilities and tagged pages. Books on desk. Nothing exact. Finally got through to Basil. Is this guy for real? He listened to my summary, asked some good questions. Said he would call YOU and let YOU know. Thinks a lot of himself. I'll be back in the morning!

I call Jabari, and it goes to voicemail.

"Thanks for everything. Be extra careful, and if you're out, consider going back home." I know her little warded apartment is safe, but my cabin is safer. "Better yet, you're welcome to come up here."

I hang up. Standing in my kitchen, I consider going to the workshop to look at the books she mentioned. Instead, I ransack the fridge and grab stuff readily available to throw on a plate and eat. I fill a water bottle and walk out to Marlow's pen.

     M.J. HOOK

His majesty is home, already sleeping on his ravaged couch. I step out, and with the last bit of energy I have, shoot a flame into the stove, throw more wood in to heat his space, then sit down on the end of the couch he is not occupying. As I put my head back and clear my mind, Marlow rouses, comes over, and rubs his whiskers against mine, then lies down next to me. His purr motor adds comforting vibrations to my misaligned spirit.

Good ol' putty tat.

M.J. Hook

17

THURSDAY MORNING

I WAKE UP alone.

Falling asleep while sitting up is easy when exhausted. The problem is waking up a few hours later and finding your body slouched like a graham cracker left in a cup of milk too long—sodden, coming apart. Getting up is hard, but I finally pull the pieces together enough to walk back into the house. A hallway mirror greets me with a face I don't recognize, a horrific wanted poster. My hair stands out as if styled by Pennywise the clown, my red eyes look like they could shoot lasers, and my beard growth is worthy of a Rob Zombie film.

No wonder Marlow left his pen. Probably woke up and ran for high ground after seeing my state of discombobulation.

Instead of going back to bed, I decide to shower and shave.

Finished, I check the fogged mirror, and although I look better, the image I see still doesn't seem right.

I feel crooked. Unnerved.

Downstairs, just past the gym, I step into my atrium, the place I go to meditate. Opening a window, I light a smudge of white sage. Then I thank Gaia and bless the space, cleansing it (and me) of all negative energy. Finished, I sit and breathe deeply to start my meditation, but progressing to a level of insight is difficult. The emotions I've experienced in the last two days make it a chore to focus.

Normally, I would refocus and step around issues, untangling them from the backside of my meditation, but this is different. Unavoidable.

I know working this out now is what I need. Revising my intent, I focus on exploring my inner chaos and facing it.

Benny thinks I'm unshakable.

I call it stubborn.

• • •

"No. No way." Jabari sits at the kitchen counter with a cup of coffee.

I'm thankful it's not a fork.

"Look, it will only be for a week. Maybe less. I just need to know that you're safe."

"No, you look. I've finally met people who like to go out and do fun things. Some of those fun things are going on this weekend. Locked up here with you is not my idea of fun." She grabs her cup like a baseball.

"I will not be around here that much. I've got to…"

Jabari palms me to stop talking. Her eyes squint shut with wrinkles, and the cup goes back on the counter.

"You want me to stay up here? By myself? While you hunt the blotch? Your place may be better protected, but it's following you. If it loses sight of you, where do you think it's going to splat and wait."

The room is silent, and I realize she's made a valid point. Something that confirms my own conclusions from my morning meditation. Something *I* need to deal with.

I stand up, pour myself a coffee, and turn to face my apprentice. She showed up this morning with no idea of what happened yesterday, and I immediately told her to cancel her life and move up to my place for a time. So, I briefly tell her everything and finish with what I discovered about myself.

"This Void shuts me down, Jabs. For the first time since I received my Runes of Defense, I feel frightened. Disarmed and paranoid. Not so much for me, but for those I care about and for innocent people who have no control over the brutality this thing pushes them to do. The angst I have toward myself is not understanding how to fix it. In two days, I've witnessed and felt a ferocity that has shaken me to the core."

Jabari stands up, then rushes over to give me a hug. I hold my cup out of the way before setting it on the counter to return her offering. A hug heals. It gives one person purpose to care and another to know they are not alone. The momentary bond can strengthen spirits on both sides of the gesture.

                        M.J. Hook

"You could have started with that, Teach, rather than coming off like a bloody warder." She pulls away and grabs my arms, looking up with eyes full of confidence. "If you need me to be here to keep researching, to give you peace of mind, I'll do it."

I touch her cheek and smile. "Thanks, Jabs. Hang with me and let's see what happens."

We bring our coffees to the bottega. Pointing to her stack of tagged books, I think out loud. Running stuff through your head is productive, but after a while, you need to spit it out and hear it to put it in some kind of order.

"Great job researching. But after reading through the notes you left me, I don't think we're dealing with a common spirit or demon. Entities you found have similar characteristics, but I'm guessing this is something older. And for that, I am counting on the illustrious Basil, whom you had the pleasure of meeting on the phone, to offer some insight."

Once the magic switch flips on in a gifted child, they realize that the things they've seen or read about in fairy tales and ghost stories exist. Makes having the spiritual sight scary. If lucky, a newbie will have someone to teach them that the stories are mostly fiction.

Ancient groups worshiped Nature, giving names and personalities to the sun, moon, earth, and water. The deities—recognized, worshiped, and thanked—manifested, became real, showing benevolence. Unfortunately, a few bad eggs hatched as well through man's belief in power and control.

The balance between light and dark is an internal struggle in man as it is in nature.

Stories were told to explain why bad things happen, to keep kids from misbehaving, or to dictate order to small groups. Fear is a great motivator. Once those cultures developed into societies, communal beliefs followed. So, belief in the existence of gods, goddesses, demons, and other entities solidified.

With belief comes faith. Belief allows an entity to manifest. Faith gives it power to exist.

Get enough of a belief-vibe in a god like Zeus and poof… Zeus appears. So do all the other deities and offshoots that go with the beliefs. Most remain unseen until one of the faithful requests an audience. Then shit hits the ethereal fan.

All organized religions are occult in practice, which is why I dislike using the word. Its definition got twisted once cultured man started conquering tribal man. Tribal deities and their holy men and women became evil in the sight of the cultured man's religion.

Many of the ancient beliefs still exist, some through hidden conventions, others through stories. So the ancient bad eggs still pop up occasionally. Not that I've dealt with any oldies, but I have run into demons, which are manifested through some of today's popular religions.

But some are as old as dirt.

Blessed as a defender of Gaia, I have a responsibility to deal with the adverse offshoots of organized beliefs and abusers of Nature's gifts on a supernatural scale—to maintain balance and harmony within Earth's spirit.

Right now, it feels like a curse. When a curse is involved, protection is the only way to approach it. Breaking it gets rid of it.

"While we wait to hear from Basil, let's make you a little something that will give me peace of mind and you a social life."

"Really? I don't mind moving up here." Jabari's face beams with happiness. If I could bottle her smile, it would make a fantastic antidepressant potion.

"No need. That was me being overprotective, paranoid, which I'm trying to *not* get used to. Let's get busy."

Since the Void likes to use its crushing tone as a tool for discombobulating a spirit, the ingredients to make a protective spell against the sound need to be unique representations of the four elements. I put my little stew cauldron on the altar, then Jabs and I hunt to fill it.

For spiritual protection, I add powdered orange agate for Earth, chrysoprase for Water, crushed lapis lazuli for Air, and powdered peridot for Fire. Pouring in some enchanted moon water for defense, I light a small flame under the cauldron and give the mixture a stir.

To find earthly items that represent sound for each element, Jabs and I explore my junk tubs. I collect stuff that had either some purpose or some use that can generate an elemental catalyst in a spell mix. It all comes down to intent: If you believe it will work, when you apply it, it will.

"This could work for Air," Jabari says, holding up a trumpet mouthpiece.

"Perfect."

I find a small wooden flute that can work for Earth and a small crystal glass that can work for Water.

"How does the glass represent Water?" she asks.

                    M.J. Hook

I fill it with water, dip my finger in the water and rub my finger around the edge. A beautiful tone fills the room.

"Now that you see how water relates to the item, you can give it the proper merit for adding it to the pot." I'm glad she asked. If she just assumed I was right, her spiritual addition to casting the spell would fail.

Finding an object to represent Fire becomes difficult. Then an idea hits me. I leave the room and come back with a CD from my music library.

"Ohio Players and their 1974 album, *Fire*. Great song. Ever heard it?"

"As a matter of fact, I have. Thanks to me mum." Jabari jumps up off the floor and starts dancing while singing the lyrics.

Her dance moves look like something from the techno-disco era. She finishes the verse with a smoking twist and laughs.

"Awesome. Guess no need to convince you of this item's intention. I saw an Earth, Wind & Fire CD in the collection, but that would be cheating. Each element deserves its own object." I toss the CD and case into the pot with all the other pieces and start a slow mix.

Increasing the heat, Jabari and I spread our hands over the pot while we recite a powerful spell of awareness and protection—she speaking Tswana and I Gaelic. The steam meets our fingers, and I feel the power expanding, pulled into the cauldron and agitating the elements within. We complete the spell and allow the pot to boil for several minutes. Lowering the flame, I cover it to let it stew.

"Grab a couple of vials out of the bin and clean them, then bless them. I'll coat and fill them in a bit. When you're done, meet me in the kitchen."

"Yes, sir."

● ● ●

Jabari enters the kitchen and announces she's finished.

"Follow me," I say.

"What do you need me to do now?"

"I need you to take part in a ritual dating back to the days of primal man and woman, when Earth and Nature were honored. Joy came from a good hunt, a bountiful harvest, and a meal cooked and consumed around a roaring fire." I walk into the living room and over to my stereo.

"What? You want me to pick fleas out of your hair?"

"Nope."

I turn on the stereo and start playing the song I chose off my playlist earlier.

"Dance."

Ohio Players' "Fire" booms over my speakers. Jabari and I were born Fire children, filled with creativity, spontaneity, and competitive spirits. Dancing is a way to immerse oneself into the vibration music offers, whether it be from a skin drum or a '70s R&B group.

Plus, it's fun, a way to direct energy into a positive spin, which we do. Twirling, smiling, and laughing our asses off, we dance, surrendering ourselves to the moment.

 M.J. Hook

18
THURSDAY AFTERNOON/EVENING

VIALS FILLED, WE each take one, seal it with wax, and bind the potion to our spirits. Jabari uses her power language and also sign language to enhance the binding. Her mother was deaf, and Jabari learned to sign so she could come home and tell her mom how her day went. The finger tutting she uses to cast spells is incredibly powerful because of the connection of love she has toward her mother.

Once she receives her defensive tattoos, it will make her a major force to reckon with.

I have my own tutts that I've developed over the years for both offense and defense casting. The finger movements add focus and direction, on top of the intention behind the spell. I discovered the hard way during our training that Jabari's finger work also adds a power boost.

Once I bind my vial, I place it inside my totem bag. The power washes over me, inflaming my tattoos with its added energy.

We walk to the door and hug. This is not something we do often, but today has been a special day with my apprentice.

"You dance pretty good for an old soul," she says.

"Old? I'm not that old, young lady."

"I mean in spirit, dude. Listening to music from the '70s and the '60s. Can't say I've ever danced to The Apes before."

"The Monkees. My parents' music that became mine. Thank you, Jabari, I feel much better now. Strong and balanced."

"Well, thank *you*. I got to see a side of you I like. I mean, it was fun seeing you cut loose and smile."

Guess I need to do it more often.

Jabari leaves, and I do not regret letting her out of my sight. If the Void is watching and follows her, I believe she can handle herself well enough to make an impression and skedaddle. The vials we carry will give a solid warning and, I hope, a powerful deterrence against its twanging onslaught.

I hope.

Deciding to be proactive, I attempt to figure out ways to lure and trap the Void. No doubt I will be the bait.

My phone rings with Benny's ringtone, and much of the good vibe I had dances right out the room. If there is another murder involving innocents, I'm not sure what level of madness I will hit before hunting and destroying the cursed blotch.

"No murders, no statues, no missing kids. Calling to see how you're doing. You were a mess last night."

"Fine. Figured some things out. Getting ready to figure more things out."

"Good. You sound more like yourself. Wondering if you might want an evening off. Maybe a Cristo at Muff's, then Billy's band's playing at a new place called Little Tycoon. Someone renovated an old church on Bijou Street. I hear they make good mules."

Billy Bross, Benny's brother-in-law (his departed wife Celia's brother), is a member of The Folkin' A's. He and two talented musician friends play gigs up and down the Front Range. I wasn't a big fan of folk music, but listening to the A's brought me around. Billy claims they play "rulk," meaning rock, funk, and folk.

Having heard them a few times, I understand the mix. The A's sound is unique. Fun to listen to over a couple of mules.

"Not sure I can take time off, Benny."

"Red, one thing I've learned in my business is that taking time off for yourself, to just have fun, is benny-ficial. No talk about murder or evil floating Rorschach tests. Just a moment to clear your head. Afterward, pending hangover, plans and *ah-ha* moments reveal themselves much quicker."

Thinking about the dance session with Jabari, I knew he had a point. The movement and sharing of energy with her healed me like a karmic back adjustment.

"OK, Detective. Let's put it to the test."

I decline the dinner, saying I'll meet him later to listen to the band. That gives me time to consider plans and spells to use in case the Void joins us.

• • •

The Catholic parish previously named Christ on the Peak looks no different as I drive by. The Lyons Red sandstone building sits on a big corner lot, the large arched doorway facing West Bijou. A simple Victorian-style church, presented with white lights in front, changes to something dramatic as I turn to find the parking lot in the rear: The ground lighting, in various colors, directs a diffused glow on the stained-glass windows along the side.

Turning the church into a venue for live music is a tasteful alternative to it being vacant or revamped as a different house for organized religion.

The parking lot is relatively full. Walking toward the building, I notice the office section behind the church is a separate business: Chaney's Costume Emporium. Signs and pictures let me know it is a shop for stage costumes, makeup, and Halloween gear. A grand opening sign informs me it opened only last month, just in time for Halloweeners buying spook gear.

The church's original glass-covered letter board out front displays a logo for Little Tycoon Bar & Grill, along with lists of bands playing over the weekend. Billy's band headlines tonight, Friday, and Saturday.

The two large oak doors at the entrance, adorned with original ornate iron hardware, look recently stained and polished. The left door has a chalkboard attached listing daily grill specials. Opening the right door, I step into an incredible revamp, from a house of worship into a club of visual entertainment.

In place of the narthex, there's now a host station and a large display detailing the building's history. Then my eyes take in the aesthetic transformation the owners applied to the interior.

What used to be the sanctuary, still introduced by what must be the first few rows of original pews, opens to several tables already filled with customers, with the middle aisle leading to a small dance floor in front of the dais where the pulpit used to be. Pool tables are located off the right transept, while a long, beautifully carved bar occupies the left transept.

The colored lights from outside shine through both sides of the building to highlight the stained-glass windows, the colors dazzling the acoustic panels that hang from the ceiling. Most of the windows show vivid images based on Bible stories, but the two front frames are different in style and story—likenesses I recognize. One is of the Hunchback of Notre Dame and the other is from the Phantom of the Opera, both depicting the characters from the silent films starring Lon Chaney.

The glass work is brilliant. Pieces of glass in various shades of black and white, placed within thin lead calmes, create beautiful images of the historical monsters. The shading of the various grays, enhanced by the colorful lighting outside, is magical to behold.

"Red!"

I look over and see Benny waving at me from a table near the bar and the stage.

Still vigilant, I switch to 3E just to make sure the Void is not hanging around the bar sipping black and tans.

"Glad you made it. What do you think of this place?"

"Charming. I'm impressed with how much of the original interior's used." My eyes switch off duty as I pull up the chair next to my friend.

"Billy says the new owner is a big Lon Chaney fan. Senior, not Junior. Guess Lon grew up here in the Springs. Did you know his grandfather founded the School for the Deaf and Blind up on Institute? Guess Chaney's parents met there as kids."

"Lon Chaney's parents were deaf?"

"Or blind, not sure. But the owner intends to honor him with this place, according to Billy."

Chaney's Costume Emporium around the corner makes more sense now.

"I won't talk business, but I want to make sure you're doing OK." Benny pats my back.

"Order us a couple of mules, and I'll let you know."

The mules are excellent. I make a mental note to ask what kind of vodka and ginger beer they use. Benny keeps to his word, and the conversation is no business. We talk about bro-in-law Billy, how he's done well since his sister's death, and how the band's booked solid for touring until the middle of next year. With two CDs out, they are working on a third.

Benny is listing the cities they will visit when the band hits the stage. Billy plays a variety of stringed instruments. He opens with a mandolin, playing a soft, Renaissance-like piece. The other members stand quietly, one on an electric bass cello, the other holding an acoustic guitar.

Billy breaks into a beautiful love song, the others adding harmony. They pause, then kick into an upbeat tune familiar to their fans in the audience. I

M.J. Hook

switch my sight on as the song continues, happy to see no sign of the Void. The mule kicks in, and I relax in normal viewing pleasure.

After the second song, Officer Williams, dressed in civies, shows up with Inspector Emiko Omori.

"You guys made it!" Benny exclaims. Already on a second mule, he's feeling no pain.

"Yes," Omori replies, hanging her backpack on the chair before sitting next to Benny. "John arranged an introduction for me to meet the USA Judo coaches this afternoon. It was wonderful."

Officer John Williams—young, tall, and built like a lean, mean swimmer—blushes like a healthy beet. "Yeah, when we went to the Olympic Museum the other day, I got some names and made a few calls to arrange it."

Mention of the museum delivers a jolt of regret to my heart.

"Good job, Williams," Benny says, then talks about Billy's band. He tries to continue as the band starts their next song, then waves it off to listen to the music. Williams orders drinks for himself and Omori without asking her what she wants. Looking at their auras, I can tell they have already had a drink or two. I can also see their amorous spirits share some warm fuzzy shades.

The song ends, and as I clap, my neck starts hackling. My totem bag vibrates like an off-center washing machine. It beats against my chest while my tattoos release a burn of immediate protective energy. I try to move, but something is pressing me to stay seated. A clamp on my body. I can feel it trying to attack my spirit.

Slamming my hands on the table, I shout, *"Daemon a tharraingt amach as!"* activating a repellent spell to throw off the attack of possession. The new vial in my totem bag releases its energy, and the oppressive burden releases.

Before I can move to throw down on the evil puppeteer, Benny grabs my wrist.

"You son of a bitch, you let my wife die at the hands of that monster. You could have saved her."

I stare at my friend, wounded by his words. They cut me with a blade of sorrow.

As Benny frees my wrist, Williams stands, grabs the front of my shirt, then pulls me to his face.

"You let your adoptive parents die, Wood. Just let them drive off that road to crash and burn. You were supposed to be with them, weren't ya? But you lied. Sounds to me like you planned it." I grab Williams's hand and squeeze, causing him to release. Pushing back from the table, I stagger. The words from these two men throw me off balance.

I switch my sight to see the Void leaping out of Williams and jumping into Omori's body. She stands up and points a finger at me, yelling.

"You killed those two kids *and* poor Jimmy's mommy. How can you live with yourself?"

I grab Omori's arm. The black parasite twists out of her body. She shakes her head violently, like she's trying to dislodge cobwebs from her hair. She looks at my grip on her arm. I immediately let go to look around the bar for the Void.

It's like trying to follow a fruit fly.

A massive fist hits me just under my right ear. It hurts, the pain throwing up a blanket of stars as I fall to one knee.

"You fucked my sister, asshole," the owner of the fist yells and follows his claim with a large boot to my ass, which also hurts. If my butt can see stars, I'm guessing they're brilliant. The powerful kick launches me across the floor, rolling away from my attacker. Crawling like a gimpy spider, I make it to the bar and pull myself up.

Fighting with my sight on is difficult. Too many stimuli to consider: Who's angry, who's scared, who wants to gouge out my eyes with a pool cue? I see the Void jumping from one person's body to another.

The hollow fucker is taunting me, throwing me off balance with gleaned information. Private details. From me? Benny? It's giving random vessels bullshit excuses to attack me. I switch off my vision, deciding to defend myself, and consider one of my plans for capture.

Only none of them involve being in a public space.

The big moose that kicked me glares at my face like I'm some sort of freak. He charges, raising his fist.

"Did you really screw my sister?" the lummox growls as he launches his five-fingered sledge. I block it, which only makes him angrier. With my back to the bar, I block two more punches, then pull his third punch past me, grab the back of his head, and slam his face down onto the bar.

The moose came with a couple of friends, who are not as large but are just as eager to defend the guy's sister. They both rush me. Grabbing the

     M.J. Hook

moose to interrupt his stargazing, I spin and throw his body down to the floor. His buddies' feet are in prime position to trip. Guy on the right goes down; the one on the left falls into my arms.

"I didn't even know he had a sister," he says as I shove him down to the floor. Switching sight on, I watch the Void jump into Billy's body on stage. I can hear people screaming, looking at me. Benny moves to rein me in.

Billy shakes and steps up to the microphone.

"Why did you let my sister die, Wood?" I freeze, the words sending another ache to my heart. The proclamation stops Benny in his tracks. I watch the Void release Billy, which causes him to stumble into his bandmate with the cello. The collision sends a strum of chords over the room, followed by a piercing shrill of feedback over the speakers. Everyone in the space covers their ears.

The Void freezes in front of the glass Hunchback image, vibrating to the harsh pitch of sound. It hammers its own twang to the noise, but the effect of its chord on my spirit is minimal. I switch off my senses to avoid any more of *that* pain.

The guy at the soundboard back by the pews looks flustered. He attempts to correct the shrill sound. I rush toward him, developing a public-friendly plan to contain the Void, albeit a painful one to the ears. Unfortunately, he finds the right switch. The feedback dies.

"Shit," I say. I don't want to, but I turn back to the stage, preparing to switch on 3E and probably a world of hurt.

A voice fills the room with an operatic tone of melodic beauty, a spiritual song of power.

As the song progresses, the room shrouds in magical calmness. My protection keeps me from reacting to the spell as I watch everyone else fall into a crowd-mind of contentment. Listening to the soothing notes, I turn to the vocalist.

A medium-height woman with exotic dark skin and shoulder-length black hair, wearing a form-fitting white T-shirt and jeans, steps out from behind the bar. Her eyes are beautiful, except for the frown of concentration causing them to crease. Her mouth, with its full lips, releases the alluring song as her glowering eyes follow something around the room. I risk switching views to witness the magic coming from her voice.

Her power is overwhelming to view. The current of energy radiating from her vocal anthem of magic follows the Void relentlessly across the room.

The song silences its destructive twang, pacifies its twitchy movements.

A border flares on the walls surrounding the inside of the building.

Wards scripted in Latin.

Her arms rotate, a constant flowing motion, like spinning a pizza vertically, always following the Void's movements.

Her Air magic captures the Void, holding it in stasis like a sparkling tornado.

"Keep it there!" I yell, but she pushes the energy toward the front doors, carrying the slouching black mass with it. The doors fly open, and she throws it out like a bouncer that's had enough of some asshole's shit. More wards flare to life around the doors as they slam shut.

"Well, that also works," I say, filling the quiet space with an echo of disappointment.

 M.J. Hook

19

THURSDAY NIGHT

"HEY, YOU, GINGER giant."

Still staring at the front entrance, I know the woman who threw my nemesis out the door is talking to me. Her voice is like a strong, cool breeze on a hot day: refreshing and capable of blowing a stack of ceramic plates to the ground.

I just spent the last minute trying not to hurt anyone, sort of, but with the power this lady used against the Void, throwing down with her could cause some serious collateral damage.

I turn and stare at her, still using my 3E. Her aura is brilliant, displaying a spirit of tremendous power. The colors radiate beyond her mortal roots, glowing with the energy of a small sun. As a tree's branches can show how wide its root system travels under the earth, most auras will stay confined to the personal space of a mortal vessel, unless there is an intention to share or push the field toward another.

Her vast branches explode wide with power.

I wonder if that's what people see when they view my aura. I've been told it's dazzling to look at, which hers certainly is.

"You talking to me?" I say, trying a bit of *Taxi Driver* humor.

"Of course I'm talking to you. You're the one who brought that piece of specter shit in here."

"I didn't bring it."

"Well, it certainly had a bead on your giant ass."

I pause, then reply. "Yep, can't argue with that. Except the 'giant ass' part."

FEAR

"Start helping me get these people back where they belong. Dampening spell won't last long."

"Dampening?"

"Duh, their minds are stifled. They won't remember the last several minutes when it wears off. I refuse to have my business wrecked over a moment of inconsiderate magical chaos." She moves to get people settled back in their seats.

I pick up the moose I face planted on the bar. "This guy is going to have a shiner."

"I'll take care of that. Just get him and his oafs to their table. Hurry."

I get all three back to their chairs, leading them like old men with impaired vision. It takes little effort to sit them back down. Checking my table, I get Benny, Omori, and John back in their seats. The woman is up on the stage trying to get the band back into position while I work on the other ass-to-seat tasks around the room.

"You say they won't remember?"

"Yeah, yeah. I heard most of the stuff they tongue-whipped you with. Wasn't them talking, so once they come back, it will melt away, like a dream."

By Buddha's belly, I sure hope so.

"Now sit your moderately fine ass down. I got one last thing to do."

Feeling a slight warmth build on my cheeks, I sit in my seat and watch her position the moose's head above the tabletop, tipping it sideways so the bruised side faces down. She waves her palm over his head, then gently rests it on his hair. She walks behind the bar, gives me a wink, then nods her head to watch the tables. People move and make noises. Several shake heads, others break into yawns as they pull out of the dream state.

The moose slams his face onto the table and falls to the floor.

"What the hell?" He sputters while reaching up to palm his bruise. His buddies, not sure what just happened, start chuckling.

"Damn, Tony, we can't take you anywhere," the friend I'd pushed down remarks, feeling his elbow and reacting to its soreness.

My tablemates look around, dazed, but they shake it off. Benny perks up and points to the stage.

"That was one of my faves. What do you guys think?"

John and Omori, looking around as if a dense fog just cleared from their eyes, reply with some hesitation that they thought the song was great.

Billy and his bandmates, after a moment, test their instruments. The bass player says he needs to re-tune. Realizing the sound is off, more time's spent getting everything set back up. Finished, they get busy on the next song.

Thankfully, no one brings up any terrible memories from the last several minutes. I ask if anyone needs anything, take their orders, and head to the bar. The witch is standing there, staring at me with a look and posture of vexation.

I smile, hoping her eyebrows will loosen up and her arms uncoil from under her formidable breasts.

"That was impressive. Mind if I ask you a slew of questions?"

She nods to my table, saying, "Give Rex your order, then meet me in my office." She points her thumb to a doorway behind the bar. "Down the hall, last door on the left."

After ordering the drinks and pointing to our table, I excuse myself with no explanation and head to her office. The hallway displays framed posters from Lon Chaney movies. There are only a few that ring a bell. Her office door is open. As I approach, I can feel a powerful spell of protection in place around the doorframe. Looking in, I see her sitting at a large cherrywood desk, staring at a laptop screen.

"Mind inviting me in for a visit?" I ask, knowing if I just walk in, her wards will give me a hefty shock of *you ain't welcome here*.

Keeping her eyes on the screen, she says, "Cough up an entry fee. I don't know you. Your aura's lit up like a 20th Century searchlight, and considering my performance failed to make you nap, I know you've got some power in your pockets."

As a wizard, stepping across a warded threshold leaves me with three choices. First, the aforementioned shock, which will either zap me of my power or kill me if it's constructed with a robust spell. Or I can study it and find a loophole to bring it down (which is difficult to do while the owner is staring at you). Finally, I can offer a portion of my power as a courtesy. If I decide she is a menace and try to throw down on her, she can deliver the zap without resistance on my part since I'm linked to her ward.

I choose the third option and release power to her construct. It will keep me honest and, as a host, keep her somewhat cordial. I walk in, feel my energy release to merge with hers, and seat myself in an uncomfortable folding chair on the other side of her desk.

The office smells of lavender and sage, with a hint of cinnamon. The walls are barren of any pictures or shelves. There is one photo on top of a three-drawer filing cabinet: a cute, dark-haired, tan girl of maybe four or five who could easily be the woman's daughter. I wait for her to look away from her laptop to speak. My impatience cuts the wait short.

"My name is Travis Wood."

"I'm Samantha Isabella Salviati, owner of this establishment and pissed off my customers were fucked with. Because you brought that *thing* into my place."

"Again, I did not bring it. It's following me. I'm trying to catch it and put it down."

"Are you a cop? You're sitting with Billy's brother-in-law. He mentioned some other off-duties would show up when I met him earlier." She shuts her laptop and gives me her full attention. Her eyes are the color of a cloudy day, shades of gray with hints of blue around the edges. An elfish upturned nose sits above two full lips.

"No, but I work with them occasionally. Detective Rogers is a good friend. A case we are working on, that I'm working on, concerns that thing that showed up tonight." Because she could control the Void, I decide to tell her briefly about the murders and the messages it left behind. She stops me when I tell her about my communion with Theresa, its first victim.

"So, you're a psychopomp?" she asks.

"I don't escort. I only point souls in the right direction. Gaia blessed me with the gift on my first ceremony. Some days, especially over the last couple of days, I consider it a chore."

"Still, I've never met someone who has that kind of access to the Universe."

"My teacher in the art of the union warned me to never ingress, so no, I don't consider that access part of my repertoire." I deflect her questioning and return to my recent adventures.

Her eyes furrow when I bring up the release of Darlene and Jimmy's spirit to the Universe. Finished, I waste no time picking her brain.

"My attempts to identify the Void have failed. My attempts to capture it have failed as well. You could control it. How?"

"Mr. Wood—" she starts.

"Red. My friends call me Red."

"So, we're friends now?" A small smirk forms on her lips, which are

     M.J. Hook

difficult to tear my eyes from.

"Considering I've trusted you with my power, conveyed the current burden on my shoulders, and unfortunately exposed your place of business to that burden, for which I am truly sorry, I'm hoping we can be friends and you'll help me kick this burden out of existence, Samantha."

She leans back in her chair and puts her hiking boots up on her desk. If I could risk the energy to view her spirit, I'm sure her colors of confidence would shine like the sun. I'm certain she is viewing my colors and can read the attraction I have toward her. Hard to hide something like that. But I'm also certain she can see the desperation I expressed verbally.

She smiles, bringing out dimples—another level of cuteness and attraction that trumps my despair.

"Please understand, I just opened this place last month, my theater supply shop in September. These are my priorities right now. All my energy's focused here; this is *my church* for crafting. I had hoped to never find a reason to activate the wards in Little Tycoon, but now they're up." She stops, having lost most of her smile. "But from what you just told me, I could never forgive myself for trying to maintain selfish standards. I'm not talking about jumping in your Mystery Machine and Scooby-Dooing the Front Range with you, but I can certainly offer my help, Red."

And with that, she waves her hand and returns my power to me.

"My friends call me Sam." The smile returns to her face.

By the blessings of Gaia, my heart pumps blood to places that make me feel like a dog in heat. Turning on my sight, I witness a mingling of our spirits that could lead to many possibilities. Sex magic with Sam could manifest a nuclear reaction.

As fast as the moment happens, I shut it down. Remembering the visions from Theresa and Jimmy is enough to firehose my personal feelings into a drain.

"Thank you," I say with an unexpected squeak of adolescence.

"You're welcome," she says, a little breathlessly. She recovers, puts her feet on the ground, gives me an intense stare with those stormy eyes, and slaps the top of her desk. "Now, ask me your questions. If my answers can help, it's the least I can do for my new friend."

"Your magic, I am guessing you are a child of Air?"

"Yep. I'm a scales baby. Received my fourth marks about ten years ago, stayed unbalanced for the last seven." She laughs with a pleasant chittering, reminding me of a songbird greeting the rising sun. "Then I followed my fanatical feelings for Lon Chaney, which brought me here to the Springs."

"Chaney?"

She perks up like a child, opening the one gift she's always wanted.

"The man of a thousand faces. He grew up here. Both his parents were deaf, so he would act out his days to entertain them. He took that talent to a local stage here with his brother, writing a play called *The Little Tycoon.* Thus, the name of my bar. The theater shop out back is obvious. The man was a genius with makeup and costumes."

Her enthusiasm is contagious. She and Jabari would have a lot to discuss about acting out the day for parents. I could spend all night getting to know her and Lon, but I want to stay focused on how she handled the Void.

"Your voice during the spell you invoked. It's beautiful, and the magic is powerful."

"I was a theater major in school. Lon Senior was my chief inspiration for stage performance and makeup. Singing brought me some success. My voice became a tool after I received my Elemental Runes. I had to learn how to separate its use for magic and for performance. That was tough. Kinda scary to see an audience break out in uncontrollable crying fits—"

"Sorry, I can imagine. But your song. Your magic. You held the Void in place."

Her posture changes with my rude interruption. I'm ignoring her happy story, bursting her bubble, and soaking her with my impatience. She stares me down with a glare and a moment of uncomfortable silence.

"Yeah. Right. Your Void thing. Kept emitting an obnoxious chord of decay. I heard it, came out just before it started hopping in and out of your friends. It tried to jump into you, but I think the music made it difficult. That and the protection you emit."

This sends a chill up my spine. The Void obviously made a link long enough to find some major regrets in my memory.

Sam continues, "It was using the distortion to bypass your personal wards. I watched and listened, which hurt a lot. Gave me weak knees and back pain. The feedback gave me time to try certain tones until I found the right one to isolate it. Tuned my damper spell to knock it off-kilter while calming the crowd. Two birds with one stone. The magic gave your Void a shot of valium, but only as long as I kept singing. That's why I needed to shoo it out the door. I activated my wards on the same frequency. That way,

M.J. Hook

I knew it couldn't make a return visit."

"Frequency?" I ask while my mind races to grasp everything she's told me.

"Do you understand spiritual frequency?"

"Sort of. When learning about Nature's vibrative tendency, I saw how sound can form shapes with sand on a metal plate. The unique tones would manifest distinct patterns."

"That's cymatics. Sort of the same. That uses varied frequencies. Spiritual oscillation happens with all the elements, including Fire, *sparky*." She smiles at me. Her nicknaming me for my blessing brings heat to my cheeks.

"You might consider adding a frequency to your personal wards to beef up your protection. I can show you how, but not tonight."

"I'll take you up on that. Sooner than later. It's an education I look forward to." I try to sound serious, but provocation colors my words.

"Look, there are frequencies that can manipulate each spirit element. I have an ear for it, but that Void was tough to dial in. Once I did, my spell toned its mischief down and caused it to reveal itself briefly."

My race to understand comes to a screeching halt.

"What do you mean 'reveal itself'?"

"That black mass it hides in is a vehicle of sorts. It rides inside of it, using the distortion to maintain the veil and stay cloaked. I don't know what it is. I only glimpsed it, but it is one ugly little fucker."

20

THURSDAY NIGHT

IT FIGURES THAT floating mass of jittery emptiness is just another way for the creep to hide. Goes along with Omori's observation of the Bunraku puppet handlers, manipulating without being seen.

Something else Omori said tickles my memory, but I can't nail it down. With everything Sam just told me, my brain is chewing a headful of information.

What I decide to do with it, though, will determine its impact.

"Do you think I can find the right frequency to shake it loose from the blotch? Contain it long enough to dispatch it?" I ask, hoping for a quick solution.

"I think so." Sam puts a finger up to her lips, then lightly taps them as she looks up at the ceiling. "A few things you need to consider though. You're obviously the lure, but to shake that thing loose, you'll need to be out of the containment zone, wearing some decent enchanted earplugs. Plus, do you know where it comes from? How it uses energy, maybe? And why in the Crone's name it has you in its crosshairs?"

Her questions are valid, matters I should've been looking into before now. Not once but twice, I witnessed a possessed innocent murdering and defiling a child. The physical and spiritual pain I experienced, bundled with the emotional distress and indirect blame, has me vulnerable. Clueless. Personal frustration wraps my pride in barbed wire and wrenches tight. My defeat exposed, I rub my eyes to hide the look of painful disappointment.

This is not how I normally handle cases.

A knock on her door breaks the conversation. Rex, the bartender from out front, is there with a request.

"Sam, got a sec? It's urgent."

She gives him a thumbs-up. "Be there in two secs."

As he leaves, I realize I have a lot to process, and talking to Sam any more will only add to the mix.

"Sam, thanks for meeting with me after I brought my shit into your house. Your information's helpful. A lot to think about. I don't want to waste any more of your time tonight. If it's OK, may I have your number to call? Uh, if I have questions?"

She grabs a business card from her desk drawer, turns it over, and writes a number on the back.

"No wood off my wand, Red. That's my private line, and you can call me with questions or requests."

My body flushes with a wave of encouragement as I take the card, Sam adding a light touch of her finger to mine.

"You can count on it. Thanks," I say, standing up. The extra weight on my shoulders competes with the additional pressure in my head, my balance challenged as I walk back into the bar.

• • •

"Where ya been? Thought I was going to need to dispatch a hazmat team to the bathroom to look for you." Benny's still feeling no pain as I rejoin the group. Williams and Omori are having a close, borderline intimate conversation across the table. I glance over to see how moose and his buddies are doing, only to see an empty table.

Guy probably went home to put ice on his pride.

"Yeah, sorry. Met the owner and learned all about Lon Chaney."

Benny gives me an elbow nudge. "She's a looker, that's for sure. She could whip my hunchback any day of the week." I wonder how many mules Benny has hitched to his wagon.

"Agree. Very intelligent," I say.

"Oh, that's right. You're a brain guy."

"Huh?"

"Some guys are attracted to boobs. Others, butts. But you, you're all about the gray matter. You should ask her out, brain guy."

"That other stuff is obvious, Ben. But once you discover intelligence,

M.J. Hook

it wraps the rest up in a shiny ribbon. Maybe I will call her, but not until I resolve this case. No need to bring any more people into my target area." Asking Sam out is definitely on my to-do list, but as a consultant, not as a date. I know if the Void visits her, she can protect herself, but I don't need to piss her off again.

Benny pats my shoulder. "Understood. I'm going to order some coffee. Want some?"

"Please."

Benny leaves while I watch the band play. I can't focus on the music though. My thoughts replay what Sam told me, sorting information, trying to figure out plans. Exhausted, I drift to her smile. Nice teeth surrounded by pouty lips that curve up into two adorable dimples...

Distraction, the one thing that I can't afford. But damn, she's a worthy diversion.

The coffee is excellent. Benny and I have another cup and discuss leaving. Williams and Omori appear to be needing a room. I give Benny some cash to settle the bill and head for the door. If the Void is outside waiting, I want eyes on it.

Cloaking myself, I step out front and move to the corner of the club. I shut my eyes and allow my ears to take over the search, listening for any discord above the sounds of traffic. If I can hear that infuriating sound, then dial in the Void's location, maybe I can trap it before it sees me.

My body trembles as I extend my earshot. Hunting for prey that I know can turn the tables with one sound shakes my fucking nerves. Doubt, a feeling that I am unfamiliar with, enhances the chill of the evening. A dry cold bites through my jacket and fractals my confidence.

I struck out twice before, but watching Sam control it, I decide I might have a trick or two this time to bag the spiritual freak. Rethinking my plans, my body calms.

Williams and Omori walk out the front and pass me by on the sidewalk. They probably wouldn't notice me if I were visible. Their auras suggest they may wind up in the inspector's hotel bed.

The two are almost at the parking lot when I hear it.

Twang.

I tune my eyes to sound, sighting the demented inkblot as it drapes itself over a house roof across the street. The Void appears weak, sliding down the shingles rather than skipping across the air like a nasty leaf.

Sam's song must have slapped the obnoxious out of the creature's personality.

Running toward it, I reach out with my left hand, tattooed with the force for Air, and send a whirlwind ahead of its path as it leaps off the roof's edge.

The vortex captures it. I release a powerful blast of flame into the tornado with my right hand. The fire quickly travels up the twister and engulfs the Void, causing it to release a satisfying scream.

I'm just increasing the heat of my flame when its disruptive chord shakes the night. My limbs shatter, causing me to release the spell and crash down to the pavement.

The Void collapses as well, slapping the street like a burnt pancake.

A small creature, no bigger than an infant, pops out of the dark blotch like it's climbing from a hole in the pavement. The creature collapses on the ground. Still unable to move, I stare at the piece of shit. The skin is black and slick like old motor oil. The face looks like a slit-nosed newborn baby. Two small horn nubs protrude from the forehead. Stubby arms and legs end in three-digit extremities.

I move to destroy the evil-birth with a banishment spell, but only destroy myself as pain ruptures my spirit when I attempt to cast. The magic arcs through my soul, short-circuiting channels like a bad transformer.

The demon rests for a second, then floats up above its frayed rug of gloom. Shaking its little horned head, it sinks back inside the inky threads of darkness.

The blotch reanimates. Disregarding me, it takes short hops, then jumps through the car door of a vehicle pulling out of the parking lot.

Before passing out, I see highlights of Williams's and Omori's faces inside the car. As it drives away, I crawl into my own defeated darkness.

● ● ●

Hushed voices are the first things I hear as consciousness returns. My eyes open to a dim light. Focus comes back with the faces of ghouls, vampires, and other monsters staring down at me. I try to move, only to discover a monster of pain attacking my body. Shutting my eyes, I decide to let the ghouls have their feast.

"Woah, partner. According to our friend here, you need to sit still." Benny's voice is a welcome sound.

"Our friend?" I mutter, hoping he doesn't mean a werewolf trying to

  M.J. Hook

decide where to bite first.

"That would be me, Mr. Wood." Sam speaks, a small tinge of angst evident in her tone.

"Where am I?" I open my eyes and figure out that the horrific faces are latex masks. Sam's costume shop.

"Where you are is in my store. How you are is in awful shape." Sam's face fills my vision. Her tone softens as she touches my face with her palm. "You're lucky I am a trained healer, Red. That splotch hit you with a spiritual whammy. Your wheels are out of alignment; your kundalini took a terrible blow. I patched things up as best I could, but you'll need to heal the rest. Soon."

My chakras. Gyroscopic disks of energy that need to stay tuned, balanced. And it all starts at the root drive of my soul. After a quick inventory of all my well-beings, I understand why a tune-up is in order. My body's not fit for the road.

"I saw Miss Salviati rush out the door. I followed her, and we found you on the street." Benny, always one to find trouble.

"I heard that obnoxious sound again. If my wards had not been up, you would probably be getting a bill for several expensive shattered windows." Sam smiles and stands, turning to Benny.

"Not sure I could have pulled you in here without the detective's help."

"Must be all those mules I drank. Gave me adrenaline-mom power. Glad it was just moving you in here and not lifting a car off your ass first."

This makes me laugh, which also flares the pain. Then I realize something.

"Sam? Benny knows you're a witch?"

"He does now, after he guessed what put you down. I think his exact words were, 'that fucking demon hit him with another whammy.'"

I look at Benny to give him stink-eye.

"Again, the mules. Sorry. I saw her waving her hands over your body as she sang her delightful tune. Knew it was more than a holistic treatment for rheumatism. Besides, I told her I've kept your secret for a few years now. What's one more zipper on the lips?"

Wanting to sit up but deciding the view from the floor feels safer, I look at Sam and smile. "Thank you for your song of mending. Let me guess, I have my own spiritual frequency?"

"Good guess. As each chakra may respond to certain crystals, oils, and herbs, they also have their own frequency. I couldn't heal the damage completely; that would take time. I can only achieve a temporary balance by removing most of the mystical static."

Nodding, I force myself into a sitting position in front of a glass counter that contains fake mustaches, teeth, and eyeballs.

"Thanks. I have routines that will help."

"That noise did a number on your Muladhara."

"Sure as fuck did. My legs cracked like glass." Rubbing a fist into my eye, I stop. "Ow," I say as a new pain introduces itself to my face.

"Forgot to mention the shiner the street gave you," Benny says.

My mouth opens to say something, then shuts. The evening's highlights zip through my mind.

I remember.

"Benny, you need to call Williams. I saw the Void jump into their car as they drove off."

Benny pulls out his phone. "What am I supposed to say? How's your evening going, and by the way, did you notice a spot of doom in your back seat?" His joke has no punch line as he dials the number.

"Ack, yeah. Just make sure they are both fine. Start with that, then find out where they are or where they're going."

I lean my head against the case as another ripple shoots up my body. An undulating pain follows with the realization that I don't know what to do. The fake eyes in the display case stare at me like dead peepers looking for answers.

M.J. Hook

21

THURSDAY NIGHT, OFFICER WILLIAMS

OFFICER JOHN WILLIAMS reflected on the past couple of days and smiled.

Taking Emiko to the Olympic & Paralympic Museum on Tuesday was a great icebreaker. Taking her to the surprise meeting with the USA Judo team coaches (many of whom recognized her and remembered her performance at the Rio Games) was a stroke of genius.

Melting the leftover ice, Emiko now shared a seat on her cloud nine with "Johnny."

Normally, he hated that name, but from her lips, it sounded exotic.

Officer Johnny, well known for his organizational skills and keen eye in the Colorado Springs PD, was feeling a tad tipsy as he drove Emiko, back to her hotel. After spending an event-filled afternoon with the coaches, followed by an evening of drinks and flirty conversation, John was also feeling twitterpated over his adorable passenger.

Tasked as her unofficial escort by Detective Rogers, Williams had not expected the level of attraction he developed during their time together. Finding things to discuss was easy: comparing police work between their two cities, differences in culture, even workout programs. Williams had even missed his afternoon bike ride today on one of the many trails available throughout the bike-friendly city, but it was worth it.

She'd been holding his hand during the short drive back to her hotel. As he pulled into the parking lot, she ended her tender grasp with a jerk, like whipping off a glop of undesired dog shit.

Williams pulled up to the front entrance of The Antlers Hotel, staring at

Emiko with confusion. She avoided his stare and opened her car door.

"Thank you so much for your time today, Officer Williams. I will see you tomorrow."

Omori shut the door before "Johnny" could spit "what the fuck?" off his twisted tongue.

After watching the petite detective walk through the front entrance without even a single glance back, Williams drove forward to park along the curb and spend some stupid time to figure out if what he had just experienced was because of something he did, like some cultural faux pas he might be unaware of.

Stupid time for Williams normally meant talking to himself, preferably in a mirror.

After adjusting the rearview mirror for a hard look at himself, he began a moronic dialogue. "I've been the perfect gentleman. All day. I made no advances. Hell, she's the one who grabbed my hand first. So, maybe she realized when we pulled up to the hotel… maybe she overstepped her own personal bounds?"

He stared at his recently discarded hand. "Would have been nice to be part of that conversation before she decided to stay in-bounds."

Williams considered browsing Japanese courtship practices on the web but realized that would reveal nothing. Just something else stupid to consider during stupid time.

Staring into the rearview, Williams knew what needed to happen.

"Park the car. Go to her room. Ask her, one, did I do anything wrong? Or two, did I misunderstand her attraction? Let her know you need to know. Make sure that, starting tomorrow, you are aware of her boundaries."

Good job, Johnny, he thought as the one-sided conversation ended. But this needed to happen fast, before she was ready for bed. Might appear too convenient for jumping a boundary.

He was pulling away to find a proper parking space when his phone rang. Hoping it was Emiko, he saw Detective Rogers's name and pulled over again to answer.

"Yes, sir."

"Look, just want to make sure that you and the inspector are okay. Not sure how much you had to drink."

"We're fine, Detective. Nothing happening to cause a twisted tale between our two cities."

                M.J. Hook

"What? No, I don't care about that shit. Well, I do, but that's not what I'm talking about. You sound like you… Is Omori being, uh, like Omori? Shit." The detective's voice went distant with the swear, then immediately returned with a tad more volume. "Look, what I'm asking, does Omori seem like herself?"

Williams, bewildered by the detective's question, kept his answer simple.

Professional.

"No, sir. She switched to decaf as soon as we pulled into the hotel parking lot. Can you fill me in on what's going on, sir?"

"No, I can't. Because I'm not sure myself. Where are you at?"

"Sitting out front of the hotel. Should I go up and check on her?" Williams figured it was as good an excuse as any, even if he didn't know what the reason was.

"No. Stay there. I'm heading over right now."

"Yes, sir."

Well, Williams thought, *I didn't join the force to experience normal.*

Pulling up a browser, he typed in *Japanese courting practices* to fill the time and distract his mind.

22

THURSDAY, LATE NIGHT

LETTING SCOUT FOLLOW Benny, I spend my short time in the driver's seat eating the last two shockra bars I'd stashed in the back, drinking two bottles of water, then finishing with two healers. A tidal wave of relief floods my system.

Sipping on a tall to-go cup of bar coffee Sam gave me, I can't help but think that she would have jumped in Scout with me had I asked for her help. I also know if she had come, her physical and spiritual presence would be a distraction for me.

I don't need distractions and don't need to add her to the potential victim list.

I pull into the hotel's turnabout. Benny parks behind Williams's SUV. I park behind his Pontiac as he jumps out and heads to the VIP parking attendant, flashing his badge and pointing to our cars.

Williams walks over to me and quickly points a finger at my face.

"Wow, what happened to you?"

"Had a disagreement with a sidewalk. Turns out I was wrong."

"O…K. So, can you tell me what's going on? Detective Rogers won't fill me in."

Deciding it's a bad time to explain the existence of the supernatural to Williams, I keep it simple, using an impromptu excuse Benny came up with as an explanation.

"We think Inspector Omori may be under the influence of a mind-altering substance."

Williams looks at me, his face resembling a blank screen—nothing identifiable.

"Care to elaborate, Wood?"

Benny returns to save my ass.

"OK, cars will remain untouched. Williams, you and me go to the front desk, find out what room she's in. We'll meet you," Benny points at me, "by the elevator."

"I know what room she's in, sir. 217." Williams's face turns a shade of embarrassment at his announcement.

"Great, let's go," Benny says.

Williams rakes Benny over the coals with questions. Stepping into the elevator, Benny finally answers the lovesick officer.

"Look, I believe someone may have been spiking drinks at the bar. That's all I can tell you right now." Benny looks up over his shoulder at me, his mouth twisted as if he had just sucked on a lemon. Lying to a fellow officer doesn't agree with him.

"I noticed a suspicious guy by the bar, John." I say this to help my friend out. "He bumped into the Inspector when she was bringing your waters to the table. Just want to make sure she's fine."

Williams gives me the blank stare again, adding clenched fists to the glare. The doors open on the second floor.

Benny knocks on 217. "Inspector? Detective Rogers. Can we chat?"

I lean against the facing wall, my legs trembling. Thinking about the Void's beatdown earlier makes the idea of a repeat daunting. A cold sweat sheets my body as I reach into my jacket and grab a vial of blackout powder to throw on both officers in case the Void answers the door. If they're passed out, at least I don't have to worry about the evil thumper threading its way into their souls.

Risking my own, I switch to 3E. The damage from earlier keeps my energy at a diminished level of efficiency. The bars and capsules I consumed are helping, just not fast enough.

Benny knocks again and raises his voice. Still no answer.

Williams fidgets, a look of worry covering his face as he paces back and forth.

"I didn't walk her to her door, sir. I would have, but…"

"I understand, son. Call her room. Maybe she's taking a shower."

"She has one of the department loaner phones. I can try that."

        M.J. Hook

Benny pulls out his phone. "I'll call the hotel to ring her. Hopefully, she'll hear one of them." He asks for her room; I can hear the phone ringing clearly behind the door. Nothing else.

My vision pushes through the door. "She's not in there," I say. Benny gives me his signature raised eyebrow, acknowledging that I'm probably doing something magical to back up my claim.

"She's not answering, sir," Williams says, staring at his phone as if the device has betrayed him.

"Shit." Benny says before heading back to the elevators.

Back in the lobby, hotel security is at the front desk talking with the manager off to one side. Williams notices what the security guys are holding.

"That's her jacket and purse!"

We run over. Benny interrupts the conversation officially by showing his badge and claiming the items as Inspector Omori's. The taller of the two guards, built like a gorilla stuffed in a nylon jacket labeled "Antlers Security" on the back, grunts for attention.

"Yessir, Detective. Someone saw her being kidnapped in the garage. Todd and I ran down and found her purse and coat by a car. We already put in a call to you guys. Just heading back to the camera room to view the footage and confirm."

"Don't let me stop you," Benny says. "She's my responsibility."

Williams nods, affirming *ditto*.

I grab Benny's arm to pull him aside. "I'm going back to her room. Call and text me what you find." He gives me a thumbs-up, then leaves.

Unlocking her door is an easy electrical-pulse spell. The light turns green, and I enter. Shutting the door, I rotate the privacy latch to buy me a moment in case anyone else attempts a visit.

If I want to find something containing Omori's DNA, the bathroom is the obvious place to start. The inspector keeps her toiletries organized in a hanging bag behind the door. Her electric toothbrush on the counter might work for spit, but dilution with water and toothpaste causes problems, making it unreliable for accuracy when casting a location spell.

Her hairbrush has a few strands of black hair, which I pull out and place in a clean baggie from one of the many pockets in my leather jacket. It will have to do, but more hair would be better. As I turn to look in the tub, something in the trash can catches my eye.

Putting a glove on, I inspect the trash and find, wrapped in a piece of blood-stained toilet paper, a used tampon filled with the inspector's menstrual blood.

Placing the wrapped tampon in a new baggie, I breathe a sigh of relief. The blood will give me the strongest, most direct connection to her location. Blood is the purest link to an individual's soul.

Omori's kidnapping in the garage probably means the kidnapper drove off with her. I head directly to Scout. If she's still in the hotel, I can do a different spell to find her inside. I'm guessing the Void is involved.

If not, I can use the break.

Buckled up, I text Benny and let him know I have what I need to find her. Not waiting for a response, I peel the plastic bag back from the tampon and rub some of the blood onto the quartz arrowhead hanging from my rearview mirror. Below the crystal, embedded into the dash, is a circle made of twined copper. Reaching inside my jacket, I remove one of my most common vials: location powder.

Sprinkling a portion into the middle of the copper coil, I speak a location spell, "*Scrúdú agus cuardach.*" A field of energy surrounds the coil, expanding up and around the arrowhead.

"OK, Scout. Time to hunt down a bad guy. Save the damsel."

The engine starts, and Scout pulls away from the curb. The arrow inside the field points south. Scout shifts to second gear, the wheels squealing with excitement as we head for the interstate.

There are other spells I could use to find the exact location of the inspector from Japan, but the time it would take is probably time she doesn't have. One day, I'll have to design a magical map app to add to Scout's repertoire. My ride whips onto I-25 as I double-check the cache of weapons, both magical and physical, inside my coat.

A sewn-in bandolier carries various small bottles of potions I use often. In addition to the knockout and location dust, I carry a memory wipe (great for crowds), a few types of summoning powders, and a couple of paralytics. Most one-on-one spells I can perform using my cog coil with an individual. If there is more than one person I need to enchant, set a trap for, or cast at from a distance using an air spell, powders work best.

A text arrives from Benny. Attached is a series of videos.

A tall man walks in from one side of the frame, then out. His face, seen at a downward angle, reminds me of Karloff's Frankenstein monster, only sporting a long, dark lumberjack beard. Wearing a black trench coat, he strides across the back of four cars in four steps. The next video starts with Inspector Omori shutting her car door, then pushing her fob to lock it. The lights flash once, then she collapses by her car, dropping her purse, jacket, and backpack. Immediately, the bearded monster walks up, picks the petite woman's body up, cradling her in his arms, grabs the backpack, and then turns back, walking out of frame.

She looks like a small child in the big man's arms.

The next video shows the monster loading her body into the rear of his car, a large SUV, shutting it, and then climbing in to start the car. One more video shows the SUV driving out of the garage. The last image is a great enhancement shot of the license plate.

Benny's text follows.

APB out on Darren Shoemacher. Chvy tahoe rental. Guest at hotel, part of funeral convention going on.

That was quick. Benny knows how to push people to make things happen.

My line of thinking is not healthy. The Void likely possessed Omori on the drive to the hotel. Then it jumped from Omori to Frankenstein (aka Shoemacher), using his vessel to take her. Another threat to someone innocent.

Innocents.

Shoemacher was probably heading up to the bar to swap funeral stories before blanking out. Surprises me the guy is an undertaker, unless he's in the business for the spare parts. Can't imagine Franky would be a decent consoler to the grieving.

As Scout keeps driving, my thoughts circle back to one daunting question: Why does this Void keep hurting others after admitting it wants to fuck with me? And why me? What did I ever do to it?

The questions continue to branch, blossoming into a headache. The Void is playing a game with me. I hate games. Baseball, football, basketball—my life never afforded me the time to learn, let alone watch, sporting events. Trying to be analogous analytical makes my head hurt worse. I redirect and finish my weapons check while developing a plan of action, or two, or four. All previous attempts to put this thing down failed. Three strikes—not in my playbook.

FEAR

Knives. Always essential, various sizes tucked away in various places. Check.

Ball bearings. Propelled by air, great for a quick distraction or use as magic bullets. Check.

My enchanted yawara stick, carved to my grip from a specially cultivated and enchanted European mountain ash. The wood wards off evil. The carefully engraved runes add one heck of a wallop. Check.

And a small kit I prepared earlier in Scout's cargo. I'm ready.

Looks like I'm about to get another chance at bat. Start a new inning. Whatever the fuck. Swallowing a couple more healers followed by two more bottles of water, I try to relax and meditate as Scout follows the blood.

One thing I know about these games. These sports. They are all based on competition.

Now *that* is something I can get my head around. I close my eyes to focus on healing.

M.J. Hook

<h1 style="text-align:center">23</h1>

<h2 style="text-align:center">THURSDAY, LATE NIGHT</h2>

WTF IS GOING ON? Send location. Do what you do, don't get caught doing it.

Benny's message is nothing new. What not to do at potential crime scenes is a big deal to Benny.

First, if there are cameras that can record my use of magic, I need to magically corrupt the security system. Always best to do it before anything happens in case of off-site recording.

Unfortunately, slinging magic can also alert another magical practitioner to my presence, always tricky to manage.

Burning or knocking down a building is efficient for destroying magical evidence, but not a good first choice. I'm not always responsible for razing a structure, but the bad guy might have left the walls intact if I hadn't shown up.

Don't leave personal evidence. No problem. My DNA doesn't exist. I've never learned why, but if I lose blood, hair, spit, or a broken nail, the sample will read wrong every time, compromising the test with inconsistent results. When I use my blood for personal spells, the markers hold for some mystical reason. I would suck as a magic practitioner if they didn't.

The final, most important *what not to do*—put innocent lives in danger.

The reality of my current situation is that the Frankenstein monster knockoff is not my enemy. The Void has possession of Darren Shoemacher, so there's a life I need to consider. No more Karloff jokes; keep a focus on that fact.

FEAR

It's a few ticks before midnight as Scout pulls off the interstate and heads toward the COS Airport. After several minutes of breaking the speed limit, my trusty ride slows down in the middle of an industrial area. Pulling into a business complex with two long rows of metal office buildings, I see one building with a light on. It's the only building with a tall chimney sticking out of the roof.

Shoemacher's Chevy is parked in back, lit up by what appears to be an open garage door.

I manually drive and park across the street behind a powder coating shop. Texting Benny the location, I mention the smokestack, then silence my cell and double-check the wards on it. Nothing like shooting energy at a bad guy and frying my phone in the process. When using magic, all digital devices are at risk.

A daily maintenance pain in the ass.

Opening Scout's tailgate, I grab a capped tube with a sling—my kit, my big plan—to catch and kick the Void's pesky ass into oblivion. I put it together this afternoon; would have been nice to apply what I learned from Sam tonight.

Work with what I've got. I just hope it's enough.

Wishing there was another shockra bar, or three, I settle for slamming a bottle of water to ease my hunger and then switch to 3E to observe my spiritual condition. Sam's healing appears to be progressive. My wheels are still out of sync, but her song continuously vibrates, mending the damage.

Her gifts are impressive.

Placing the tube strap over my head, I turn off my sight to conserve energy and protect myself from the twang of spiritual havoc. Time to sneak across the pavement toward the rear of the building. Old school. Hiding in shadows.

The Chevy's parked in front of a large bay door, a convenient cover for me to duck behind and look inside the large, lit area. The temperature is cold enough to show my breath, so my gloved hand covers my mouth to direct the steam down as I look.

A three-tiered scaffold stands to the left just inside the bay door. Beside it, a large metal door stands wide open to a room with several metal gurneys inside. Most are empty. A few appear to have sheet-covered bodies lying on them.

The creepies spindle up my back as I watch Shoemacher, dressed only

      M.J. Hook

in tighty-whitey underwear, come rolling out of the freezer with two naked bodies on top of one gurney. Fortunately, neither is Omori.

A large erection tents Shoemacher's briefs as he breaks into song and dance.

"Country roads, taking me home, to a place, I belong," butchering John Denver's hit in a voice like a goat being castrated with a butter knife. Shoemacher launches a showy kick in the air with a long, hairy leg as he turns the gurney—which twists so sharply that the top body rolls off onto the concrete floor. He stops to look at the cadaver, then continues to sing and dance as he rolls on.

Shoemacher is tall, built like a linebacker, and covered in so much thick, dark hair that he could be a gorilla extra from *Planet of the Apes*. Moving behind the SUV, I track him as he pushes the gurney across the space.

He parks the cart next to two others, both mounted with a bundle of bodies and sheets. At this angle I can see two ovens set out from the back wall, the grates open and insides cold.

A crematorium.

Reminding myself that it's not Shoemacher the undertaker but the Void grabbing a body and stuffing it into an oven, I move to the end of the Tahoe to see what other attractions await in this freak show.

Inspector Omori lies passed out on her own gurney across the warehouse, next to a desk with a computer monitor and a pile of clothes on its surface. Omori, still dressed, is alive. Her green backpack, placed on her chest, rises and falls with each breath.

The singing stops. Remaining behind the Chevy, I watch Shoemacher finish stuffing a third body through the open grate. He walks over to the body he dropped. He stands above it, prepares to bend down to pick it up, then pauses. Looking out into the darkness, he lifts his heavy brow with anticipation. A smile causes his beard to expand and expose an extensive set of white, happy teeth.

"Mr. Wood. The mighty shaman. Defender of… what do you call her? Gaia? Whatever, so glad you made it to my party." His voice booms across the barren parking lot. "I was just about to start a fire. Nothing like the crackling of skin and bones to warm a cold body on such a frigid night, right?"

No cameras are on the outside of the building, but I can see a few mounted on the inside. I make my move and step out from behind the Chevy.

"Why bother with a fire? That fur coat Shoemacher wears should keep you plenty warm," I say to announce myself.

The Void sees me, claps, then exposes even more of the impressive dentals. His brow rises, giving his face a Muppet quality as the whites of his eyes enlarge. The erection in his underwear points straight at me, a disturbing visual garnish to the entire scene.

To remain calm, I force myself to see the Void *as* Shoemacher; otherwise, the brief-clad protrusion would have already been blasted to a nub. Keeping 3E off, I can only see and hear Shoemacher, an unwilling vessel for the Void.

"It's such a dry cold here, Wood. Where I come from, it's wet. Wet cold, wet heat. But your Rocky Mountain weather is so pleasant. I hope you brought some marshmallows to roast." Shoemacher leans down and picks up the body, turns, and then walks back to the ovens. No care at all about having his back to me.

This pisses me off.

Keeping my distance, I follow, angling to the other side of the warehouse. To Inspector Omori.

Instead of creating a power surge to knock out the cameras, along with the lights, I cast a glamour blur to warp my presence for the lenses. Hairy-backed Shoemacher messes with the controls on one oven after stuffing the retrieved body inside. An arm and two legs hang outside the grate as he succeeds in getting it started. Jets of flame fill the oven, searing the bodies inside.

"This may take a moment. Meat's kinda frozen," he chortles.

Shoemacher moves to the second oven and starts tossing in the remaining cadavers. I quick-step toward Omori on the opposite side of the room. Shoemacher turns to see me walking in her direction. I stop, still several feet from her.

"Yes, dear little Emiko. Was preparing to take her out tonight. Help her find a small child she could manage to stuff, pose, and mount. Make her the main suspect. But then I realized all the hardware stores are closed." He starts beating his chest. "Then this fine puppet showed up. After I got a glimpse of his well-traveled mind, I dumped Omori and decided to make her the main course tonight, Red. But needs tenderizing before dropping her on the hibachi. I plan on being *very* tender to her. So, no touching or you'll spoil the meat. Whoop-hoo!"

        M.J. Hook

I can't turn away quick enough as he grabs his boner and starts gyrating and slapping his ass. My disgust carries me closer to Omori.

My tattoos flare with protection. Shoemacher crosses the floor in a blink, grabs me by my arm. Before I can react, he lifts and throws me back toward the bay door. Landing on my left shoulder, I feel something pop and then a surge of pain as I slide and crash into the scaffolding. The structure flips as poles and platforms fall to the floor in a noisy pile.

This fucker is supernaturally fast and strong, which would have been nice to know. My tatts are great for warning me when cursed spells are thrown at me. They also buffer my body to a degree when I slam into hard surfaces. But there's no red flag for my stupidity.

Rolling over, I look up to see the hairy vessel clamping his hands over his ears. Once the scaffold poles cease their clanging on the concrete floor, he releases his ears and offers me a large bearded grin.

"Time to pound the Kobe Omori with my mallet. You can enjoy the show. Sorry, I don't have any popcorn for you to chew on, Red, but this shouldn't take long." Shoemacher pulls down his underwear and kicks them across the room, then grabs his stiffy as he turns toward Omori.

Forcing myself to get up, I grab two poles with my good hand and throw them to the floor. The noise startles Shoemacher, causing him to cover his ears. Before I can grab another pole, he's across the floor again, speed-thumping me with his shoulder. I cast an air spell to buffer my back and head before I hit the wall.

It's hard to tell if the cushion helps when the back of my head hits. As I slide down to rest my ass on the concrete, I reach up to feel for cracks in my skull.

The scent of burning flesh from the stuffed ovens fills my nose. Like beef burning in a pan or a slab of pork charring on a grill, marinated in rot. Unpleasant. Worthy of a gag as I try to focus.

While using 3E, I suffer spiritual and physical damage from his ethereal thrum. Turned off, I can still feel the devastating twang, just not as acutely. Doesn't matter. I'm still getting a severe beatdown, reduced to watching the hairy, naked man named Shoemacher dance a disjointed jig. His large erect bobber only adds to the eyesore.

Trying to stand, I forget about my dislocated shoulder. That pain above all others puts me down hard on my ass again. The burning stench causes me to cough, which stops the Void from dancing.

The heat from the ovens adds to the oppressive smell as I change my mind.

He is no longer Darren Shoemacher. It is the Void. As it makes exaggerated steps over to me, like a twisted marionette with a stringless third leg, I accept that poor Darren may not make it out of here alive.

"I've truly enjoyed the opportunity to get out and see your part of the world, Red. Being isolated for so long with only forlorn spirits to play with tends to make one feel despondent." It approaches me, the edges of its hairy body glistening like a spiky halo. "Fortunately, my master wished for me to leave my little thicket of despair to evaluate your abilities."

My shoulder throbs, but the Void's latest reveal shelves the hurt. I decide to buy into the bad-guy monologue, see what I can find out. Even if I put this shit stain down, sounds like I got another one waiting in line.

"Your master?"

"He speaks!" Shoemacher twirls, waving his arms up and down as if a black monolith just threw him a bone. "I was told you'd be a force of nature, but you've been nothing but a weak fart."

So many questions fill my head. I need to feed its ego to discover answers.

"Obviously, your master chose well. But why you?"

The furry twirl stops.

"Fuck if I know. He gave me the tapestry so I could travel. Get out of my rut. I didn't care. Also souped up my rig to fly with grace. Guess he figured my talents would prove worthy against one so formidable. Ha!" With his jibe, the twirling continues.

I get to my knees, moaning as if my shoulder is in distress—which it is. I crawl toward the Void to improve the angle and shorten the distance I need.

"Then, why me?" I ask, kneeling again, putting the Void behind me.

"Never said why. All I know is that I love the Rockies. After you're gone…"

With my back toward Omori, putting the Void's happy feet between the desk by her gurney and myself, I tuck tight, arms out. palms cupped, and yell, "*Siodean gaoithe!*" to release a powerful surge of air.

My shoulder burns as the blast shoots me back into and through the Void's legs. The monologuing ape flips over my head as my enchanted gust catches him, blowing him up and out of the crematorium. I continue my slide across the floor to the unconscious inspector. As I lower my arms, my

     M.J. Hook

back hits the desk, stopping my progress.

I lift my dislocated arm up and over my head, then slam my shoulder against the desk, popping my humerus back in place. The satisfying pain rouses me to my feet.

Just in time to see the Void launching high off the floor to attack.

I squat and use my good arm as a halting fulcrum, the hand grabbing a chest full of hair and skin. My free hand punches and sticks into the Void's stomach. I rotate, then push, releasing a frustrated scream to send the creep over the desk. He slams headfirst into the corrugated metal wall. The crash echoes throughout the space.

"Tenderize that, you piece of shit." I spit the words out while shaking chest hair off my hand.

Omori remains passed out as I reach her gurney. Trying to push it out of the warehouse fails. Locked castors keep it in place.

Reaching for the tube to put my big plan in motion, I grab nothing but air.

The obvious place it would be is by the open bay door. Throwing Omori's backpack strap around my neck, I pick her small body up and run. I hear the Void moan as I spot the tube sticking out from under the pile of scaffolding. Slinging the small inspector over my shoulder, I lift a plank and remove the tube.

Tearing the cap away, I reach in and touch the rolled piece of glassine tucked inside. Timing is everything. The Void is back up. It hurdles the desk, sees Omori gone, then spots me.

"Right, guess I'll pound you first, Red," it roars. The head knock slowed it down. Thankfully, it also caused the erection to wilt. It staggers toward me like a drunk gorilla, then trips on a loose pole and lands headfirst on the floor. The pole adds to the slapstick as it clangs across the concrete.

While the Void's distracted, I pull the glassine sheet out of the tube and toss it on the floor at my feet. With an adhesion spell, it sticks to the concrete. The translucent surface is hard to see. I hold tight to Omori, still draped over my shoulder, and take two steps back.

Then I laugh. It's genuine. Watching the ape fall was hilarious.

The Void pushes up off the floor and glares at me.

I can feel its power thrumming throughout the warehouse. The crippling twang has little impact against my wards while my sight is off. I laugh harder, then point to the inflamed bald spot next to its left nipple.

"Sorry about the wax job. Not that it made any difference." I continue to chuckle.

The chord comes in subtle waves. I feel the power with each vibration. Ignoring the slight crack in my spirit, I give the shit stain my best smile. My lack of reaction pisses the primate off. Its fists clench as it releases an impressive roar, complemented with a fine spray of spit and blood.

Time to twist the fucker blind.

"I saw your true form, runt. You're nothing but anal spawn from a ruined harpy." I smile again and add a wink to enhance the jibe. When your enemy is angry, they get sloppy. When you infuriate them, sloppy gets downright stupid.

The Void rushes at me—the stupid move I hoped for. I step back. Before his hairy foot lands on the glassine, I spring the trap.

"*Tá sé gafa!*" I yell. The circle of containment brushed on the glassine with a mixture of enchanted gelatin, salt, and some very special minerals, plus my own unobstructed blood, ignites to imprison the brute.

The ring of magic forces Shoemacher to stop in midair, then fall to the floor, constraining his body inside. The spell propels a wave of power across the large bay, causing the overhead lights, and happily the mounted cameras, to spark and die.

The best part: The containment is spiritually soundproof with special runes etched into its construct. I can hear it speak, but that destructive, unearthly twang will remain quiet.

The fires from the two ovens fill the darkness with a token glow of hell.

Not wasting time, I lay Omori down on the concrete. Time for the Q&A segment of the evening.

"Answer my questions, whelp, and I'll consider dismissing you kindly. Keep refusing and I'll snuff your black hide out for good. No one will ever have to hear you butcher another John Denver song. Who sent you? And why me?"

No answer, just a lot of groaning and small yelps as the Void tries to break the spell walls. The large body has no room to move. With each touch, the Void's skin burns like a sloppy Brazilian hair treatment.

With my true blood in the mix, I control the magic and give the field a small squeeze.

"AHHHHH! You ratshit fuck." The Void stills its efforts to escape.

"Wrong answer," I say.

     M.J. Hook

A hard-pressed threat to fulfill, destroying the Void. Making oblivion for the little shit possible means destroying the vessel, Darren Shoemacher. Still, getting answers is my first priority.

Then I'll snuff it. For what it did to those kids, those families…

I am in no immediate rush, so I act relaxed and squeeze the cell walls tighter. While the Void screams, I remove Omori's backpack from around my neck. I look inside. I see her gun, a wallet, some tampons, and a wad of rags.

The totem around my neck goes heavy, yanks my head down. My tattoos, already tingling with protection, burn like fresh brands. I switch to 3E, and a potent glow of energy radiates within the rags. The magic in the backpack disrupts my concentration.

The Void makes a solid crack in my containment field. I turn off my sight, but not before getting a solid earful of its thrum. A cruel vibration wrenches my body. The Void rips through the containment, scorching hair and searing skin.

It's almost free.

Her backpack in hand, I dive toward Omori, throwing my body on top of hers. I cast a shield for protection from possession around us, if only to buy some time. But instead of attacking us, the naked undertaker races across the bay and leaps into an oven. After a moment of quiet, screams of realization fill the space and then quickly die away in flames meant for the dead.

M.J. Hook

24

FRIDAY, EARLY MORNING

EVEN THOUGH MY sight's fragged, I use it to look for the shit stain. No Void. No thrum. I turn it off and wait, still holding the protection around Omori and myself. Once I hear the sirens, I look again.

Still no Void.

Figuring it needs a life source of some type to feed on to build strength, maybe I hurt it enough that it tagged out to go find a rat to possess. The idea gives me little satisfaction as I release the field and try to stand up. I settle for kneeling as I check Omori's pulse.

She's alive. Strong beat, but no way to rouse her.

I summon Scout to pick me up. Probably making a terrible decision, I grab Omori's backpack and leave her for Benny to rescue. Scout pulls up and swings open the passenger door. I drag myself in. Pulling away, my faithful ride finds a grassy incline to four-wheel up and out of the complex and back onto a city street.

"Home," I say, knowing Scout will get us there.

Texting Benny, I let him know Omori is passed out but fine and that Shoemacher is in oven #2. Before putting the phone away, I add one more text Benny will understand.

You may need to check for camera in the cloud. Oops

On the way home, I throw the backpack in a protective bag I keep in Scout for enchanted objects. Once home, I take it to my bottega, throw the damned thing in the middle of my six-foot ring of copper and cast a potent wall of defense between it and me.

After eating a quick, healthy meal, taking a hot and cold shower, then swallowing a few healers, I leave my Benny-pinging phone in the kitchen to charge and head to bed to crash.

• • •

Waking up hurts.

Attempts to ignore the day fail as memories from the night before hit my brain like a runaway recall locomotive.

"Shit and sorcery." My voice sounds and feels like a dry boiler. My head screams like a steam whistle as I sit up and examine the damage the Void railed through my body and soul.

I soak in the shower and allow the heat and steam to lift me onto a new track of thinking. After drying off, I throw on my robe and head to the kitchen for coffee.

By the time I finish my first cup, Jabari has shown up, and I give her the scoop on last night's romp in the crematorium. We take our mugs to the bottega and stare at the backpack. I feel stronger in body and spirit, but my thoughts play like a scratched record, skipping parts I know are important to a song I need to hear.

"Whaddaya think it is?" Jabari asks.

"Bad news, for the moment. I do know what's in that bag is important to the shit stain. It made a point to grab it, leaving her purse and jacket behind. The power radiating from whatever is in there distracted my enchantment. I swear it was emanating a similar spiritual timbre to the Void. It happened so fast. Kicked my ass, what little I had left to twerk."

"You did not just say that," Jabari smirks.

Mork from Ork starts blasting from my phone. My head lowers with guilt, realizing I've ignored Benny's texts and calls all morning.

"Watch it, Jabs. I doubt anything will happen. The containment is strong, and I refreshed all the home wards when I got up. But—"

"You never know what evil may be up its sleeve." She finishes my sentence with a statement of lesson.

"Good girl. Thanks," I say, shutting her in the botegga.

Instead of going through all the texts and messages from the dissatisfied detective, I listen to the one he just left.

"I'm almost at your place right-the-fuck-now. You better be there." I can almost hear him slam a receiver down when he hangs up.

Pulling out another cup for Benny, I refresh mine as I hear gravel crunching out front. I pour his brew and greet the disheveled officer outside.

"Morning, Benjamin," I say after he slams the Pontiac's door.

"It's still last night for me, you ass. That mug better have my name on it."

I hand him the full cup, which settles him down so he doesn't spill the hot liquid on his already stained overcoat. He takes several sips, shuts his eyes, and groans.

"You're lucky I have a forgiving heart. This mug buys you a few moments of reprieve until I've tanked up on caffeine."

"Come in, Detective, and let's fill each other's cups with information. May not be sweet, but I dare say it should clear the froth from last night's activities."

We walk inside, and before he can ask anything, I ask the question nagging me. "How is Omori?"

Benny takes another sip, then sets his cup on the counter too fast, causing it to splash a new stain on the sleeve of his blemished coat.

"Yeah, yeah, she's at Memorial. Still KO'd by whatever Shoemacher gave her. They should have tox results back soon. Her vitals are all good." He takes off his coat, lays it over the stool next to him, and decompresses. His shoulders slump as he rubs his face. "So, you start with your evening's activities, and I'll finish."

"Well first, the Void *was* in control of Shoemacher," and from there I tell him everything, except about finding a magical surprise at the bottom of Omori's backpack.

"You look pretty chipper for getting your ass kicked again by the noir musical smear of shit," Benny jokes, but when he's tired, his wit can be a tad brutal. "Sounds like it was going to have its way with Omori before roasting her."

"No doubt." The disturbing reminder flashes by as I redirect the conversation. "Your turn."

"We showed up. Williams ran to Emiko like a white knight while I tried to turn off the body cookers. Had to use a gurney to slam the doors shut before I could even look for the off switches. Smelled like a pig roast gone bad. Turns out the body grill is a commercial outfit used by local funeral homes that don't have their own facility. Owner is over there right now trying to sort through the ashes and identify who all got flamed."

"Security footage?" I won't be recognized, but other shit happened that would make for questionable viewing.

"You lucked out there. System wasn't recording. Owner is probably going to be cited by the Funeral Directors Association for that faux pas. He's unlucky most of his grand poo-bahs are in town at the convention." Benny picks up his coffee and takes a large swallow. "One guy who came in to help sort ash claims they're backlogged on stiffs. Everyone's partying at the convention. Also, our kidnapper, Shoemacher, happens to be one of the owners. Big outfit out of L.A. That bit of news justified going to that particular hot spot first, luckily. Didn't have a clue how to justify your map tag."

"Makes sense. The Void not only controls the person, it pulls information from their memories." I shudder, remembering its brief touch at the bar last night. Hearing my skeletons revealed through the mouths of acquaintances rattled my bones. "Anything else, Detective?"

"Yeah, I need ten hours of sleep and a vacation to follow." The angst Benny brought up the mountain has vanished, replaced by weariness. He finishes his cup and prepares to leave, then goes wide-eyed with a thought.

"You didn't happen to see Omori's backpack anywhere? Williams is worried about it. Thinks her gun, ID, and other important stuff are in it."

I look my friend straight in the eye and lie.

"No, but if I did, I can guarantee I wouldn't have noticed."

• • •

"Did *Coffee Time with Badges* reveal anything about the prize in the Cracker Jack bag here?" Jabari is reading a graphic novel of some sort, her point of sight at the backpack just over the top of the pages.

"No and yes," I reply. "I may have forgotten to mention that I had it when he brought it up. But mentioning it offered a moment of clarification." I step up to the edge of the circle and stare at the neon lump in the center. "We need to get whatever is inside out."

"You said 'we,' as in I am going to help?" The sunny tone of Jabari's voice is evident.

"Yes, and you are going to do most of the work."

We position ourselves shoulder to shoulder on the ground outside of the constraining ring, in front of a smaller ring embedded in the floor next to the larger coil.

"I'm going to create a portal in the shield, and you're going to use air fingers to open the bag, remove the object, then retrieve the bag through the portal. Understand?"

"Sure do. Only you said it's wrapped up. Don't you want me to unwrap it?"

"One step at a time. I cannot keep the portal open very long, so get it out, then grab the bag and pull it through. Her gun is in there. No idea if the safety is on, so avoid pulling the trigger."

"Gotcha." Jabari's enthusiasm becomes a sharp focus on the small ring.

When constructing the larger coil, I placed the smaller coiled ring on the outside for moments like this. A thin line of copper runs under the floor and emerges flush inside the main ring, attached to another coiled circle of copper. This allows me the ability to pass items to and from the containment field. The size of the open portal is only big enough for small items.

For a prisoner, I can pass nourishment through. With potentially enchanted items, I can run limited tests without risk of harm outside the protective walls. For handling objects, though, it helps to have someone else who knows how to manipulate air with precision.

And Jabs has the best air hands I know.

Opening the portal takes little effort. Keeping the portal open and manipulating items inside at the same time is tough. It's a mess having to close the portal on a sandwich when a vessel-possessing spirit realizes the conduit is there and tries to escape. A knee-jerk reaction staining the floor with mustard.

With two people, I only need to focus on keeping the line open.

The food and sleep last night helped put my disjointed spirit back together. Switching to 3E, I notice Sam's song is no longer present. My energy slightly unbalanced, I can still maintain a strong visual of my containment barrier. The azure glow of restraint emits from the embedded ring, generating a circular wall of magic confinement. Colorful sparkles of power flash throughout the field that domes near the ceiling.

Opening the portal, my magic pushes through the small ring between us, follows the lead through the field, and opens inside the barrier.

Jabari tutts her fingers as if signing to the element, then moves her magic through the portal. I watch a small dust bunny wisp away as Jabari's air enters the ring. The bag lifts, then stops.

"Really? A zipper? Couldn't you have unzipped it before throwing it in?"

"Good practice. Keep going."

It takes a couple of grabs on the puller before she can finally get the zipper started and open the top.

The real trick of using air fingers is being able to feel what you touch. Touching air to texture and recognizing it is a level of concentration I rarely achieve unless it is something obvious, like corduroy or hair.

Her eyes close. Jabari takes inventory. "That's... the gun. That's, that's... Does she have tampons in here?"

"Probably. Also, a billfold. Find the..."

"Found it. I can feel the energy pulse. The vibration is quiet. Dormant."

A hump travels through the bag and appears at the opening. A small rag-wrapped object appears. With a steady pull, the ball of cloth floats out of the backpack. Verdant swirls of energy snake around and through the wraps.

"I don't think it enjoys being outside of the bag, Red."

The green swirls increase their undulating movement, the lines of power multiplying, looking like a nest of eco-angry centipedes.

A tail of the rag catches on the zipper as Jabari sets the lump on the floor, causing the pack to fall over.

Breathing steadily, I keep my knees jerk free.

"That's good. Now grab the bag and pull it out," I say, watching the energy in case a swirl beelines for the portal.

Portal magic has size limitations determined by the entrances available. The backpack should have no problem squeezing through. A spirit can certainly size itself to fit. Jabari starts with a slow scoot, moving the bag towards the ring. The cloth stuck to the bag pulls. I see the pile move and knee-jerk.

"Pull it!" I yell. Jabari extends her arms above her head, like a fisher who just caught the big one. The bag disappears from inside the field, and I close the portal. A section of rag pulls through before being cut off.

The backpack flies out of the small ring and up into the air, then lands at Jabari's feet with a heavy thump. Inside the containment field, the lump of cloth rolls, unraveling because of the quick pull. A small green jar spools out of the wrappings, rolling a few inches before stopping near the field's edge.

M.J. HOOK

"What? What is it? Did it come through?" Jabari kicks the bag aside and launches to her feet.

"No. The cloth caught on the bag and made it wiggle loose. At least it wasn't a turkey sandwich."

"Huh?"

"Never mind." The jar has my undivided attention.

Lying on its side, it's no bigger than an eight-ounce squatty jar of mustard. The green tendrils of energy cycle around the container. Tightening like desperate vines, the coils pull the jar upright and away from the containment field. Standing on four small round feet, the tendrils rest in place on the surface, mimicking carved designs of vines and leaves.

"Is that jade?" Jabari asks, referring to the material of the jar.

The polished teal surface shines with brilliant reflection and energy. Carved around the outside is a detailed relief: patterns of roots, vines, and leaves from bottom to top. The lid, resting in a beveled inset, crowns the jar with a beautifully carved camellia flower, the petals in a perfect pattern of phyllotaxis.

"That would be my first guess. The artwork is exquisite." Shifting my sight to look at its spiritual properties, the energy tells another story. "Look at how the magic bound to the jar protects it. Jade is an earth stone, and I guess that whatever is inside is some type of earth energy." Staring at the ornate totem, I feel puzzle pieces click into place.

"Um, Red? It's pretty. But I think you should check out this piece of rag I yanked out. Looks like some sort of tapis."

Wearing her enchanted gloves, Jabari releases the piece of material from the pack's zipper. She carries it over to the altar and lays it flat on the surface. No magic appears attached to it, but that's a supposition that can kill. My apprentice seals the rag in a small containment field and casts a series of tests. All pass with no results.

"It's clean. But there's some type of pattern printed on it." She looks closer, keeping the fragment contained.

Observing, I turn back and look at the remaining piece inside the field with the jar. A small tendril of energy releases from its side and taps around its little ball feet.

Using the portal again, I send an air spell inside, blowing the remaining piece of fabric toward the jar. As it falls back down, a piece drapes against the jar. Several vines of energy loosen from the carving and wrap a portion of the material around the totem's base.

The jar and tapestry are bound.

Moving to the altar, I release the spell and touch a corner of the remnant.

The fabric feels like silk, the once-white surface stained with grime and dirt. The fragment's about seven inches long up to the chop and only four inches in width. On the surface are blemished images of trees, dyed in the material with light grey ink. Down toward the severed end, in the same light ink, is a row of brushed Asian characters, most clipped in half.

"His master gave him the tapestry," I mutter, remembering the Void's boast in Shoemacher's voice.

"You need to speak louder if you want me to hear you the first time, Teach." Jabari moves closer to look inside the containment ring.

"This belongs to the Void. I bet once we get the remaining part of the rag out of containment, we'll be that much closer to putting it down. My Japanese is rudimentary at best, but I have a member in the Donum who'll be able to translate this for me."

"Will I ever get a Donum membership card? Your little group of intellectual shamanites appears to know a little bit about everything." Jabari's earnest stare gives me pause.

"Once you earn your Fourth Mark tatts, I have no doubt that you will not only get a card, but also learn the secret handshake." I return her stare.

"You're joking."

"Only about the handshake. You're basically a member now, through association."

"Sweet." Jabari smiles, then points at the jade jar snuggling against the other piece of tapis. "I'm all about sharing knowledge and kicking ass, but what about the pretty green can of energy? We going to pull that out for a looky-look?"

"One step at a time. Let's admire the wrapping paper before we see what's in the box."

     M.J. Hook

25

FRIDAY MORNING

JABS PULLS THE remaining piece of tapestry out. Little vines from the jar reach for it, then settle back on the surface when they find no purchase. I reinforce the protection around the circle as Jabari floats the piece over to the altar next to its missing part.

"Ah, bloody hell. Boss, you need to see this," she says. "I lowered the shielding, dropped the rag in, and set it up again. Then this fucking shit started."

Four quick steps to the altar and I see what caused her to swear.

The two pieces of tapestry are moving, scooting separated edges next to each other. As we watch, threads from both pieces reach out to reattach, creating a seamless fix to the tapestry.

"Well, that's a new one on me, Jabs. It would appear this thing has a mending spell applied to it. I've got some socks that could use a good mend."

"You're not serious!"

"No, I'm not," I reply. Jabs hits me on the shoulder.

"Is everything a joke with you? This Void thing has been kicking your ass up and down the front range, killed people, and has *you* in a bullseye—and you joke about darning socks?"

I turn and look Jabari in the eyes. "Listen, my dear pupil, humor is one of my defenses to deal with my own fears. It releases endorphins, which counter the cortisol and adrenaline pumping through my heart right now. I use laughter to fight my demons. I use wit to fight the demons that cause it.

Right now, I need a clear head, not an anxious one.”

Jabari holds my stare as she listens. Her look of concern melts as understanding enlightens her gaze.

“Balance,” she replies after a moment.

“Exactly.”

She smiles. “I’ve got some holey jeans that could use a darn or three.”

I chuckle. “Nice. Now let’s see what magic keeps this piece of cloth together.”

Manipulating the containment circle with words of protection, I cycle through several new enchantments to determine the type of magic woven within the material. All appear inactive until I use an old incantation that causes the ink drawn on the silk to glow. As the images shine in pearlescent blues, the tapestry lifts and stretches, bowing at the edges where it meets the containment walls.

“Jabs, take pics.”

She pulls out her phone and takes a shot, checks it, and lowers it to her hip.

“The characters aren’t showing up.”

“That’s OK. Now that I know the magic involved, I think we can lower the field and try some other things to get pics.” I take a breath, then lower the protection. The silk falls to the table.

“What kind of magic is involved, boss?” she asks, taking a few steps back from the altar.

“It’s not a curse. More like a blessing.” I put on my protective gloves and spread the tapestry out straight. Four inches wide, and with the two pieces together, it spreads out to just over two feet. “Mythology in all cultures has stories of blessed objects given to warriors to help with their quests. The armor of Achilles; the golden coat of chain mail Sigurd took in Norse mythology; Dubán, the shield of Cú Chulainn… tons of stories with tons of objects.”

Jabari, keeping her distance, points at the cloth. “Are you telling me some sort of god blessed this rag?”

“Remember your teachings with Dr. Tinibu, Jabs. A powerful belief in something can cause manifestation. Sometimes, devout belief may cause someone to think they see, hear, and feel the *something*. If there is a true spiritual link to the entity through Nature…” I pause.

“It can manifest. Become real. Yeah, I remember. But that was like

 M.J. Hook

elemental spirits, not gods with a capital 'G.' Even after all his discussions about the fae folk, if and when they ever existed, he never talked about real gods ruling the heavens."

"True, but it doesn't take a god to bless or curse an object. You and Benny wear blessed medallions that allow you to step into my home, avoiding my wards and still having my blessing. It's all about power and the intent behind it. If this rag displayed a curse, I would not have lowered the protection."

"So?" Jabari steps a little closer to look at the silk.

"So, we need to get the images to show up so I can take pics and send them to a Donum member that can read them. The ink's faded, or it may be a light tint for a purpose. Here, look." I point to the finished characters mended by the cloth's self-restoration. "These looked like Japanese characters, but seeing the full ideogram, they are something else. I'm guessing an older writing system. And look here, does this scene look familiar?" I move my finger past the line of characters to the center of the tapestry.

Jabari moves her head up and down to allow the light to hit the fabric at different angles.

"It looks like an enormous mountain surrounded by little trees."

"That mountain is pretty iconic, if it's what I think it is."

When Jabari's eyes get big, they shine.

"Is that Fuji?"

"I think so, considering the characters framing the image. I may be going out on a limb here, but we found this in the bag of Inspector Omori, who arrived from Japan around the time this shit show started."

Eyes still shining, Jabari looks over at the tossed backpack.

"Guess you're going to the hospital and return her backpack, huh?"

"And then some. While I am gone, I need you to try shining different lights on this thing to make the ink clear enough to read. Shoot pics I can send. I have several lamps and bulbs in the closet by the sink."

"You sure this rag is safe?"

"Sure enough, but wear protection."

"Brilliant. You sound like a cool parent."

• • •

To avoid a conversation with Benny, I text.

Meet me at Memorial. Found Omori's pack in Scout. Go figure. Need escort to bring her gun in hospital. Also, look up flight from LA Tom Hutchins was on. Then look up flight Omori arrived on. Can't talk, I'm driving.

After a long moment, he replies.

I call bullshit on pack and your driving. Thinking about ratting Scout out to Traffic Div. Meet me east entrance.

I park next to his Pontiac. Standing on the curb, I see Benny in a clean shirt and somewhat pressed pants, meaning he put them between his mattress and box springs the night before.

"How did you know?" He asks as I step out of Scout.

"Same flight?"

"Yes. How did you know?"

"Got a lot of magic stuff to explain to you. Or I can give you the short version."

As we walk to the entrance, I hand Benny the neon backpack. He stops, turns around, looks around, then pulls out Omori's gun and puts it in his coat pocket. We continue walking, and he says, "Short version."

"Inspector Omori brought the Void over from Japan. Don't know why, and I still don't know what it is exactly, but I need to chat with her. Maybe she can enlighten me with answers."

"You don't think she's in cahoots with the damn thing, do ya?" He stops me just before we get to the door.

"Honestly, no, I don't. I'm thinking she got picked as a mule to smuggle it into the Springs. I'm hoping she's got a story to tell. Do you know if she's awake?"

"Woke up this morning. Williams stayed with her all night. Sent a text around two hours ago."

"Good. If he's there, take him down to the cafeteria and buy him an attaboy meal."

It took Benny a moment to get Williams out of Omori's room. As soon as they hit the elevator, I walk in her room.

"Mr. Wood?" Her small body is covered with several blankets.

"Inspector."

"Detective Rogers was just here, returning my backpack. He and John went down to get some coffee. You must have just missed them.”

“I wanted to come in and talk to *you*. How are you feeling?”

“Better. The doctor said I have no drugs in my blood. They did a scan, a…,” she struggles with the word. “It reads my brain. Said my brain was…” She goes quiet, trying to put a word to the diagnosis. “Anyway, they did another scan this morning and everything is better. Said I can leave later today, maybe.”

“Wonderful.” I consider continuing the conversation about her health, but my patience is worn down to a desperate nub. “I need to ask you a few questions, if you feel up to it.”

“I told John and Benny everything I remember about the kidnapping, which was very little.”

“Not about that. I need to know why you came to Colorado Springs.”

“I don’t understand. My department selected me after I put in a request. I wanted to visit the Olympic Training Center.”

A thought occurs to me. “And the Olympic & Paralympic Museum?”

“Yes. Very much. But I also wanted to experience an American police department, too.”

My questions are getting honest answers. Knowing how the Void entraps its vessel’s mind, I know I need to dig deeper. Reaching into my coat, I pull a vial, uncork it, and put a small pile of the dust on my palm.

“What’s that, Mr. Wood?”

“Here, let me show you.” I put my palm with the powder in front of her face. “I’m into natural remedies, and I’m betting if you take a sniff of this, your headache will go away.”

“But I don’t have a…” she begins, then I blow the powder in her face.

Her eyes dilate as I say “*brionglōid*.” She falls asleep.

Sleeping powder is a good thing. Who doesn’t need a good night’s rest occasionally?

Mixing the powder with a knockout spell may seem redundant, but it mimics general anesthesia. I’ve sent Inspector Emiko Omori to la-la land, where I need her to review her memories.

Without her permission, I am a voyeur—a Peeping Tom of the lowest order. But with no time to explain the magic, I settle for being an asshole. I throw an enchanted lock on her door and pull the curtain to hide my mental eavesdropping.

This is the only way to find the answers my gut says are hiding in

Omori's memories. Magic with bad intentions can hide simple recall. Magic with good intentions can remove the blocks.

Sometimes good intentions can have terrible consequences. I'm too spooked to reconsider my desperate actions as I coil my spirit with hers.

If I am linked to a spirit entity in a baddoon, I'm at the mercy of the tethered soul to show me their past. When connected to a living spirit, I can normally view their memories like watching streaming video, with control to reverse or forward through all memories and, if I choose, the feelings attached to each one.

In Inspector Omori's case, instead of trying to explain to her that she most likely transported a murderous entity in her baggage, it's easier to check her memory manifest for proof. A discussion is a waste of time.

My spirit coil laces with hers. I easily make my way into her mind. Accessing her memories happens quickly, and I rewind immediately. Catching glimpses of recent moments that I may touch on when I move forward, I continue until I find her back in Japan.

She finds out she is going to Colorado Springs. *Rewind*.

Several images sweep by that I must see once I find a place to start. *Stop*.

She parks her car on a trailhead to a massive forest. Two other officers meet her. She turns and looks at the sign near the path. I recognize what I read: a suicide warning for Aokigahara Forest.

The suicide forest.

She discusses the car found abandoned by the other two officers. I understand enough of the Japanese spoken to figure out the owner has been missing for several days. *Forward*.

Walking by herself in the forest. Unhappy. They didn't select her for the trip to Colorado. Fiancé broke up with her. Was looking forward to getting away. *Forward*.

Darkness.

Stop. Play.

She is not in control. Her spirit is contained by another. No audio. *Slow*.

I recognize the trembling darkness as I work to push through the possession, which could cause a serious fracture to Omori's psyche when she wakes. Her memory is blank. The Void holds her.

I see the forest again. I turn up the sound. I hear the devastating twang of the Void's presence. Fortunately, being inside the possessed vessel seems to damper it. The effect does not shatter me, but to watch and listen nauseates

M.J. Hook

my spirit.

I recognize the intonation and patronizing tone of the Void's voice speaking Japanese: "Poor, sad child. You are welcome here, girl. In this beautiful garden. This is the place kind souls come to find happiness. I feel the disappointment you've had. I see your failures after trying so hard. Be strong, child. Use your gun, join us here. Leave the darkness behind."

Omori is reaching for her gun when another voice speaks in English. "Wait." A woman steps into view from behind a large formation of moss-covered rocks. She is tall, dressed in black slacks, a black button-down shirt. Her face is tough to define through the Void's shadow. Angular, with short, spikey white hair.

"My father has use of this one. Has need of you too, forest fiend."

The scene goes black and silent. I consider fast-forwarding but remain patient.

Omori is sitting on a rock, dazed. She notices an object in her hand as her view becomes clouded with black mist. The silk tapestry, wrapped around what I assume is the jade jar. The bundle goes in her coat pocket, and the darkness clears. Her gun is on the ground. Confused, she picks it up.

The woman in black is no longer there when Omori looks up.

Omori's radio announces her name. She answers, claiming she has found nothing so far. She stands up and continues her search. *Forward.*

Walking out of the forest with no success. *Forward.* Back to the office. The shadow returns as she pulls out the concealed jar and places it in her backpack, then it clears. Home. Next day in the office, while Omori's filling out paperwork, a man appears to let her know she is going to Colorado. Officer Takahashi had an accident and is in the hospital.

Omori is happy. *Forward.*

Every time she opens her backpack, the mist appears. *Forward.*

Packing her bag, mist appears. She places the wrapped jar in her suitcase. *Forward.*

Plane ride. Through her eyes I cannot see Thomas Hutchins, but I feel the Void coming and going from her vessel. *Forward.*

Nothing. *Forward.*

The crime scene where we meet. *Forward.*

She's at the USOPC museum, noticing Jimmy Shurter and his mother Darlene racing. She smiles as a moment of darkness covers and lifts away.

I can see a change in Darlene. She grabs her son with a forceful hand

and leaves. *Forward.*

Forward.

Stop.

Before I remove my coil, I examine Omori's spirit. With no idea if my actions inside her mind opened fresh memories, I check her aura. She reads fine. Still in a deep sleep.

Removing the spell, I let the sleep dust keep her in dreams. Pulling the curtain back, I wave my hand to unseal the door, then leave.

26

FRIDAY, LATE MORNING, JABARI

WORKING IN ALMOST total darkness, Jabari tried several bulbs in a small lamp she found in the closet.

"Who knew bulbs came in so many colors?" she said to herself, replacing a green bulb with an orange one. After trying several colored bulbs, she pulled out different lamps to test. A black light seemed to shed some light on the ink, but not enough to get a decent picture.

Picking up a small lamp, the bulb housed in a shielded container, she clicked it on, and the ink appeared in fluorescent shades of purple.

"Oh wow. Finally." She held the lamp above the tapestry and took careful pictures, overlapping sections as she moved down the table.

Turning on the lights, she took a picture of the lamp so Red would know what worked and sent all the images to his phone. Cleaning up the bulbs and lamps, she put them away, then folded the tapestry, putting it under another containment spell on the altar.

"Better safe than stupid."

Finished, she texted an update to Basil, Red's research friend in Amsterdam. Considering the evidence appeared to be Japanese in origin, it might help the pretentious-sounding analyst dial in his information.

A scream outside the workshop caused Jabari to jump. Hearing it again, she realized it was Marlow.

"Arrrgh. Damn cat." Storming out of the workshop and hiding the entrance, Jabari ran down the hall to the door leading out to Marlow's pen. "What's got your big, ugly testicles tied in a knot, lion?"

Marlow crouched, facing the opening that led outside. Jabari knocked on the glass door, then stuck her toe into the large pet door beside it so the cat could hear her complaint.

"What's got you spooked? You got a bear wanting to come in and try out your couch?"

Marlow crouched tighter, preparing to attack. The growl emanating from his body was enough for Jabari to remove her toe.

"What is it, buddy?"

Unable to see anything moving outside the pen, Jabari switched to 3E and saw a black, twisting form up on the ridge, twelve feet from Marlow's door.

"Bloody fuckety shit."

27

FRIDAY, LATE MORNING

MY PHONE CHIRPS with Jabari's text. I scroll through the images, zooming in on a couple. The last image raises my eyebrows like two excited caterpillars.

"Damn. A Woods lamp," I say out loud.

"Huh? What? You got a crime scene you need to scan for blood and semen?" Benny walks up behind me in the parking lot.

Before answering, I forward the tapestry and jar images to Yui, my sigil teacher and a Donum member in Japan, tapping a quick note asking if she can decipher the tapestry.

"Sorry, important magic stuff. No. No scene. But I gotta tell you something about what I found in Omori's backpack. It's the reason I needed to question her. The—"

Jabari's recorded ringtone, saying, "Answer me now, dammit," interrupts my confession to Benny.

"Hold on," I tell him and take the call.

"Red, it's here. The Void is here. Outside the house, and it's trying real hard to get in."

"Damn it. I doubt it can get in, but keep your sight off. Turn it on only to check wards. I'll be there as soon as I can."

"I bet it's here wanting to get its jar of peas and fancy toilet paper." Jabari's using humor to mask the fear evident in her voice.

"Just stay inside. Sight off." I hang up.

"What's happening?" Benny yells at me as I jump in Scout's open door.

FEAR   161

"The Void's at my cabin."

"I-I-I'll come with, give you backup." I can hear the doubt in Benny's voice. He means it, but I know he questions his ability to help.

"No. You'll only be a tool for it to work against me. Drive over to the Little Tycoon. See if Samantha is available. She handled the piece of shit last night. Maybe she can do it again."

"Will do!"

I know I will get there long before Benny, but maybe I can stall it at home until Sam arrives.

Racing across town, I drive to keep my mind focused on something life-threatening. I call Jabari after running a red light.

"I'm on my way."

"Good. I got Marlow inside. He's the one that warned me the shitty thing was outside."

"He could see it?" I know cats are sensitive to the spiritual world, but I've never tested the theory.

"I didn't ask him, Red. But when I opened the door and told him to get inside, he bolted in like a fur-covered rocket."

"OK, let's keep the line open here. Tell me if anything happens."

"You and your cat will be first to know."

Driving through the Crystal Heights entrance without stopping, I ignore Boris trying to get my attention from the gatehouse. Having driven the switchbacks up my mountain since I first learned to drive, I take the turns without touching the brakes.

Pulling up to the front of my cabin, I stay within Scout's wards, switch to 3E, and pull my phone close.

"Jabs?"

"Yes, sir."

"I'm here. I don't see it out front. About ten feet for me to make it to the front door. Get down there and be ready to open it. Inside, we can figure out a way to squash this thing." Holding the handle to the car door, I look every which way to see if the vile spot is around.

"I'm at the door, boss. I see you."

Pulling the latch, I jump out and race three steps before an earsplitting twang hits my spirit. Working on an adrenaline rush, I kept my sight open, exposing my ears.

Stupid.

   M.J. Hook

My sore shoulder hits the ground. I roll off it and onto my back. Above me, trembling like a nervous piece of tar, is the Void. I try to turn off my sight, but it's locked open. Panic stitches through every inch of my spirit. My body seizes as the Void slams me with another thrum of discord, grinding my back into the gravel.

I can't breathe, my lungs trapped in a vacuum of terror. An attempt to blast the trembling darkness above me away with an air spell fails as its music violates my senses. I stare into the Void's darkness. The emptiness is so deep that it warps the field of energy around it.

"You surprised me last night, Red." The vocals grind into my soul like the gravel digging into my back—rough with sharp edges. It strums again, causing my skeleton to rattle in my skin like a bag of scrying bones. A searing pain, as if my groin splits and continues to tear through my body. What remaining breath I have chokes out.

Covered in sweat, my body shrieks from every pore as the pressure recedes. Nerve endings tingle as I inhale a whisper of blessed air and open my eyes.

My sight exposed, I see the small demon spawn emerge from its darkness. Resting a dark elbow on the static edge of its floating hollow, it cups its pudgy face in a tiny three-clawed hand. Smiling down at my helpless form, the Void sighs.

"You ruined my date with that *chīsana meinu* Emiko. You wasted my wonderful cadaver fire." The empty eye sockets of the creature fill with orbs of flame. Its brow furrows as it sends another chord of ruin through my soul. My groan sounds so distant.

"But the cock-shocker of the night—you took something of mine. I know it's inside your *yōsai*. Have your bitch bring it out, NOW!" With its last word, a rage of sound vibrates throughout my spirit.

I scream as the Void's emptiness fills my vision.

A large blur, emitting a roar of animal anger, hits the Void. I see the sky. To my left, Marlow is ripping into the black patch with teeth and claws. Every tear mends itself, but Marlow's shredding keeps the black blanket of torture occupied.

Trying to get up, I manage to roll to my stomach. Inhaling deeply, I push myself up on an elbow. My head feels like a sack of bowling balls, jumbled weights of pain banging inside my brain as my neck strains to lift my eyes up.

The Void arches and rolls itself into a wave, launching my loyal cat into the air. Landing on his feet, Marlow rushes to my side and guards my body with devoted growls.

The Void rises off the ground. The effort looks agonizing while it's repairing the damage Marlow delivered. Both the Void and I shudder when we hear Jabari scream out a spell of flame. The jet of fire catches the Void on its bottom edge. The patch of darkness flips, then flies right at her.

"Jabari! No. Get back inside," I scream with what voice I have left. Turning my head is a burden. An icy chill runs down my back as I watch Jabari run back to the house.

Before she can make the warded entry, the Void slaps her body, causing her to spin, lose footing, and fall hard to the gravel. She tries to get up. The oily blotch wastes no time. The Void hits the back of her neck like a rock hitting water. Her skin ripples as the darkness disappears inside her vessel. Her personal wards cannot keep it out.

She becomes its toy.

A powerful toy.

Jabari's head arches back. A loud twang of discord erupts from her open mouth, the muscles on her neck straining with the effort. Her body begins to fill with darkness; a pool of dirty oil pours down her skin and clothes. The flow stops as Jabari screams. Her hands start scratching where the darkness resides. Twisting left, right, she spins and falls to the ground, silent, as the jittery filth blankets her body.

"Oh, fuck no." I try to get up, but the vibration sucks my remaining strength and puts my face down in the gravel. Marlow shakes his head as if a mass of fleas has flown into his ears. One last swipe of his paw, he turns to my apprentice. He knows Jabari, but he knows evil now controls her as he postures to attack.

"Marlow. No." The wind it takes to push out the words burns. "Leave. Alone," I say, hoping he understands. My cat holds position.

Jabari's empty, twitchy silhouette stands up, moving like the powerful athlete that she is. She admires her arms and hands as she turns toward me. Tears swell my eyes as the recent litany of events streams through my head.

It's not her. It's not Jabari. It's the Void.

"This will do. This will do just fine." It's her voice, but not her tone.

Thoughts fill my head as I search for new solutions. Must separate the Void from Jabari. Leave Jabari safe. Destroy the Void. Spells and

M.J. Hook

containments. Frustration and anger. My body and my spirit.

Broken. A cracked toilet filled with waste.

The Void laughs as it heads to the open front door. It makes the threshold as the wards around the door ignite with power. The force sends the dark form flying back through the air. For a moment, I see Jabari again. The Void fills her back up with its murk as it hits the ground.

It rolls with the impact, landing back on its feet. The Void turns to stare at me.

"Well, this is one massive disappointment." The Void looks up in reflection, touches its chest, then looks around on the ground. As if it just remembered something, it turns and looks through the door. I follow the gaze and see Jabari's ward medallion, the one that allows her entry into my cabin, hanging on the stair's banister post inside.

"Smart girl. You stupid, beautiful, smart girl," I say. Tears leak from my eyes.

"No problem, Wood." The Void walks toward me, then stops when Marlow growls and crouches. It stops. "Tell your puss to back off. Would hate for this new sleeve to be damaged before I have time to test-drive it."

I touch Marlow's leg. He backs up to stand beside me.

"Tell you what, *boss*. You got my number." It pulls Jabari's phone from a pocket of blackness. "Call when you are ready to hand over my stuff. I'll trade her back for it."

"You. Better not. Harm. Her." I try to sound angry, but my voice only whispers threat.

"Harm? She's got a powerful soul, Red. I'm going to feed on it for a while. Then, when the plate empties, I'll see how many men she can fuck with this fine physique. After the fucking's done, I'll switch sleeves and tube her up into a sculpture as a useless whore."

It walks to her car, gets in, finds the keys in the console, and starts it. Rolling down the window, it shouts, "Call me!"

As it drives away, it waves, then flips me off with an empty, twitchy finger.

Yep. Fuck me royal I think before I pass out.

M.J. Hook

28

FRIDAY AFTERNOON

MY EYES OPEN to sky in normal view. Passing out turned off my 3E.

Feeling like a snake hit by a lawnmower, I drag myself to Scout and prop myself up against the rear wheel. Marlow comes over and rubs his head against my face, then licks dried tear salt from my cheeks. Purring, he lies down and rests his head on my feeble leg.

Scout honks. The hatch opens and Marlow jumps inside. After a moment, the big cat jumps out and drops a bottle of water beside me.

"When did you two become such good friends?"

With a lead weight in my hand, I lift it and pet my hero cat. Twisting off the lid and taking my first gulp of the water is a chore. I savor the hydration. My head rests against the tire. I want to sleep. Pass out. The image of Jabari's violation shakes me awake more than once.

Eventually, a car pulls into my drive. I know it's Benny's Pontiac. Marlow gets up and starts pacing back and forth as two car doors open and close.

"By the power of Grayskull… is that a mountain lion?" Samantha's nostalgic He-Man quip gives me a smile. Hearing her voice lifts my spirit a few inches out of the dirt.

"That's Marlow," Benny says. "Red's house cat. He's a sweetheart, long as you don't smell like wabbit." He pauses, then yells, "Red? Red, you inside?"

"Here," I croak. Raising my arm to wave, I fall over and expose myself behind Scout. Marlow quits pacing to nudge his nose into my neck.

"Oh, shit." Benny runs over to me, scratches Marlow behind the ears to move him, then lifts me back up.

Samantha squats beside me, touches my face, places a palm on my chest, then hums a song—a beautiful, healing tune. I feel her mage magic immediately as its warmth courses through my spirit.

"What happened, bud? You're pale as a milk bottle," Benny says.

The vibration from Sam's tune is like a gentle purring session with Marlow, touching my spirit with a sweet tremor of healing. Briefly switching to 3E, I witness her magic as its color and energy examine my broken spirit. My sight snaps off like a dead bulb.

"Void. Possessed Jabari," is all I can force out.

"I'm going to get you some water." Benny moves, and I grab his coat.

"Give Sam. Medallion." Then point to the open door. I know Benny will recognize it. He has one just like it.

Floating on Sam's medicinal cloud of recovery, I pass out again.

• • •

Waking up in the front entry, a cushion under my head, Marlow lying at my feet, and Sam burning a sweet-smelling smudge while still humming her beautiful tune, I take a full deep breath without pain. My sight is normal as I watch her wave the smoke above my body.

I see Jabari's charm nestled in her cleavage.

Then I remember and attempt to sit up.

"Woah, buddy. You need to stay put. According to Dr. Salviati here, you're in need of a major tune-up." Benny puts a hand on my shoulder to keep me down. "And before you start telling me what happened, know that I've put out an APB on Jabari's Honda. Possible kidnapping, with a do not approach but call in. Also, got a trace started on her phone."

By Gaia, my friend is good at his job.

"Thank you," my voice cracks. "Cancel it."

"Why would I do that?" Benny says, exasperated.

"If I need to find her, I have plenty of her DNA here to locate her." I stare up at the entry light. The globe remains dark, and I see the husks of dead insects inside.

"The Void's controlling her body, Benny. If her car's pulled over, I can only imagine the scene the patrol video would capture. She doesn't need that." It amazes me that the light can be so tantalizing to bugs. It draws them

      M.J. Hook

in—a glowing ambush to death.

"It will keep her phone off, turning it on to see if I've called. And I can't call until I know I have some idea how to save her." I should clean the globe, give the dried insects back to Gaia.

Sam interrupts her tune. I miss her vibe immediately. How strange that one sound can cause my soul to crack and another can feel like a warm, soothing balm to put me back together.

In a gentle voice, she says, "If you're going to talk, only move your mouth and stay focused on your breathing." Her eyes shine like two brilliant emeralds affixed in the face of an angel. The radiance of her stare sends a wave of ease through my body.

"I have a lot I need to fill you guys in on. So… you understand. So you can help with ideas. My body, nerves… my soul… fuck. My brain. All marinating in pain," I say, as a tear for Jabari leaks from my eye.

"In that case," Sam says, pulling her hand up. She touches a charm on her bracelet, then looks under her arm. She reaches into a magical space. Her hand disappears, then reappears holding a vial.

"What the…" Benny starts at Sam's display of magic.

"Pantry charm," I say. "Nice. I tried to make one once. Ended up with a hole with no bottom. Tossed a rock in. Never heard it land."

"I'll show you how to build the construct for the spell. But not now." She unscrews the vial lid and puts the bottle to my lips. "If you need to exert yourself, drink this. The potion will work with my healing. Just try to stay still until it has time to spread."

I drink it. Sam continues her song.

The tastes divide on my tongue as I swallow. Lavender, ginger, gingko… there are other flavors I recognize as each taste spreads to distinct parts of my body. Her tune generates the directions. The elixir is more for my soul, aligning the levels of my spirit.

"You'll have to give me the recipe for that as well."

She stops long enough to say, "It only works with an air spell of healing," then continues her song.

My mind clears, so I decide to use it, but keep myself horizontal.

"OK," I say, and tell them about the jar and tapestry, what I scried searching Omori's memories, then the fight outside. I choke up when I tell them what the Void did to Jabari and its demands for her return.

Benny steps over to crouch down beside Marlow, giving my cat scratches behind the ears. "I've never understood why you adopted this fur ball, but seems like you two are meant for each other." Marlow purrs in agreement. "Good thing he could see the bad guy. Think he's got your sight?"

"Animals are sensitive to spirit energy. And I suppose hanging around me, he's developed a sense for good vibes and bad." Marlow licks my hand with a scratchy tongue. His ability to damage the Void fills my head with ideas. Too many to consider right now.

"Never a dull moment hanging around you, Red. So, you got a plan?"

"Sort of. A lot of it may depend on *you*." My gaze turns to Sam, and she meets it with a reluctant smile.

"I figured you wanted me here for my good looks and charming personality. But if catching this splotch of yours means I don't have to keep healing your ass, count me in." She continues her humming, changing it to *la-la-la*. The medicinal magic intensifies.

"You had me at looks," I smile and drift off under her spiritual tones.

• • •

Sunset comes early on the Front Range in November. Seeing the last glow of day running to hide behind the mountains scares me; time is a bitch-monkey jumping on my bruised back.

With Samantha's spiritual healing, plus a few of my own enchanted home remedies, I feel better. When I try to move, my legs wobble like a newborn colt's—each step like learning to walk again. My anger refuses to let me sit down. Using a staff for balance, I pace back and forth to think and talk.

The movement focuses my mind on solutions, rather than on Jabari—what she must be experiencing.

"All you need is a tall pointy hat with that stick, and I would label you a stereotype," Benny says.

"Funny, but I think I need a robe to pull it off."

"Don't think they make 'em in your size, big guy," Benny laughs. Relief shines on his face hearing me join in with his banter.

"They do," Sam replies. "But I'm sure the sticker price is high."

Benny and I both laugh. The costumer would know.

"Good one, Sam," I say. Then I become serious. "Last night, you held off and pushed the Void out of your bar by using your song spell?" My training as a Fire baby encompasses some Air magic discipline. But Sam, being an Air tot, surpasses my knowledge on so many levels.

"The right sound, the right frequency, and a big burst of pissed-off Air. Excuse me, speaking of my bar, it's Friday evening, and I'm not there. I need to make a couple of CMA calls." She stands up with phone in hand.

"CMA?" Benny asks.

"Cover my ass." She walks out of the room. Both Benny and I follow her with admiring eyes, undoubtedly thinking about what covering her ass might entail.

Reality snaps me back to urgency.

"You know anything about frequency, Ben?"

"Our old department radios worked on frequencies. They used high and low bands. Since we've gone digital, I'm not sure. Not my forte. Radio stations are subscribed channels, which I think are frequencies of some sort, but don't pin me to the bulletin board with that thought."

I pour a fresh mug of coffee, then refill Benny's. After a few blessed sips, I realize who I need to talk to about this shit. The bitch-howler on my back hurts my head when I consider the time it will take, but I need to get it right. Jabari's life is at stake, and I refuse to let the Void go unpunished. I want to call to see how she's doing, but I know she won't be the one answering the phone.

Her voice, but not her spirit.

I'm feeling helpless to save my apprentice, responsibility weighing heavily on my fractured soul as Sam steps back into the kitchen.

"I'm covered for a few hours, Red."

"Great, I need you to take a drive up to Divide with me. I think between you and my friend Rick, my learning curve on understanding how to capture the shit spot will level out." I look at Benny finishing his last chug of brew. "Benny, let me know if you hear anything. Hopefully, the Void will stay out of trouble."

"I will. Jabs would be relatively obvious if her profile comes across. *Nubian warrior* is a dead giveaway."

"That she is, which worries me."

I look at Samantha, trying to smile without appearing desperate. "Sam, I know it's a lot to ask, but please, I need your help."

"Already made the time, Red. Let's go visit your friend."

Benny leaves. Before Sam and I follow, I grab a small iron box from the closet in my bottega. First, I release the silk tapestry. Squatting beside the containment field holding the jade pot, I set the iron box down, release the field, and toss the tapestry in. Desperate vines of energy extend from the ornate pot and grab the silk, pulling it close. The vines manipulate the fabric to wrap around the little vessel. Within a minute, the wrap is complete and the green whisps of power swirl in and out of the ball of fabric to keep it in place.

Wearing my protective gloves, I carefully pick up the package, place it inside the box, latch the lid, and activate a spell to lock and contain the energy inside. As I recharge the wards around my place, Sam notices the box.

"What's in the box?"

"The Void's battery pack. Not sure what's in the jar or what the fabric has to do with the magic, but the little shit wants it back. Bad. It's the only bargaining chip I've got to save Jabari." I finish up, already feeling exhausted by just doing basic maintenance magic.

"Let's go see if I can add some more chips to the pile."

29

FRIDAY EVENING

SAMANTHA TURNS DOWN my gentlemanly effort to assist her into Scout, thanking me while making use of available handholds to climb up and in.

"This is quite the ride you have, Red," she says as we head down the mountain.

"He's been in the family since brand new and modified to fit my size and needs over time."

"He?"

"Sam, meet Scout." I pat the dash and smile. "Enchanted, warded, and enhanced to get me where I need to go. Quick and safe." With that, Scout honks his horn in a perky welcome.

"Uh… Hello. Scout," she says, not sure where to look. I notice her switching to her own 3E and visualizing much of Scout's magical bling. "Wow. I don't think I've ever experienced magic like this."

"It's been a process. Some upgrades have taken on a life of their own." Scout honks once, sounding like a strangled goose. "That was meant to be a compliment, bud."

"Impressive," Sam says. "So, who's this friend Rick?"

"Hold on, I'm going to call him and give a warning for the visit." I let go of the steering wheel as we approach a curve. Sam makes a move to grab the wheel, then stops, watching Scout handle the switchback with ease.

"This is one smart car. Dang." She sits back in wonder.

"Yeah, and he knows it." I get two perky honks for the comments.

Rick answers my call after one ring.

FEAR

"Red, long time no audio or video. Happy to see your name pop up." His voice is robust, in tone and memory.

"Rick. It has been too long. Me and a friend are heading your way."

"Is she cute?"

"And intelligent."

"Well, shoot, I'll break out my special stock of Tab and Crystal Pepsi. Think I may still have a case of Screaming Yellow Zonkers in storage." Hearing the names of long-lost sleepover snacks we ate as kids brings a needed smile to my worn face.

"Hold off. But I'll take a rain check on the Zonkers for a proper visit."

"Hold you to it. Your gate code is still good. I'll be in the studio."

"Fun-fuckin-tastic," I say from a plucked memory, then hang up.

"Zonkers?" Sam asks.

"Junk food fave we munched on as kids. He stocked up on them before they disappeared off the shelves. He has a cellar of bad cuisine. Rare and probably stale."

"I must say, Red, meeting you is like falling down a hole to Gotta-Wonder Land. I would ask questions, but I think just sitting along for the ride will offer enough information. Take it in bits, rather than bites."

"Probably a good idea. I'm not thinking straight right now. Bruises, worry, failure, and the pain related to all the above have me discombobulated."

Sam chuckles. "Well put." She turns serious. "I'm sorry about Jabari. I want to help, but understand, I have limits. Magic is a big part of my life, but secondary to my current personal endeavors."

"I understand. Call me out if the mercury gets too high."

"I will."

My own limits blew to pieces last night at the crematorium. I've never encountered an entity that took me down like this. I've prided myself on serving Gaia by being tactful, resourceful, and powerful enough to extinguish all abusers of Nature's gifts. Fast and efficient. But in less than two days, I have had my ass handed to me multiple times. The frequency of injuries to both body and spirit have left me progressively ill-prepared. To learn that the Void's evil, inflicted on innocent people, is all about calling me out—it's a mindfuck to start, then continues to get more twisted.

The shit originates in directives by some master of magical mayhem I still need to discover and deal with. And now Jabari…

Maybe it's time to find a new line of work.

                    M.J. Hook

"So, tell me about Rick. He sounds like a personality," Sam says, obviously trying to lift the veil of mental darkness clouding my thoughts.

"That he is. Met Rick Denny on the first day of first grade in Manitou. He was the short, wiry, snot-nosed kid everyone picked on. I was the burly brute no one wanted to piss off. We became buds when I scattered some bullies teasing him about his tie and shiny shoes. Right away, we had lots in common and several differences that balanced into becoming best friends."

The talking is good, keeping my mind away from self-deflating bullshit.

"Back then, I went to school, then came home to spend afternoons and evenings training for my First Rune Marks. My parents insisted I take one weekend day and night off to be a normal kid. Since Rick was the only kid-friend I had, that meant an afternoon and overnight at his house. His dad was some kind of wealthy oil refinery exec. His mother was a germaphobe who hovered over Rick.

"He was a brainiac. Would have advanced a grade or two in middle school, but while biking home one day, got hit by a drunk driver in a truck owned by a major beef distributer. His dad used big-shot lawyers to fetch a huge settlement while Rick slowly recovered. The boy that stepped out of the hospital was a brand-new, agoraphobic musical genius. He'd never touched an instrument in his life and, out of nowhere, could pick up and learn any instrument he touched in a day, write and score wonderful songs, and sing with perfect pitch. But scared shitless to leave the house."

"I've heard of people with head injuries suddenly developing supernatural-like talents," Sam says.

"That was Rick. His mom kept him home with private tutors, and I was the only friend he would, or could, have over to goof around. His parents divorced my senior year, giving Rick and his mom a load of cash on top of what he got from the accident. He started a radio station, KRCK. Had a studio built and began broadcasting nowhere. No tower. His format centered on Midwestern rock and roll, playing famous bands like Kansas, Styx, and REO Speedwagon. He would also play solo acts—Bob Seger, Joe Walsh, Glenn Frey—any artist born in one of the twelve states considered Midwest in America. Obscure to popular. Even offered tickets to acts coming to town, if you were the right caller."

Sam puts a hand on my arm. "Wait, he would DJ a station, but not broadcast? I don't get it. How would anyone know to call in?"

"I went to several concerts, since I was the only one who ever called him.

Not broadcasting had something to do with his agoraphobia, not wanting his voice to leave the house. Anyway, he still has tapes from all his shows and recordings of all the songs he's written and produced. No one except me, I think, has ever heard them. I haven't listened to all of them, but the ones I have are incredible.

"A few years back, he started listening to podcasts and made it his next project. Turned KRCK into *The Kick*, gaining a huge following of listeners in its first month. Since they were recorded, posting the episodes did not freak him out. Actually helped him open up and meet new people over the phone and online. He's had interviews with several Midwest bands and artists. His knowledge and unique banter are entertaining."

"That's incredible. Wait, does Rick know what you are? Magically speaking?" Her question is tough to answer.

"Sort of, but it never comes up outright in conversation. When we get together, it's like we are still kids. We'll have grown-up talks now and then, but we revert quickly." I wonder how to approach him with my current grown-up, fucked-up magical situation.

"He must be lonely."

I laugh. "If he is, he doesn't admit it. Or show it in his aura. Over the last few years, people have come to his house to play and produce music, party a little, and shoot guns. He has a little arsenal with a range out back. His house is like a fortress, but he opens the door on rare occasions."

I pause, then look at Sam. "Thanks."

"For what?"

"Prompting me to talk. A moment of distraction. I appreciate it."

Samantha touches my arm again and smiles. "I'm guessing you don't allow yourself much time for distraction."

My phone rings.

"Not lately."

30

FRIDAY NIGHT

"YUI, THANKS FOR calling me back. I'm putting you on speaker so my friend, Samantha, can hear our discussion about the pot and rag pics I sent you."

"You always have the most interesting baubles to send me, Red. But it would be nice to have a conversation with you about you, sometime." Yui Kimura's voice is soft and lilting. Her magic, specializing in sigils and symbology, is powerful and fierce.

"I agree. Unfortunately, the situation involving the images I sent has turned into a life-or-death affair."

"They always are with you, Red. And after examining the images, I think you may need to find a new line of work."

"Bottom line, Yui," I demand.

"The tapestry is a divine pass, Red. Scripted in the ancient language of the *Kojiki*, the characters grant whatever entity that's confined to a specified region, which is obviously near Mount Fuji based on the illustrative image, a spiritual liberation."

"Meaning what, exactly?

"Meaning it can go wherever it wants to go while maintaining its spiritual force tied to that limited region."

"So, destroy the tapestry, and the entity gets a one-way ticket back to its hole in the ground?" I grab an obvious straw.

"No, no. Don't do that. The tapestry… its magic is divine, Red. The deity that created it used its spiritual gamete to write the pass. By destroying it outright, you would unleash the spirit. And my guess is you would only strengthen it, make it able to root its energy anywhere."

I silently thank Gaia that cutting it earlier did not open Pandora's box. That's one problem I don't want to add to the list.

"Excuse me, this is Sam. I have a question," Sam says.

"Hello," Yui replies.

"Hi, can you explain what a spiritual gamete is, please?"

"Certainly. It's spirit semen. I'm not an expert on the subject, but according to some lore, it's the stuff that allowed gods to impregnate mortals. I have only seen it used as an incorporeal binder, like the substance on the tapestry. Rare, but not unheard of. Some claim it's a spiritual protein made from the consumption of mortal spirits, but it's hard to put otherworldly cells under a microscope."

"That is so rad," Sam exclaims.

"Also, very powerful magic. But Red, I need to mention, for the pass to work, the entity must have something of its origin in place. I am guessing dirt or dried leaves and rocks from its regional confinement."

"The jade jar," I say. "So, if I destroy that?"

"The spirit should weaken enough to dispatch. But without having the jar in front of me, I cannot tell you what wards are in place to seal and bind it to the tapestry. Consider the source of the gamete, Red. It will be difficult to break a deal like that. Deadly is my guess." Yui finishes. The long pause of quiet that follows rakes my nerves with misery.

"Any suggestions, Yui?"

"Two. Do what you always do, Red Wood. Your focus, drive, and power are your strongest weapons."

"And?"

"Be careful."

I thank Yui and hang up.

"So, the ethereal spooge brush belongs to a god?" Sam asks. "You're having to deal with magic dispensed by some sort of all-powerful celestial deity with a hard-on?"

"Yes. Well, sort of," I say, thinking about the spikey-haired woman I saw in Omori's memories. The one that mentioned her 'father.' "It just means magic thrown down by something that has had a millennium or two to exist and practice. If the so-called god is nearby, there might be a bigger problem."

          M.J. Hook

"Glad to hear that. Whew, for a second, thought I might need to say *adios* and hitch a broom back to my warm and comfy grill."

My thoughts circle back to Jabari as we pull off the highway and head up to Rick's place. What kind of messed-up power is violating her soul? I begin to worry that even if I separate the Void from her body, there will be permanent damage left behind.

Ancient magic is some of the strongest, purest energy ever wielded. I've heard stories and read books of elder craft, but I have very little experience dealing with it. I wish the Oracle would have clued me in. I hope Basil finds something in his giant library.

Bottom line, I need to make sure my warrior apprentice has a fighting chance to survive. Whole in body, pure in spirit.

• • •

Rick lives in a mountainous neighborhood nestled in the Pike-San Isabel National Forest on the west side of Pikes Peak. A light snow falls as we head up the road. After the second switchback, Scout stops to allow a herd of elk to cross the drive. Their large bodies move through Scout's beams as if we don't even exist. A large bull, taking its time to cross the road, stops to look in our direction. Satisfied we are not a threat, it continues its crossing.

We pull up to Rick's entry drive. Sam examines the large, iron-barred gate that blocks our way. Mounted on each side to twelve-foot walls of natural granite, Rick's welcome mat looks like an entry to a prison.

"He takes his privacy seriously," she says.

"All the stone came off his property, and the wall completes a large circle around his cabin. He has cameras everywhere, motion sensors, razor glass and barbed wire mounted on top of the wall, and he kids about having computer-controlled machine guns to cover all sights."

"*Is* he kidding?"

"I've never tested the joke."

I roll down the window and plug my code into the panel, 8888. My birthday. The gate slides to the left at a slow, lumbering pace.

We drive through a grove of aspens, then approach Rick's cabin, lit by subtle, warm lighting around the outside.

"That's a big cabin. Looks more like a Norse lodge hall for the rich and plunderous," Sam says.

"When you live in the same place 24/7, you spend your vacation time in different wings." It's an old Rick joke, but saying it myself doesn't bring much joy. My friend lives a happy life, I know, having looked at his aura plenty of times, but I still feel moments of sadness for him.

We walk up to the door and go in. The front entry is a wide hall, stretching from the left to the right. The side facing us is decorated from ceiling to floor with concert posters and memorabilia of Midwestern rock bands: signed pictures, autographed T-shirts, bumper stickers—all items either sent to him as gifts or purchased online.

"Hello, nurse," Sam says, quoting a beloved catchphrase from the *Animaniacs* cartoon as she approaches a Smashing Pumpkins poster, a big Billy Corgan signature scrawled across the top.

"That was a smashing year for the Pumpkins." Rick walks out from the side, speaking in a lousy cockney accent. Still trim, but muscled up under a loose sweater and pressed blue jeans, his long, blonde hair pulled back in a tight ponytail, he displays a smile of shiny white teeth.

"Samantha Salviati, meet Richard Denny."

"Call me Rick," he says, extending a hand to shake.

"Call me Sam," she replies, taking his offered hand.

"Salviati. That's quite a family name. Some archbishops and cardinals in your genetic line. Even some links to *la famiglia Medici* if I'm not mistaken," Rick says, switching to an even lousier Italian accent.

"Think there may have been a bastard or two in the mix way back then." Sam waves her hand to showcase Rick's wall. "You have quite the collection here. Red told me you're a fan of Midwest bands. I didn't realize there were so many."

"The region deserves its due," Rick says with a tone of pride.

"And you never listen to any other bands?"

"Only if a member was born in any of the Midwest states. I am a purist, but sometimes you've got to add salt to the audible."

I'm staring at the floor, thinking about the call with Yui, when Rick invades my brooding.

"Red Wood, you look like someone stole your Blockbuster card."

I offer a weak smile. "Stole it and abused it by checking out all five seasons of *Blossom*."

"Ouch," Rick replies, switching to Ren's slight south-of the border accent, "now look stupid, Stimpy, and put on your happy helmet and tell me what's up."

     M.J. Hook

I can't keep up with our retro-convo. As my shoulders slump and my fists tighten, Rick drops the voice and comes over to put a hand on my shoulder.

"You look like the Terminator just before his last scene under the press. Something bad's going on, huh? How can I help?"

"Tell me what you know about frequency."

Rick smiles and grabs my arm with a gentle grip. "Follow me to my office. This may take a moment or five."

• • •

Rick's office of the day is a large living room with a long, ornately carved cherrywood bar on the left side garnished with lit shelves full of various liquors. At the front of the office is a large-screen television with theater seating and, to the right, a computer workstation with several monitors banked to display images from security cameras. A large monitor is front and center, with a computer keyboard and an electric piano keyboard on the tabletop below it.

The room smells of freshly popped buttered popcorn from the Red Carnival popper machine in the corner. Styx's *Crystal Ball* surrounds the room in quiet volume as we sit down on the leather couches in the middle.

"So, what type of frequency are we talking about? Transdimensional? Subspace? Light? Sound? Or are you interested in natural frequency?" Rick's intelligence leaves me staring like the bull elk in headlights we saw earlier.

"Sound." Sam speaks for me.

"Sure. Audio frequency still covers a wide gamut of characteristics." Rick turns to me and gives me the stare I've known for years to mean *get to the point*.

I don't discuss magic with Rick directly, and I've learned to beat around the bush. He knows I chase bad guys, like a private detective, and enjoys my modified stories when I visit. I know he wonders about what I'm not saying, but I've never discussed an active case with him.

Until tonight. My friend is a wealth of information, and I know he can help me.

"There's a bad guy in town," I say, "from Japan. He has some sort of instrument that when he plays a chord, the vibration's amplified somehow. Strong enough to slap me down to the ground."

FEAR

"Damn, that's hard to imagine. Weird, too. Most things are with you, though. Sounds like some sort of comic villain, strumming a guitar to break windows, locks, and I guess necks. So, what? It's some sort of augmented Asian stringed instrument?"

Sam and I answer "yes" at the same time.

"Hold that thought," Rick says as he heads to his computer. After he pushes a few keys on the computer keyboard, a smaller monitor behind the piano keyboard comes to life. The voice of Tommy Shaw gets louder over the speakers, then turns off.

"OK." Rick finishes mousing and clicking around, then looks at us. "Does it sound like this?"

Rick pushes a key on the piano, and a loud twang fills the room. I open my 3E and ask him to play it again. I can see and hear the vibration as it fills the room and immediately know it's not the same.

"No," I tell him.

"It has a deeper tone. Very distinctive quality of sound," Sam says.

"That was a yamatogoto, one of the oldest Japanese instruments. Too reverent? So, let's try something a bit more common. Heavier. How about this?"

The speakers pulse out a vibration that is lower, richer in tone and thrum. My body feels a minor quake of recognition as I immediately switch off my sight in reaction.

"That's it," I croak, my voice slightly shattered from the memory of the Void's power.

"You're sure? I've got a whole list of Asian instruments I can play through."

"That's it," I say and see Sam nodding next to me.

"Good. So, your villain's armed with a sonic shamisen, which means 'three strings' because it only has three strings." Rick is reading the monitor. "Let's see… Its origins are from a Chinese instrument, but the Japanese adapted it to accompany kabuki theater, but a larger version with a lower pitch and fuller tone is commonly used in bunraku…"

"Puppet theater," I interrupt. "That's definitely it, Rick."

"Does this guy use some sort of device to augment the tone to shake things up?" I see Rick searching again on his screen.

"That doesn't matter, Rick." Anxious feelings increase my blood flow, and I realize that coming to Rick, even though it is taking time, will save me

     M.J. Hook

time if he answers my next question correctly.

"What matters is, do you have equipment that will allow me to… I hope I say this right… to play a range of tones to offset this guy's three-stringer?"

Sam grabs my arm with a firm grip, then clarifies my sophomoric attempt at a request. In a confident voice, she asks, "What he means is, do you have frequency modification equipment we can use to put the smackdown on Japan-man's ass?"

Rick's smile shines across the room. "Interesting. And strange. A regular battle of the bands, a la frequency. I just might. Follow me."

Thank Gaia. I look at Sam and realize the infatuation I may be feeling toward her is based on a foundation of respect.

31

FRIDAY NIGHT

RICK TAKES US to his warehouse, a large wooden barn behind his cabin. It's two stories of eclectic stuff—kid's toys and games, video arcade game consoles, musical instruments, old computers and peripherals, recording equipment—organized and arranged on shelves with room to grow.

When he turns on the overhead lights, the abundance of gear visually defeats my concentration.

"Before you fill my head with every possible piece of equipment that I don't know how to use, Rick, I have a plan I need to discuss. Hopefully, if my thoughts make sense, you can lead us to the right components." Overwhelmed and desperate, I grasp at what Yui told me: *Your focus and drive are your strongest weapons.*

She left out *your friends*. It's time to focus.

"Spell it out, captain. I'm here to help," Rick says.

"First, we need to figure out how to release Jabari from the posses—uh, clutches of the bad guy."

"Woah, wait, my Jabs is being held hostage?" Rick's jovial attitude turns into a serious stance. Jabs and Rick hit it off immediately on her first visit to what she calls "Rick's Shanty." She loved the games, guns, and goofiness hanging out with my friend. "You left out that detail. Maybe we need to visit the armory."

I cut him off. "No. Beating this guy is going to take sound, not bullets."

Rick paces, distraught by the news I should have left unsaid. I suggest that he go get us some Crystal Pepsi while Sam and I discuss the plan forming in my head. He nods and leaves. I check his aura on the way, radiating colors of discouragement and worry.

"Is he going to be OK?" Sam asks.

"He will. I should have paid attention to my mouth before I started talking. He loves Jabs, and I feel like an ass right now. Probably just threw him a head full of piss-a-phobia—wanting to leave to help but won't, can't." I put my face in my hand, thinking maybe I should slap myself.

Instead, I look up at Sam. "You need to hear my thoughts and tell me what you think, whether I make any sense." I lay out my plan, rough as it is, and she nods, never interrupting.

"The only problem is that I don't know how or where to set it up. Needs to be clear of people, clean of wards, no immediate sign of magical containment."

"I have just the place, out east of town. Big storage building off Highway 94. Buddy of mine lets me use it for grill junk. He's in Europe right now. And your plan sounds great, but it will only work if Rick has the equipment to step through the modulations quickly."

Rick returns with three frosty bottles of the ancient soda.

"Here you go." He hands us each a bottle. "Still refreshing."

I take a taste and am flooded with memories of sitting in front of Rick's television watching horror movies at two in the morning. Sam takes a swig, and her mouth twists.

"Never had this before." She continues to drink.

"I keep the stuff almost frozen and am always surprised how well it keeps."

"I'm not sure if that's good or bad," she says after finishing half the bottle.

"So, I know you sent me on an errand to discuss your plan. Figured out what kind of equipment you need?" Rick takes a pull off his bottle of transparent soda.

Sam takes over and starts discussing amplifiers, oscillators, and synthesizers. The two walk over to a set of shelves with several cardboard boxes, black-cased components, speakers, and ancient computers. Rick hands Sam a tablet of paper and a pen. She draws what I know is the layout we discussed.

"I'm going to go get Scout and hook up one of your trailers to it to carry this stuff, Rick."

Rick gives me a thumbs-up and says, "Get the green one, Red. It's a five-by-ten and should handle what you need here. Plus, it has a hitch adapter to reach Scout's height."

Outside I look up at the sky as the cool air fogs my breath. I feel the phone in my pocket and resist the desire to yank it out and call Jabari.

32

FRIDAY NIGHT, JABARI

SHIT, SHIT, SHIT.

Jabari knew what she was doing when she rushed out to help Red.

She knew the Void was after the jar and rag.

She knew she needed to leave the medallion behind, just in case.

She now knew that Marlow was one badass pussycat.

What she hadn't known was that the trembling splotch of shit would jump her bones so fast, invading her body like a superworm on an apple. The stain crawled through her skin and took control. Too quick. The core protection she and Red made had bought her a precious moment to hide and shelter her consciousness, but not before the smudge stole a glimmer of recent memories.

Shit.

Trapped and unable to control her body, she could still see through her eyes. She could also hear the fucking stain talk. In her own voice, which was weird. An incessant, nasty garble of threats, stupid observations, and confusing gibberish about suicides, tasteless souls, wasted time and effort.

It also rattled off tirades in Japanese.

She could tell it was weak. Bastard tried to feed off her soul before she secured it. She wasn't sure just how she'd managed the protection, but she was damn happy it'd clicked into place.

While the stain jabbered and drove around the city, Jabari explored her spiritual core. Her sight was continuous, allowing a look at her own soul. The display fascinated her, a ladder of energy and color that marrowed

FEAR   189

through her mortal vessel. She wondered if she could accomplish this feat without the motivation of an ensuing incorporeal rape. Hopefully, she would survive to find out.

Taking the time to tour Jabs Spirit Land was a holiday she could not afford. The jitterbug infecting her body would not allow her the time or freedom.

The car stopped. Jabari prepared herself for another onslaught of internal combat. The shit stain banged on the energy field as she secluded herself inside.

"Bitch, I know you can hear me. I'm going to abuse your body in ways that would make a lunatic blush. Give it *all* up, or I swear I'll tear you up." The Void's rants, frequent at first, were getting less threatening in strength. Jabari could tell it was losing steam. She could only guess that the stain needed her soul to feed on to sustain its life force.

That and its little jar of jade peas.

"Splotch fucker. Ain't gettin' no more of me." She spoke for the first time in captivity, and the words came through her mortal mouth.

"There you are. You think so, bitch? We'll see about that. Let's go find you a gangbang of bikers to play with."

She was arguing with herself, but not herself.

Jabari could feel a hand moving to start the car. She jerked it to her face, causing a loud slap followed by "fucking bitch" from the Void.

"If any harm comes to me, you piece of shit stain, Red's going to toss you out of existence, where all bad voids belong." Jabari enjoyed hearing her own voice coming from her own mouth.

"Maybe, you skank whore, but you'll be dead, your soul just a morsel resting happily in my gut."

Jabari did not respond. Instead, she continued to explore the space inside her captive soul a little more. If she could see her face, her real face, in a mirror, she knew it would have a big, nervous grin reflecting back.

M.J. HOOK

33

FRIDAY, LATE NIGHT

AS I HOOK up the trailer, my phone rings. Looking at the caller, I feel a glimmer of hope.

"Basil Rusu. How are the pastries in Holland today?"

"Fresh, flaky, and sticky, Red Wood. I had taken down just about every reference here at the library these past few days since your caustic apprentice called me with a copious list of lavish evils to explore. Hours, days even, discovering spiritual entities that classify as possessing pranksters, all on your dime."

Most of the time I enjoy hearing Basil talk. His Romanian accent, laced with an elaborate vocabulary and a hint of bother, can make my day. But not now, especially being eager for information.

"Well, Basil, bill me."

A long silence ensues. Not sure if he is checking his notes or reluctant to mention he has no notes.

"You sound irritable. Your girl updated me. Told me to focus on Japanese entities. I tried calling her back, but she won't answer. So, I call you."

Bless *my* girl.

In the past, Basil has been essential in identifying many of the evil spirits, demons, ghosts, and entities the Donum pursue. Knowledge is wealth, and Basil is full of it. Knowing what your enemy is can mean the difference between defeating it or it defeating you. Hopefully, he's come through with a valuable nugget to enhance his historical ego.

"Irritable is the icing on my overbaked cake. With some help from my *caustic apprentice*, Jabari, and others, I haven't figured out what it is, but we know it is a forest entity of some type. Likes to prey on suicidal souls. Does that ring any cymbals in your Roma brain?"

"Nice joke, big man. I may have to add to your bill the cost of hearing it. There's a ghost called a *yurei*, a spirit from suicide that can cause problems on the physical plane…"

"Not a ghost. Elemental forest critter of some sort. Can take complete possession." I explain the Void's dynamic, letting him know about the memory capture and the degree of awareness the vessel retains while doing unspeakable acts.

"Vile. You always find the choice evils in the world. Here's a vengeful soul called a *shinigami*. Can possess humans and make them suffer, want to die."

"That may have possibilities. Make me up a list with any banishment information and text it, please. I appreciate your efforts, Basil." I pause, knowing my gruff response sounds nothing like appreciation. "This… this chase has turned into a mind-fuck fiasco. So anything, any info you can offer, will be helpful, my friend."

I refrain from discussing the spikey white-haired bitch from Emiko's memory. Basil could have insight on what jerk-off god hired the Void to put a hit on me, but I bite my lip. Need to stay focused on the task at hand.

"In all the years I've known you, Red Wood, I've never heard you sound *so* distraught. I have some other findings that may assist you with your fiasco. Will send right away. Take care, *ádh mōr ort a laoch millteanach*. And I appreciate your donations to the library. I'll send the bill with the info."

Good luck, giant warrior, he says to me in my own power language. If only I could feel the power of his blessing.

• • •

Rick shows me the diagram he's drawn for the frequency trap, as he calls it. Using colored electrical tape, he marks every cord and component for plug-in and setup. While charging a laptop, he takes Samantha through the program used to set the trap.

Rick knows I have no patience for such details, so I load the trailer with everything they set aside: several speakers, coils of cable, tarps, power strips, a rack to stack the components in, and several crimps. I also grab a

M.J. Hook

fire extinguisher.

After making sure everything is secure, I look at Rick's workbench and notice a sixteen-pound sledgehammer leaning in the corner.

"OK if I take this too?"

"Whatever you need to save Jabs, Red. Can't say I understand your situation, but that's nothing new. I know you, and I trust Sam." He leans in a little closer and whispers. "Between you and me, bro, this one is a keeper."

I smile at my friend. Even with all his idiosyncrasies, his judgment of the few friends I have introduced him to over the years has always been sound. We both smile at Sam as she walks up to the trailer with the laptop.

"What?" she says.

"Nothing," we say in unison, then laugh. It feels good.

I give Rick a hug and climb into Scout. He knocks on Sam's window, so she rolls it down.

"Samantha, it was an immense pleasure to meet you. Please don't hesitate to come back."

"It has been a pleasure, Rick."

Directing his stare at me, he lets his smile vanish.

"Red, you call me. You let me know. Understand?"

"I will."

We drive out and make it back to the highway before either of us says anything.

"It's a good plan, Red," Sam says.

"Thanks. No way it could happen without your help. I'll get you back to work. Send me a map to your friend's place and I'll start setting up." I sound distant in my rattled head.

"I'll need to give you the keys." She looks at me, sighs, then asks, "What are you thinking about?"

"Plan B. And it sucks."

M.J. Hook

34

SATURDAY, EARLY MORNING, JABARI

JABARI KNEW IT was turning on the phone again to check for messages.

"Shit. I know your man is planning something. He better call soon, or you and I are going to visit a dive bar with motorcycles parked out front driven by skank-drunk assholes wearing beater T-shirts and week-old underwear."

I don't talk like this. It was weird hearing herself toss out ugly threats to herself. Her voice, but not her lingo.

It texted a message. Then another.

"I like this city. I like this climate. Maybe your giant will make a mistake and allow me to stay here. Suck up some Rocky Mountain souls. Yum."

The Void was distracted. It no longer beat on her containment, which she'd been able to reinforce some as the night wore on. Her internal chain of power glowed with her conviction. She remained silent, knowing the quiet only frustrated the stain more. Weakened it, maybe. Better to keep it occupied than let it jump into some other poor soul.

Jabari realized that her decision reminded her of Red. His convictions. His sacrifices for others.

The realization surged more colorful energy throughout her soul.

The Void turned the phone off as Japanese started spewing from its mouth. Her mouth.

Red, she thought, *please hurry.*

35

SATURDAY, EARLY MORNING

SAM'S DIRECTIONS LEAD me to a gate just off the two-lane highway. The rough fence surrounds a large plot of land. The road inside splits. Up a hill to the left is a small house, lightly lit with a small picket fence around the perimeter. Go right into the hilly acreage covered with plain brush and the dirt track leads to a metal-sided barn toward the back. I shut the gate but leave the lock off and drive to the barn.

I unlock the door and turn on the fluorescent lights. A large tractor sits in front of the garage door. Finding the keys in the ignition, I get it outside and park it to the side with no problem. I leave the garage door open to allow fresh air to fill the space as I move boxes, tools, and equipment around to create an open area to accommodate Rick's equipment.

The Void possessing Jabari makes this face-to-face dangerous. She is, even at her level of Rune Blessings, a powerful force. Will the Void be able to tap into that power? Will it have learned all that she knows about how to use it?

I sweep the floor. Scout backs the trailer in, and I unload.

Any sign of magical containment will be obvious if the Void uses Jabari's sight. The Void's fast, strong, and capable of jumping hosts. It doesn't care if we meet in public, compromising the lives of innocents. It will kill anyone, including Jabari, to get its precious jar and spooge rag back.

Yes, out here in the flatlands is best.

Once everything is out of the trailer, I send Scout to park around back. Spending a long moment staring at Rick and Sam's plans, I push the doubt

FEAR

away and get busy with the set up.

The physical work feels good, but I move slow. My body still shakes. My legs and arms make doubtful moves and lifts. Each effort tests my coordination. Not needing to use 3E, I still switch it on for brief moments to check for deficiencies. Opening all my senses, I step outside and expose myself to the star-filled sky.

The auras surrounding the distant suns and planets radiate colors unique in the spiritual spectrum: hues unrecognizable to regular sight. Listening to the night sounds, I hear a symphony of songs above and below the ground. A chill breeze fills my nose with the rich smells of life and the natural smells of decay and death. As I let the wind touch my face and arms, I feel the caress of faint wishes and ancient thoughts from obscure spiritual residue, emotions that cling even though the hearts and minds have long passed.

Turning it all off, I take a deep breath of the night air. As my lungs fill, my stomach grumbles.

While eating some food I picked up on the drive across town, I feel the vibration of my phone inside my pants pocket. I look at the screen to see who I've been ignoring for the last couple of hours.

A couple of texts are from Benny asking for updates.

One long text from Basil.

His methodical notes give me a few more entities to consider. Japan is rich with monsters, demons, shapeshifters, and ghosts. How many are real? Or were real? Hard to say. Even the shinigami he mentioned are obscure in story and purpose. One story cited seems to fit: the demon, or spirit, that thrives where repeat deaths or suicides occur.

That fits the Suicide Forest. The Void might just be a reason, if not *the* reason, why Aokigahara Forest has such a terrible reputation. Maybe getting rid of the creep would clean up the area's character. Maybe not. The reputation, built over time, is a force of its own.

All the banishment suggestions related to that region are like the ones I use. I need to catch it first, and Basil adds nothing to help with getting past the Void's chord of destruction. The demon no doubt uses the thrum to beat down the living spirit to accept suicide, even welcome it.

My experience viewing Darlene Shurter's spirit, and Omori's memory while they were both possessed produced little noise. I can only surmise that while under the influence of the Void, the ruinous thrum joins their soul in a type of harmony. To please. Seduce.

         M.J. Hook

There are several texts from Jabari's phone. All of her, or *its,* messages are rants, impatient threats to do Jabs harm if I don't reply soon. I worry about what the Void's doing to Jabs.

I worry…

I need answers. Shutting the Void down solves one immediate problem but leaves bigger problems open: Who the fuck is after me? I would have discussed the spikey-haired woman and her father with Basil, Jabs, even Benny, but to what end? Especially now? I can't beat the hired thug, why add the mob boss and his runt to the equation.

Keeping the Void corporeal long enough to get answers is important. To me.

But that might mean… I refuse to let worry and anger turn into impatience.

There's a plan in place. Set it up. Make the call.

It's a sound plan. Ha!

The instructions are easy to follow: where to put things, what to plug in where. I stay focused on the work, only allowing myself to consider the second plan when I stop to hydrate.

Using 3E exposes me to the Void's discord. My spirit and body cannot take any more abuse, but I need the sight to follow the Void once it releases Jabari's body, the first focus of Plan A. The plan uses minimal ethereal magic. It primarily uses the science of sound, which is certainly a type of magic.

Plan B ends with an act of magic I do not want to conjure. It would mean destroying the vessel, exposing the Void to more powerful, direct magic.

It would mean killing Jabari.

Something I cannot accept.

I get back to work.

M.J. Hook

36
SATURDAY, EARLY MORNING

SAMANTHA ARRIVES AS I finish concealing everything inside the barn. Her headlights fill the space, which looks like a regular workshop once again. The tools and equipment I moved earlier are back inside, set up in front of several tarps that cover components of the trap.

The front space, where the tractor was, remains clear.

After parking in back, Sam steps through the bay door. She's changed clothes. Dressed in formfitting black workout pants and a long-sleeved fleece top with a black knit hat and gloves, she looks prepared to cat-burgle a jewelry shop.

"You looked dressed for a night of clandestine activities," I say.

"This old thing?" She poses, draping her hand up and down the outfit. "This is my casual Yule celebration attire. Minus the ugly log sweater. I didn't want to overdress."

"I'm sure your sweater would cause coven envy in any circle you dance in."

"Such a flatterer." She comes close and looks me over, using her sight. "Your healing is still progressing. Needs more time, but good to hear your sense of humor is on the mend. So, how are things going with the trap?" She walks around, lifting tarps and blankets to peek at all the items I put in place.

"Just finished. Need to test it, which I'm not qualified to do. Also, need to set up the light and prep the runes." Having an obvious *concealed* circle to ignite for containment will let me know if the Void is using Jabari's sight. If it's noticed, I'll have other trap sigils planted. If it's unseen, the showdown should progress quickly.

Sam walks over to the table and component rack I set up behind metal roof panels and boxes. She boots up the laptop. As the screen comes to life, she hands me a pair of earplugs.

"I enchanted these for you. Should help keep the spiritual noise down some. If I had more time…"

"Thank you." I say, putting them in my pocket. "I appreciate your effort."

Next, she hands me a cassette tape.

"Rick gave this to me. Said reel-to-reel would be better, but next to 8-track, cassettes project a good, crisp sound."

I wondered why a cassette deck was added to the setup. I look down at the tape and see the artist name and song written on the label. It's worthy.

"Leave it to Rick to find a good ol' Kansas boy to put the cherry on top of this mess."

Sam looks up at me, and her hand comes to rest on my chest.

"Rick told me about Jabari, about her energy and joy. Benny told me about how much of a pain in your ass, and a delight to your heart, she is. The mercury is high here, Red, but from everything your two friends told me about you—a lot of good and some potentially lousy—I think I can handle the fever you're dealing with."

She grabs my shirt and pulls my face down to hers. The gentle kiss she pulses on the side of my lips sends a shot of energy throughout my being. We part. I look into her eyes to gauge her commitment. I consider making the kiss more substantial, but right now, her being here to help is more significant than the momentary jolt from my libido.

"Glad you're here, Sam. We just met, and right now, you are the only one I can think of to have my back in this situation. Normally it would be Jabari, but…" I squeeze her arms. "Thanks for the mercury read. And if they told you the good and bad about me, I'm sure you understand why my fever reads on the high side. A lot."

"Yeah, Benny made that point very clear." She gives my chest a firm slap. "Air feeds fire, so let's test this sucker out. Get ready to save Jabari and burn the little shit to oblivion."

"Let's," I reply and grab a ladder to set up the lighting.

• • •

　　　　M.J. Hook

With sunrise still a few hours away, Sam and I are ready. I pull out my phone and dial Jabari's number. It goes to voicemail, so I hang up. Opening the text thread, I ignore the dozen rants the Void has sent and send my location to Jabari's phone.

After fifteen minutes, my phone rings. The sound is turned on now so I can hear Jabari's recorded voice telling me to answer.

"It's about time you called. Got everything ready to kick my ass, *boss*?"

"You got the map. I got your stuff. Jabari better be unharmed, or…"

"RED, REVERSE THE POLARITY AND WIPE THIS DAMAGED FUCK OUT OF EXISTENCE." Jabari's voice blares through the phone. I know it's her. She's using a movie trope we both find funny.

"Shut up, you fucking whore." Her voice again, but not her.

"You got the map," I say with confidence and hang up.

I look at Sam and smile.

"What?"

"It would appear Jabari is living up to her pain-in-the-ass reputation." I tell her what I heard.

Plan A has a bonus. Plan B goes off the burner and sits on a hot pad to cool.

Sam and I test the trap one more time, review our cues, then wait. We each eat a shockra bar, sip water, and work on staying relaxed and focused.

"These bars are good, Red. I must get the recipe. The energy boosts are brilliant."

"Ingredients are simple, but the magic to pull it all together takes time. That's why I usually make a big batch. Trade you the recipe for your pantry charm construct."

"Worthy. And delicious."

We sit. We talk. We wait.

Headlights show up at the main gate. The only light on in the barn is a small overhead bulb I hung from a rafter, shining down on the tapestry-wrapped jade jar sitting in the middle of a small, active containment circle. The car drives through the gate, pauses, starts heading for the house, reverses, then drives toward the barn.

Sam heads back behind the table to hide behind the metal bunker. She has several gun holes to look through as she disappears into the shadows. The computer screen and component lights remain hidden under a pitched blanket.

When I turn on my 3E, anxiety builds: Exposing myself to the Void's thrum will suck nails. My nerves spark like exposed wires, making it difficult to maintain my spiritual healing and dial down the sound.

A quiet hum fills the room, a sign that Sam has the sound system turned on. I sit on a stool, centered and as far away from the bay doors as needed.

Jabari's Honda parks. The headlights shine on my face. As she, no *it*, steps out of the car, I send a flash spell to kill the lights. The Void flinches and stays by the car.

"What's wrong, Red? 'Fraid I might see something I'm not supposed to?" Jabari's voice sounds rough, as if the Void has deprived her vocal cords of water.

"The only thing you need to see is right here." I point to the wrapped jar on the floor in front of me. "Besides, you know I'm going to protect it. You've got Jabari's memories in your head, so I'm guessing you already know most of my tricks."

Hoping I'm wrong and that Jabs has somehow concealed her powers with her consciousness, its next move will reveal a lot.

"Of course," it replies, looking around the bay door, possibly searching for wards. It puts its hands out as if feeling for hidden cobwebs. Now I know it has no access to Jabari's sight. The larger concealed circle of the demon trap is only a few steps in front of it.

How Jabari blocked the Void is something I look forward to hearing about later this morning when she reacquires her own lips.

As the Void steps into the building, I pull the sledgehammer out from behind the stool and rest it easily in my palm. The Void reacts with one major chord of chaos. It hits me. My reaction stays limited to a genuine grimace of pain. If I wasn't sitting, I might have fallen.

"Really? You planning on bashing in the head of your dear apprentice?"

"No, I plan on smashing your precious little compost jar from home, then mixing it with a bucket of grade-A prime Colorado cow shit." I point to a 5-gallon bucket I filled with dirt over to the side.

The Void stops, realizing I know what's inside the jar. I understand the contents' purpose, even though I don't know whether they are rocks and dirt from its forest. Or even panda poop.

"Release Jabari, then you and I can talk." I raise the sledge to my shoulder.

"You wouldn't. You destroy that," it points to the jar, "and you destroy her."

                              M.J. Hook

"If it means killing you, then so be it," I say with confidence.

The Void smiles. It takes several more steps into the building, points a finger at me and screams a torrent of Japanese words I don't bother translating. The vibrations from its chord-of-ruin strums reach my spiritual core as I watch the tarps around the room ripple from the distortion.

Long as I don't actively listen with my 3E, which is becoming less of a choice, I can manage the pain. But it's time to play my cards.

To make my bluff convincing, I open my hearing to a blast of the Void's puppet music, letting the vibration take me off the stool and to my knees. My nose shoots out a nice spout of blood. I can feel blood dripping from my ears too. I'm not sure, but I may have blood coming out my ass; my jeans immediately feel warm and moist in the seat. Blood or shit, my bluff may be too convincing.

I wipe my mouth and hold up my bloody palm to signal a stop to the Void's noisy tirade. Using the sledge, I force myself back up to sit on the stool, then wipe my face with my shirt so I can talk without spitting blood.

"Here's an offer to consider. You let Jabari go, stop playing your greatest hits tracks, sit down with me, and have a happy chat concerning who gave you the golden cum ticket to travel here and trial my ass. Tell me who the spikey white-haired bitch is that pulled you from the Sea of Trees, give me the name of her master, and I might just let you take your baby demon-food jar and wipe rag and bounce away."

Revealing knowledge with enough detail to put you in a dominant position to deal also makes it much easier to hide your true hand. A tempting lie of diversion. The eyes in Jabari's face go through several stages of emotion with each revelation I mention.

"I don't trust you," it says, still smiling while jabbing a familiar finger in my direction.

I hold one card back, knowing that if I destroy the tapestry, I free its ass. It wants me to use the sledge and wreck its insulated battery. First, I need to remove the Void from Jabari, then its protective blotch. I sweeten the pot with my final offer, knowing the little black curd of evil enjoys being free from Mount Fuji's flank forest.

All the better to force its hand.

"And why should you? But here's the deal. I'm sure you can see the damage you've inflicted on me already. I can't take much more, to be honest. I care about Jabari, and I care about innocent people getting murdered and hurt. All for your purpose of testing me. So, bottom line, you win! You can tell your divine benefactors I failed. I'm a wimpy wizard. Just release Jabari. Then tell me who your sponsors are, and I'll give you your stuff and call it a night." I wave my bloody hand toward the package.

The Void, slack-jawed and enticed, takes a few steps closer, putting it inside the inactive circle.

Standing stoic, hands to the side and the smile gone, the Void tells me a truth. The aura of possession relaxes, so I know the words are fact. "I cannot tell you who they are. Part of the covenant is that if I speak the names, the tapestry unravels."

The confession sucks. But the good news is that it must think that if I burn the rag, I will be breaking the covenant as well. The joy of watching the Void pretending to suffer from my momentary trump is righteous. I know the order of things. First, unfortunately, my apprentice's vessel needs release.

"Damn, that is a deal breaker. Sucks for you. *Rac agus Roll!*" Using my power language, my spell ignites the larger circle of containment, sparks a sigil to slam the garage door down, and most importantly, cues Sam to fill the speakers surrounding the area inside the barn with beautiful, catastrophic sound.

Time to show my final hand.

        M.J. Hook

37

SATURDAY, EARLY MORNING

THE VOID, CONFINED to Jabari's body, reacts in line with predictable human nature.

Me yelling "rock and roll!" is the initial shock. Seeing and hearing the garage door crash down adds a nice twist of surprise. Feeling the containment field surround the open space where the trap is set gives the Void plenty to keep it occupied for a moment as Sam emits single tones through the twenty various-sized speakers circling the trap.

A smaller circle of protection domes the jar and tapestry.

The modulating tones increase in volume, switching from one frequency to the next. Thanks to the program Rick put on the computer, Sam is able to vary the modulation quickly, along with some other carrier wave amplitudes and blah blah signals I don't understand.

Still viewing in 3E, knowing I am putting myself at risk from the Void's painful thrum, I watch its reaction closely.

"There!" I yell, seeing the Void's edges outlining Jabari's body cease trembling. Its thrum goes quiet. Jabari's form begins to emerge through the darkness as static edges poke through her skin and ruffle her clothes. The possession begins again when the frequency changes, but Sam knows to step it back, making slow key presses.

"Stop!" I yell, when the right signal disrupts the Void again.

The Void continues to vibrate, trying to stay inside Jabari. Sam turns up the volume, making it harder to maintain the possession. The vibration inside the building causes the metal walls of the barn to shake. The tone pierces my ears with sharp sound, even with my spiritual hearing cloaked. I pull Sam's earplugs from my pocket and stuff them into my bloody ears.

Jabari's hands come up to cover her ears as the Void releases another thrum. I smile as my buffered ears feel no disruption. I shake the sledgehammer at the demon puppeteer.

Payback… best served loud on a routed Gibson Deluxe electric guitar.

"You like the Rocky Mountains, you piece of shit?" I scream. "Let me give you a proper welcome." Joe Walsh's guitar riff and piano intro to "Rocky Mountain Way" blast out of all twenty speakers.

Playing at a beautiful, destructive frequency.

The Void continues to fragment, its pixelated edges tremor through Jabari's exposed skin. Her clothing lifts and shakes with exorcising trembles.

Walsh's vocals kick in as the Void continues to shudder under the heavy sound. Jabari begins to move to the music. Her body sways, her feet stomp. I never considered the song to be a dance tune, but her gyrations make it look good. The Void loses more control.

Grabbing the sledge in both hands, I step closer.

It sees me and launches a front kick. I block it, but the power of the strike pushes me back.

The lyrics boom out that ladies are crying because the story's sad.

"HIT ME," Jabari screams. Her face changes from anger to confusion. I know it's her.

Hesitant, I drop the sledgehammer and move in, punching her in the arm with the impact of a tossed marshmallow. I don't want to hurt her.

She replies with a roundhouse, her foot slams into the side of my face. Sound fills my head as the plugs fly out of my ears. I go down.

Joe Walsh sings that it doesn't matter.

"HIT ME IN THE FUCKIN' HEAD LIKE YOU MEAN IT!" Jabari screams at me.

The song lets me know that Casey is stepping up to bat as I get up and face off with my apprentice.

Jabari's dance becomes a sensuous whirl of hip swings and aggressive floor stomps. The Void shakes loose even more. It attempts to tether itself to Jabari's cognitive cord.

My adrenaline peaks as I slide over and smash my fist into her head. No holding back.

Her head takes the punch. The force hardly fazes her, but the Void releases her coil. Its response erratic.

"AGAIN! YOU'RE HURTING IT, NOT ME!"

My fist goes for purchase. She blocks, then backhands me across the face. Feels like a shovel slamming my cheek.

She blocks two more punches with no counters. My third punch connects to her gut. Jabari bends over. The Void stands her body back up, smiling, with solid black eyes. It replies with a flurry of two-fisted piledriving shots to my head, my chest, and my stomach. The sequence repeats.

Too exhausted to block, the power and pain put me down in the dirt.

The lyrics end. The instrumental begins—guitar solo, followed by Walsh using a talk box. I push myself back up to my knees. Then a voice of magical power lifts above the music.

Sam walks out, vocalizing a harmonious passage of Walsh's lyrics that stuns the Void. Her vocals project more energy than any spell I can conjure. Her voice is solid. Hard. Her range would bring any other rock diva to tears of admiration.

The Void reacts. The static splotch pulls out of my assistant's body. Hanging in the air, its trembling edges begin to unravel. Jabari falls face-first to the floor.

Remembering Marlow's attack, I force myself to get up to my knees. Casting an air spell, I surround the blotch with a funnel, causing it to spin in place. Tightening the tube, I pull moisture in to my trap, allowing it to freeze and hold the shit stain in place.

As the wall of ice thickens, The Void releases a powerful thrum. The ice explodes and my body goes down to the floor next to Jabari. My bones feel fractured. My spirit withers to a small spark of defeat.

The full tattered form of the Void falls on top of Jabari's back. Her efforts exhausted, the darkness solidifies and attempts to twist its way back into her body. A corner folds up, and I see the evil cherub face smiling at me from its hollow depths. A long, black tongue slips out from between its lips.

Another thrum of power keeps my head down on the floor. I can only watch as the snakelike protrusion moves down and wraps around Jabari's neck to lift her head. Arching her neck, straining her muscles. The corner folds down, and the Void mounts Jabari from behind as it pulls itself back into her body.

Sam continues to sing, improvising Joe's lyrics. Her voice strains the Void's efforts, but I'm worried it won't be enough.

Unable to lift myself from the floor, I lead my coil over to halt the violation to Jabari. As it nears, Jabari's eyes open wide. Her own coil shoots out and slaps mine down, adding insult to the physical injury already handed to me.

"I GOT THIS," she screams. The Void's tongue moves off her neck and shoots into her mouth.

My sight sees another vibration covering Jabari's spirit with healing power, shaking up the Void with a constant surge of musical energy. Sam's magic integrates dual intent.

Jabari lifts her shoulders, slides her knees in, and screams with effort. The Void's snake flies out of her mouth and slaps the concrete.

I put my head down and force my sight to remain on, trying to cycle energy back to my spirit with a moment of focused breathing. I need to know Jabari is going to make it.

The Void slides off Jabari's back as she stands. Its chords thrum less in frequency and strength. As it lifts off the ground, the raveled blotch hits the containment field.

Jabari stumbles out of my line of sight while Sam's vocals keep the demon's spot pressed against the magic.

Two small legs drop out from the bottom of the blackness.

The tiny troublemaker falls to the floor, covering its pointed ears as Joe begins his final guitar solo. Trying to reach the unraveling darkness above means uncovering an ear, which inflicts too much pain on the little shit. The creature huddles on the floor as its hidey hole unravels to nothing.

I release the containment field around the jar and stretch to grab the hammer, but can only get a finger on it. The sledge lifts. I look up, expecting to see Sam, but it's Jabari. Her face is full of fury, eyes open wide with hate. I glance over and see the little black demon quivering, its empty eyes staring at the jar, unable to move.

"Jabs. Burn it. First." I yell, using the last of my spirit to raise my voice above the music. I point with my finger at the shivering creature.

She screams as fire shoots from her left hand. The flame ignites the demon.

Its demonic squeal of pain is a reward in audio to my bloody ears.

The floating splotch, its gift from a cum-filled god, destroyed. The little creep torched to a cinder. I point to the tapestry-wrapped jar.

"Smash," is all I need to say.

M.J. Hook

Jabs looks at the bundle of silk, cuts the flame, raises the sledge, and brings it down on the wrapped jar. It shatters—dirt, rocks, and dried plants, along with shards of jade, burst from the tapestry and spread across the floor.

The sledge falls from Jabari's grasp. She ignites her magic again. The directed blaze ignites the pile of filth.

The music fades into its final riffs.

Sam sprays the extinguisher.

All quiet, except for a muffled hum from the speakers.

Tension releases from my body, replaced with the pain my adrenaline kept hidden.

Jabari falls to her knees and drapes herself on top of me.

"That's my favorite song, now and forever," she says as I sink into blessed darkness.

38

SATURDAY MORNING, SAM AND JABARI

"HE'S IN AWFUL shape," Sam said, touching Red's body.

"Who're you?" Jabari asked.

"Sam. I'm a friend. Right now, I need to be a healer." Sam hummed, her vibration causing the big man's body to shudder.

Jabari stepped back. With her third eye, she watched Sam and Red's spirits mingle as color returned to her teacher's aura. Satisfied that the woman was no threat, she turned to look at the small charred pile that used to be her possessor.

Her flame damaged the Void, but she could still see some energy radiating from the crude mass on the floor. Looking around the barn, she discovered a stack of iron pipes under a bench near the back. Grabbing a piece of two-inch about two feet long, she put on a pair of discarded work gloves and walked back to face the violator.

The silk tapestry, undamaged from her flamethrowing endeavors, still glowed with power. Picking up one end, she dragged it over to what was left of the Void.

"You may have some life left in your damn hide, and I'm not exactly sure how to snuff it out properly." She rolled the gooey mess into the tapestry, tight, allowing it to extend inside the silk. "So, until my *boss* is back on his feet, I'm going to give you a taste of what I felt, fucker."

Finished, she took the encased goo and shoved it into the pipe. Noticing that the ends were threaded, she headed back to the bench and found domed caps to screw on to seal it inside. Satisfied, she took an old towel and rolled the pipe inside, performing a containment spell to bind the towel to the iron prison. Then, adding a few zip ties to hold the towel in place, she walked back and placed the demon's new home on the floor near Sam.

"Is he going to be OK?" Jabari asked.

Sam stopped her song and looked at Jabari.

"He'll live, but the 'OK' part will take time. My phone is over there behind that cardboard box. Will you call Detective Rogers and tell him where we are? We need his help to clean up this place and get Red out of here." Jabari found her own phone in her back pocket and used it instead.

After hanging up, she sat next to Sam, impressed with her healing skill; Jabari watched as the tones worked to realign Red's spirit wheels. Using what she had learned trapped inside her own spirit, she reached her coil out to Red. By sharing her energy, Jabari used subtle touches to repair spiritual connectivity within his sacred alignment.

Sam stopped her song to admire Jabari, her face conveying curiosity.

"Where did you learn that? It's beautiful."

Jabari continued, seeing the positive results of her efforts.

"Something I picked up while trapped by the shit stain."

"Well, keep it up. Maybe we won't have to lift him. I've done it twice, and the third time here is no charm." They both chuckled, then Sam took the chain from around her neck and handed it to Jabari. "Speaking of charms, I think this one belongs to you."

Jabari held it tight before putting it over her head. Feeling the familiar weight of Red's ward key brought fresh tears to her eyes.

     M.J. HOOK

39
SATURDAY MORNING

MY EYES OPEN in time to watch friends loading equipment into a trailer. I remain silent as memory catches up to the moment. The smell of burnt demon quickens my recall.

Seeing Jabari, I smile.

"Jabs." My throat feels like I swallowed broken glass.

"He's awake!" Jabari rushes over and puts a water bottle to my lips. The liquid feels good. I reach out and grab the bottle, then stop when pain flares with the movement.

"Stay still." She helps me drink.

Jabari shows me a small scepter made of rags.

"I trapped its ass in here with the tapestry." When I frown, she continues. "It's not going anywhere. We can deal with it later." She lays her head on my shoulder. "I knew you would come through for me."

"Rick. Sam. Helped" is all I can say.

"Sam told me. I'll give that bloody wacko a hug when I return his stuff. You need to rest. We still have a bit to do here."

Sam and Benny are next. It hurts to even look up.

"Glad to see you're still with the living, Red," Sam says. "I'll send you a bill in the morning. Interesting magic with your blood. Never heard of magic that removes DNA markers from blood and hair droppings. Saves time cleaning up. Maybe another trade to discuss?"

I put a thumb up and fall back asleep as Benny starts a rant.

• • •

Opening my eyes again, I hear Jabari and Boris talking. I am in Scout, beside the gatehouse at the bottom of my mountain. I close my eyes when I hear Jabari say, "Well he had a rough night, I'll be sure to give him your message."

As Scout turns the last switchback to the cabin, I wake again and turn to Jabari in the driver's seat.

"Oh good. You're awake. Almost home. Don't fall back asleep. Otherwise, I'll get the dolly and dump you on Marlow's couch."

My walk inside is labored, but feeling Jabari under my arm is a crutch I'm happy to lean on.

Exhaustion and the overwhelming pain traveling through my body and spirit keep me awake long enough to take a piss, a quick shower, then fall into bed.

"So, boss. Leaving a pile of stuff on your table here to eat, drink, and heal. I'm off to Rick's, returning his arsenal of sound equipment. I'll be back."

Darkness, again.

40

MONDAY, LATE MORNING

"**SCIENCE HAS ALWAYS** been the foundation for discovering and exploring magic. Nature has offered an overabundance of discovery within itself. Humans have learned to use it…"

"Then continued to fuck it up royally," Jabari interrupts me.

"Well, yes. mankind ruined many of Nature's resources and has taken advantage of Her spiritual gifts, both arcane and common, but that's not my point."

"Your point," my zealous student continues, "is that when you are basically powerless against your magical enemy, sometimes you need to look at other aspects of Nature to beef up your arsenal."

I take another sip from my first mug of coffee since the throwdown on Saturday. It tastes like manna from Gaia, to adjust an old saying. Smells like a good start to a great day.

"Well, yes. Not exactly how I wanted to phrase it, but if you remember the lesson in your words, hopefully it will save your own butt in the future."

"You saved my butt, Red. But I get it. I saw how damaged you were. I felt it. I also touched your consciousness and felt the despair you'd been undergoing. Never thought I would ever experience something like that from *you*. But if I learned one thing, it's that even if *you* are against the ropes, hell, even on the mat, *you* never lose your fight."

The shudder up my back causes my mug to shake and spill precious brew.

"This fight was won by your efforts and ingenuity, Jabs. But there was something I needed to learn about myself: having friends to trust and back me up can make the difference."

"Speaking of friends, I really like Samantha. She's got a special something going on. Don't you think?" Jabari winks at me. I'm just glad she is across the counter so her elbow can't give me a nudge.

"She is… special. I may ask her to join Donum."

"Really? That's what you're considering? How about asking her out on a date?"

The thought of trying to turn my new friendship into something more had crossed my mind, but Sam already has her priorities. No need for my life to shake them up. But her knowledge and experience would be invaluable to my small coven of international witches.

"Maybe, Jabs. I think after filling up her dance card this last week, she may want to take a break and rest her feet."

"Maybe, Red, you just need to take a break from *dancing* and try breathing like a normal person for a while."

Normal. I don't know what that is.

• • •

Sitting down the street from Tom Hutchins's house, I see no gawkers, no official vehicles. The only sign that a murder took place in the house is the few shreds of yellow tape still stuck to the front railing.

Grabbing a tubular container from the back of Scout, I walk up the street, casually looking at the neighbor's windows to see if any auras are present to take in the view. Theresa's house still has several cars parked out front, so I make a move to the opposite neighbor's backyard, casting myself invisible behind a large pine. Stepping over a strand of police tape, I walk up to the back door leading to the basement of the late Tom's house.

Locked. I cast a simple spell to let myself in. Walking through the mudroom, I enter the man cave and head for the steps going upstairs. The workshop where Theresa's murder happened remains in the dark. I catch the stale, iron smell of old blood.

Opening the garage door, I'm glad to find all the bays empty of cars. According to Benny, Tom's wife flew back to California to get her kids and tell them the bad news. The toolbox on the workbench is gone. A rack of fishing poles and shelves filled with fishing equipment stand on the other side of the bench. I easily find Tom's favorite pole, identified from the

                M.J. Hook

pictures hanging in the man cave downstairs.

I remove a smudge from my coat pocket and light it.

Speaking a routine incantation of blessing, I direct the smoke in all four directions, asking for success and protection. Not knowing what state of reason Hutchins's spirit might be in, I do not ask specifically to remove any evil that may be present.

As I finish the blessing, the totem bag around my neck vibrates. The tattoos of protection flare on my body. I know Tom's spirit is nearby.

It's a three-bay garage. The third bay contains family bikes, lawn tools, a mower, and other outdoor gear. I move to the middle of the first two bays and unsling the tube. Inside is a rolled portable altar, teacup candles, a bag of salt, a small copper bowl, and a baggie filled with a summoning mixture of herbs and minerals.

Spreading the altar fabric out, I use the salt to create a circle encompassing myself and the small sheet. I place the candles at each point of the pentagram. Lighting each one, I call on the elements for their support. Casting a flame to the spirit candle, I meditate, allowing my spirit to open to the energy vibrating within the space.

The air becomes agitated inside the garage. Bits of paper, leaves, and dust blow around the space. Placing the fishing rod across the altar, I fill the bowl inside the pentagram with the summoning mix, then light it, performing a summoning spell in Gaelic to empower the words.

"Thomas Hutchins, *labhair leis an spiorad*. Come on out and let's have us a chat. I know you're here, buddy. I also know your soul is having a dreadful week. Maybe I can help you with that, but I need you to show yourself."

Extending a coil into the air above my head, I let it hang there like a baited hook. The one thing a spirit cannot resist is latching onto a link to the living.

Nibble. Nibble.

Who are you? My house. This is my house. What have I done?

Bite.

That noise, that awful noise. It would not stop. It would not let me stop. Poor girl. Not my fault. Not my fault.

"I know, Tom. She knows, too. It's time for you to let go. Let me show you the Universe."

The spirit refuses, wanting to haunt this plane in anger and pain, wanting

to suffer for what he saw himself do to Theresa. I talk Tom's spirit through
the denial, and eventually, with my help, he finds his life thread and the
acceptance to release his spirit to the Universe.

• • •

I collect my things, crack the garage door, and push the lingering smoke
down to the opening. Grabbing a broom, I sweep the salt out onto the
driveway.

*Some spirits prefer to suffer. Too afraid of what may be on the other
side. Feeling undeserving of the release. Comfortable in unearthly misery?
Maybe. It's how many people live their corporeal lives, eke out their spiritual
existence.*

*Evildoers want to be remembered for their acts. Innocents remembered
for evil become the blame, any good they may have achieved forgotten.*

Tom was not to blame.

Tell his family and neighbors that.

An eternal twist of fate in the mortal world.

A blessed release and forgiveness in the Universe.

• • •

The Void is deep-fried, wrapped in its wipe rag, encased in iron, and
placed on a shelf in my warded vault deep inside my mountain. When I am
stronger, I will try communicating with the little prick.

Not like he would be worse off giving me the names of spikey white-
haired chick and her daddy now.

• • •

Too damaged to perform a portal spell, I purchase a flight to Zihuatanejo,
Mexico. After I talked to my friend Sena, a bruja and a top-notch healer, she
invited me down. She is one of the founding members of Donum, so I know
I can trust her with the amount of spiritual exposure I need to recover.

"We'll go over the spiritual self-maintenance you discovered when I get
back, Jabs. Right now, I'm not sure I would like what I see."

"Yeah, you're a mess," she says. "But once you get patched up, I
guarantee you'll dig it."

Packing finished, the last item I grab is the journal I started for Theresa's
baddoon. Having filled in most of the details from dealing with the Void,

                M.J. Hook

I know I will have more to add. Some of the information will be good to discuss with Sena. I grab an empty journal, realizing that it may behoove me to start taking notes concerning the white haired girl and her spoogey father.

My head hurts to try and formulate a reason for their existence.

I scratch Marlow and make sure he knows how much I appreciate his support by giving him some raw beef I picked up earlier. He eats, and I'm an afterthought.

On the way to the airport, I text Benny that I'm leaving and will let him know when I get back. I text Carmella Frillman, thanking her and George for inviting me to Thanksgiving dinner but that I'll be out of town. I text Rick, thank him again, and promise a Zonkers sleepover when I get back.

I text because talking to anyone right now feels like it would take too much effort. Jabari knows this, remaining quiet behind Scout's steering wheel.

I consider calling Sam, then decide to text. I thank her for her help, her healing, and her time, letting her know I'm leaving to have a tune up and that I look forward to seeing her when I return.

After that message, I send her one more.

I'll leave the mercury at home in the medicine cabinet.

Pressing send, I double-check to make sure I didn't promise.

Hook 02-28-2025

ACKNOWLEDGMENTS

A confession: Tapping out these "thank-ye kindlies" for *FEAR* is exciting. For several years I've threatened so many people with plans to write a book. This is my opportunity to finally thank everyone (in published print, no less) who's stuck with me through all my blah blah.

But first, I want to thank *you*, blessed reader, for finishing *FEAR*. I hope you enjoyed meeting Red and will continue reading as the series and blogs about his story evolve.

Please leave a review to let me and other potential readers know what you think about the book.

Second, it's important for me to thank all the eye rollers who made it obvious that they thought my effort was just blah blah. Your ocular gymnastics did occasionally manifest feelings of doubt, but in the end, the peeper jitters became a source of motivation. You know who you are—thanks!

Next, I need to thank Lisa Takemura for getting me back in touch with her sister, Katherine Wyatt. *The Red Wood Chronicles* were already in development when I discovered Kathy lost her life years ago. Chatting with Lisa, and a call with Kathy's friend Martha Vestecka-Miller, offered me an opportunity to reconnect with my first-best-friend in spirit (see link below). Dedicating the series to her has given me profound purpose. Bless you both, and thanks.

Praise to my alpha readers—none of you are "beta" in my book:

"Uncle" John Rollhaus, your due diligence in reading and discussing the story (and everything else under the sun) are calls I always look forward to. Appreciate the turn-ons to new authors and ideas. David "DrumSting" Mansfield, my old friend whose attention to detail and love for the genre were immediately obvious. I'm thankful for rediscovering your focus. "Scary" Larry Hinkle, an incredible horror writer (see his author link below) of whom I can say, "I knew you when you were just funny." I know you're one busy mofo, so my appreciation for your time and feedback is unbounded. Sherri "The Boot" Wood Emmons, also an awesome author (see her link below) and old friend. Your consistent kicks in my writing ass were always an inspiration. Thank you for starting your eye rolls…they meant so much to me. Merv "BambooPunk" Velasco and Trong "Notarry" Nguyen, my brothers in mania and imagination, you guys are certainly a

 M.J. Hook

big part of this story and the stories to come—if you would hurry up and graduate and write! You guys stuck with me, and your feedback stuck to me. It's been an honor to get inside your heads and to let you inside mine. And finally, Haylee "Ninja Biker" Holt, your fresh-eyed awareness and polite badgering will always be a welcome scream to my ears. You rev, girl.

To all of you, many thanks and blessings.

Larry Hinkle: https://thatscarylarry.wixsite.com/thatscarylarry
Sherri Wood Emmons: https://www.goodreads.com/author/list/4235092. Sherri_Wood_Emmons
M.G. Velasco: https://mgvelasco.com
About Kathy Wyatt: https://mj-hook.com/kathy-wyatt/

In my attempts to start learning Gaelic, I realized not all dialects are the same. Red's Donegal region was a must. So, finding a class to learn, the time to learn, and scavenging brain cells to learn became a chore. Same with finding someone who could translate Red's meaning—not just his words. A special thanks to Mary O'Brien Fahy, a blessed soul from Gortahork, Co. Donegal. Introduced to me by a friend of a friend of my sister's friend, your life and heritage are my luck. I appreciate your time working with me, gifting Red's power language with genuine energy.

To my All Writers Online Workshop (AWOW) group, thank you so much for your feedback and tap-tap tips. I'm so glad I attend on an almost regular basis now. You guys are a *most def* game changer.

I also need to thank the DFWWW group for the conference opportunities and the few meetings I could attend. Damn the traffic-jammed distance between us.

To my S.W.I.M. brethren, I might not see you much, but it's like no time's passed when we hook up. You guys know your part in all this mess, and I appreciate those of you that gave me a place to hide, to write, or to manifest steam. Damn, you certainly knew me when!

A sweet, warm blessing to Lady Ivy, whose Higher Purpose Emporium and multileveled presence have been a constant when I take the time to visit. Always something to learn. Always something to embrace. You make magic a beautiful, natural *ambiance*.

To my editor Rebecca Brite, your redlines were an education. Through you, I've learned that commas are not my best friend and that some words should not exist. Appreciate all the comments and suggestions offered, your time spent, but most importantly your presence in my life. You are a true blessing.

A big red circle callout to Brad Converse, the reason why having an editor is so important. You're like having a conscious to point out what I really mean to shoot before I pull the trigger. Thank you for the insight, comma slashing, and wonderful questions and concerns you discovered in our journey together. Look forward to the next one.

To the numerous family and friends that have put up with my weirdness and creative obsessions over the years, I say, "Thanks, but it ain't over yet! Just look at this current thing I *gots* here!"

To SkinWalker, without you I would be permanently glued to my chair, and all that entails.

Most importantly, a wave of love and gratitude to M'Love and kids. You guys have had to build your lives around my infernal time spent on the magic screen. Know that you're the foundation for all my efforts— something solid I can always return to when things get too normal. Love you guys with all my soul.

M.J. "Happy" Hook

ABOUT THE AUTHOR

M.J. Hook was born and raised in vanilla towns across the Midwest, and discovered immaturely that if you want flavor in life, the best waiter to order from is your imagination.

After stuffing himself with fantasy and horror, then hurling the glut of his creativity onto drawing paper, canvas, and notepads, what emerged from the heartland was an artistically weird kid with an unhinged imagination.

He manages the creative day-career of *art gigolo*—designing brands, publications, brochures, illustrations for a variety of clients. But once the sun sinks, he writes, paints, and doodles on walls. Coloring them is much easier than climbing them.

He's into movies that tell a good story and reading books that force him to forget about responsibility. Currently stuck in Texas, his heart craves the Rocky Mountains and spends frequent imaginary visits to the Northwest. His wife and kids acknowledge the troll living in the cave, and frequently leave treats at the entrance to keep him alive and gruntled.

www.ingramcontent.com/pod-product-compliance
Lightning Source LLC
Chambersburg PA
CBHW032019150726
47990CB00005B/2035